Departures

Books by Robin Jones Gunn

THE CHRISTY MILLER SERIES

SIERRA JENSEN SERIES

Books by Wendy Lee Nentwig

UNMISTAKABLY COOPER ELLIS

SPACE NEEDLE WISCONSIN DELLS MONTANA

3 BOOKS IN 1

Departures

CHRISTY MILLER
NOW BOARDING AT
GATE 10

COOPER ELLIS
PLEASE PICK UP THE
WHITE COURTESY PHONE

SIERRA JENSEN
IN THE EVENT OF A
WATER LANDING

ROBIN JONES GUNN & WENDY LEE NENTWIG

BETHANY HOUSE PUBLISHERS
MINNEAPOLIS, MINNESOTA 55438

Published by Bethany House Publishers
A Ministry of Bethany Fellowship International
11400 Hampshire Avenue South
Minneapolis, Minnesota 55438
www.bethanyhouse.com

Printed in the United States of America by
Bethany Press International, Minneapolis, Minnesota 55438

Library of Congress Cataloging-in-Publication Data

Departures : [three books in one].
       p.   cm.
       Summary: A collection of stories which feature Christy Miller, Sierra Jensen, and Cooper Ellis gaining new understandings about faith and themselves during trips to various destinations.
       ISBN 0–7642–2271–6 (pbk.)
       1. Christian life Juvenile fiction. 2. Children's stories, American. [1. Christian life Fiction. 2. Short stories.] I. Gunn, Robin Jones, 1955–   Now boarding at gate 10. II. Nentwig, Wendy Lee. Please pick up the white courtesy phone. III. Gunn, Robin Jones, 1955–   In the event of a water landing.
PZ5.D45   1999   99–6738
[Fic]—dc21   CIP

To my parents,
who left Baraboo and the dairy farm
to move to California when I was five.
May your memories of summer picnics
fifty years ago at the Dells
be as bright as a sky full of fireworks
on the Fourth of July.

And to Tammi Scheetz,
with fun memories of when
we rode the Ferris wheel at Camp Snoopy
and searched the Minneapolis-St. Paul Airport
for cinnamon rolls so we could share a Sierra moment.

—Robin

To the real Penny and Brian

—Wendy

ROBIN JONES GUNN is an award-winning author of over forty books, including THE CHRISTY MILLER SERIES, which has sold more than 1.5 million copies. Other series by Robin are the SIERRA JENSEN SERIES and THE GLENBROOKE SERIES, as well as the much anticipated CHRISTY AND TODD: THE COLLEGE YEARS, scheduled for release in summer 2000. A storyteller at heart, Robin is also a popular speaker. She and her husband, Ross, have two teenagers and have lived many places, including California and Hawaii. They currently live near Portland, Oregon, where Ross is a youth pastor.

WENDY LEE NENTWIG is editor-at-large of *CCM Magazine* and has been on staff with *Virtue, Aspire,* and *Seventeen.* Wendy Lee has worked extensively with teens, both overseas and at home. She is the author of the UNMISTAKABLY COOPER ELLIS series and two other young adult novels. A born traveler, Wendy Lee spent two years in Amsterdam before settling in Nashville.

ROBIN AND WENDY LEE have been close friends for over fifteen years. While rooming together at a writer's conference several years ago, they came up with the idea of each writing short stories featuring their three teen characters and putting them together in one book. Six months later, Wendy Lee and Robin met up in South Carolina for a book signing. After the last book was autographed and the final photo taken, they jumped into their rented Mustang convertible and headed for the Great Smokey Mountains with the music turned up full blast. That weekend, at a charming bed-and-breakfast, the two friends laughed and talked and planned *Departures.*

Both Robin and Wendy Lee agree: There's nothing more delightful than traveling with an old friend. May you enjoy "traveling" with your old friends Christy, Cooper, and Sierra. And may your journey be delightful!

Contents

Departures

WISCONSIN DELLS

Now Boarding at Gate 10

A CHRISTY MILLER NOVELLA

ROBIN JONES GUNN

Chapter 1

As beads of perspiration dripped down her back, Christy Miller lifted her long, nutmeg brown hair to try to get some air on her neck. She didn't know why her parents had dashed so quickly off the plane when it landed at the Minneapolis-St. Paul Airport. They had more than an hour before their connecting flight left for Madison, Wisconsin.

"Would it be okay if I went to the snack bar for something to drink?" Christy asked her dad.

"Sure," Dad said, reaching into his pocket for some money. "Buy something for your mother and me—and take your brother with you."

Christy tried to hide her lack of enthusiasm over thirteen-year-old David's tagging along. This was the first vacation her family had taken in a long time, and she didn't want to be the one to start an argument.

"Can we play one of those video games?" David asked, pushing up his glasses. He was big for his age, just as Christy had been, and he resembled their red-haired father more every day.

"No. We're only getting something to drink." Christy led her brother through a maze of small round tables. The two of them were almost to the counter when David tripped over a girl's foot that was sticking out from under a table. She was wearing large clunky boots and had her dark hair up in a clip. David stumbled and bumped into her chair, causing the girl's backpack, which had been slung over the chair's back, to fall to the floor.

"Sorry," Christy said, apologizing for her brother and urging him to move on quickly.

The girl and her friend, who was sitting next to her, were probably a year or two younger than Christy was, yet they appeared to be traveling by themselves. At that moment Christy wished she were traveling with her best friend, Katie. A summer adventure would be so much more fun with a friend than with her family.

When Christy had graduated from high school two weeks ago, several classmates went on senior trips to exotic locations like Mexico and Hawaii. This was Christy's exotic trip—a family weekend in Brightwater, Wisconsin, population 832.

Two days ago Katie had told Christy, "You shouldn't complain. At least you're going *somewhere*—unlike *some* people we know." Katie then had flopped onto her bed and let out a sigh. "If you come home on Monday and find me here, in this same position, call the Guinness Book of World Records."

Even though Christy knew better, she asked why.

"Because I will be the first person in history who will have died from boredom."

Christy had argued that her grandparents' fiftieth wedding anniversary in Brightwater, the town Christy had grown up in, would be twice as boring, but Katie didn't buy it. She reminded Christy that more than once mystery, romance, and adventure had found her when she had least expected it.

Then Katie had lifted her head and added, "And don't forget. You happen to be very available at the moment."

Yes, Christy thought while handing David his drink, *this would have been a much more exciting trip with Katie along*. Christy directed her brother to a nearby exit she had spotted where he would have less human traffic to navigate through. With each of them holding two full drinks, Christy knew the chances of disaster with David were pretty high.

They had just made it through the café when Christy caught sight of a flash of sandy blond hair that looked so familiar. She held her breath and watched a guy enter the bookshop next to the café.

"David," Christy said, "stay right beside me. I want to check on something in that bookstore."

"That's not fair. You wouldn't let me play video games."

Christy's heart pounded wildly as she caught another glimpse of the broad shoulders and a tan neck. He wore a white T-shirt with a familiar surfing logo on the back.

"Hurry up, David," Christy said, walking faster.

"Where are we going?"

Christy couldn't answer her brother. She was too absorbed in not screaming out "Todd!" at the top of her voice and running to the guy who was now standing with his back to her, looking at a magazine.

With cautious steps and protecting the drinks she held, Christy blinked away sudden tears from her blue-green eyes. She now stood only a few feet from the person who had held a special place in her heart. Only two months ago, as they watched the sunset at the beach, Christy had said good-bye to Todd. She never dreamed she would be saying hello to him so soon.

"Hello," she said aloud before she had a chance to think of a better greeting.

When he didn't turn around, she stepped closer, her heart pounding loudly in her ears, and said, "Hi."

"Christy?" David said. "What are you doing? Who are you talking to?"

The guy turned to face both of them, and Christy nearly dropped her drinks. This guy, who stood only inches from her, was definitely not Todd Spencer. He was good-looking, but he wasn't Todd.

"Oh, sorry," Christy mumbled. She turned before her crimson cheeks painted her whole face a bright red.

"What were you doing?" David asked, following her fast stride out of the bookstore. "Who did you think that was?"

Christy ignored David, trying to calm her emotions. How could she have made such a fool of herself?

"Did you think he was someone you knew?" David asked, trotting to keep up with Christy.

"Yes," she answered. "From the back, he kind of looked like Todd."

"Todd?! He didn't look like Todd at all. You should have asked me before you went up to him. I could have told you it wasn't Todd."

Christy was about to turn and tell David to just drop the whole thing, when a voice over the loudspeaker announced, "Flight 73 to Madison, Wisconsin, is now boarding at gate 10."

"Come on, David, that's us." Christy strode through the terminal, leading the way to gate 10. When they entered the waiting area, their parents were anxiously looking for them.

"Where have you been?" Mom asked, taking her drink from Christy.

"Christy thought she saw Todd," David announced for the whole world to hear. "She followed this guy into a bookstore and started to talk to him."

"David!" Christy scolded.

"Well, you did."

Christy grabbed her backpack and started for the line of passengers boarding the plane. Mom stopped her. "We have to wait. They're only boarding rows 15 and higher. We're row 14."

David tugged on the strap of Christy's backpack and said, "Hey, look! There he is."

The guy from the bookstore had entered their waiting area and stood in line to board the same plane. Christy tucked her chin and turned her head so he wouldn't see her.

"He doesn't look at all like Todd, does he?" David said.

"David, lower your voice!" Christy pleaded.

"Come on," Dad said. "They just called our row."

Christy slowly followed as her family stood in line. The guy was only two people ahead of her mom.

"He's looking at you," David announced, punching Christy in the side.

"David," Christy threatened through clenched teeth. "Don't you dare say another word. I mean it!"

David pretended to lock his lips with an invisible key. He stood with his shoulders back, playing the role of the model child. Christy moved along behind him with her head down, avoiding eye contact with any of the passengers, especially the tall blond surfer who was definitely boarding the same plane.

Chapter 2

Once her family was seated, Christy nonchalantly began to look around to see if the guy was sitting near them. Fortunately, he wasn't. She settled back and buried her nose in a magazine.

Since the flight was short, Christy didn't expect to have any more awkward encounters. She knew it was ridiculous to have thought he could be Todd. What would Todd be doing in the Midwest? Most likely he was off on some tropical island, sipping coconut juice, surfing the world's most remote beaches, and telling the natives about God. As long as Christy had known Todd, that had been his dream. And now he was living it.

She quickly tried to push her thoughts on to other things. Her mind and heart had been over this a thousand times. She had made the right choice when she broke up with Todd. She knew it. It was time for her to move on.

The Fasten Seat Belt sign came on overhead, and Mom tapped Christy's arm. "David has been in the rest room an awfully long time. Since you're in the aisle seat, would you mind checking on him?"

Checking on David was the last thing Christy wanted to do. But since Dad was napping and Mom would have to crawl over her, Christy reluctantly unfastened her seat belt and made her way to the rest room. Of the two doors, only one had the Occupied sign up, indicating that someone was in it.

Christy self-consciously looked to the right and left, hoping no one was watching. Leaning closer to the door, she said in a low voice, "Are you almost done in there?"

When she heard no answer, Christy knocked and said in a louder voice, "We're about to land. You need to come back to your seat. You better not be playing with the soap."

The door's handle moved, and Christy stepped back to make room for David to come out. With her hand on her hip, she said, "What took you so long?"

When she looked up, she saw David wasn't the person who emerged. It was the blond guy from the bookstore.

"What's with you?" he asked, glaring at Christy.

"I thought—I didn't . . . My brother was . . . I'm . . ."

Just then the door to the other bathroom opened, and David joined them in the tight area. The guy turned with a shake of his head. Christy spouted, "David, you're supposed to lock the door."

"I got sick, Christy," he said, holding his stomach.

"Oh great," she muttered. "Do you need to go back in the bathroom or can you make it to your seat?"

"I think I can go to my seat."

Christy ushered David down the aisle ahead of her and turned him over to Mom as soon as they reached their row. David moaned and complained, but fortunately he didn't get sick again during the landing.

As Christy and her mom collected their luggage at baggage claim, Dad stood in line at the car rental desk. David sat on a bench looking forlorn, with only a cold can of 7-Up to keep him company. But it seemed to be good company for him because half an hour later, as they left the airport in their dark blue rental car and drove north on Highway 12, David started to point out places he recognized.

Christy was just glad to be away from the airport and from the blond guy, who had practically run in the other direction when he saw her at baggage claim.

As they left the suburbs and traveled down the country road, Christy watched the blur of green fields against the fresh blue summer sky. Every quarter of a mile or so a weathered barn accompanied by a farmhouse would appear. Some homesteads had kids' toys in the front yard, some had gardens along the side, and some were partially hidden from the road by huge shade trees planted long ago.

Fields of cornstalks stood at attention in orderly rows. Christy knew that in a few weeks the corn would be ready, and nothing she had ever tasted was better than corn fresh-picked, boiled immediately, and smothered with butter and salt. Her mouth watered just thinking about it.

Not much seemed to have changed since Christy had last watched all this landscape roll by. She wondered if she was right in thinking that Wisconsin had stayed the same while she had changed so much.

"Can we go to our old house?" David asked.

"Maybe tomorrow," Mom answered quickly.

Christy hadn't asked that question, even though she had thought it, since seeing the farm might be a difficult memory for her parents. They'd had to sell the farm and leave family and friends behind three years ago when it became apparent they could no longer make it financially. Her dad had decided he wanted to work for someone else rather than be his own employer. So they had moved to California, and he had found a job at Hollandale Dairy. The move had been a wise choice, even though Christy got the impression that some of their relatives still disagreed with the decision.

"Do I have to sleep on the floor at Grandma's?" David asked.

"I'm not sure," Mom said. "But try to make the best of it, no matter where we end up sleeping, all right?"

"Are we going to eat when we get there?" David asked.

"I don't know," Mom said. "I'm glad you feel like eating again. We'll make sure you get some food as soon as we can, David."

Dad drove nearly an hour before arriving in the small community where Christy's grandparents had lived all their married lives, which, by tomorrow, would be fifty years. *Half a century*. The thought sobered Christy. *What a long time to live in the same place with the same person.*

Her parents' old farm was only a ten-minute drive from her grandparents' home in Brightwater. She watched David look at the turnoff as they passed it and kept heading straight on the country road for town.

"Our old house is down that road," David said.

"That's right," Dad agreed, but that's all he said.

They were only a few blocks inside the city limits when Christy saw the flagpoles and then the front of George Washington Elementary School.

"That's my old school!" David announced.

"Mine too," Christy said softly. So many memories collided at once. First days of school and Mom taking Christy's picture every year in her back-to-school clothes. Fire drills with the students lined up on the grass. The harvest festivals with the school transformed into a wondrous carnival of clowns, ring-toss booths, and cakewalks. She even remembered the cafeteria's aroma on pizza day and the table where she and Paula met every day for lunch.

And Christy remembered her first crush. Her heart skipped a happy beat when she silently mouthed his name: Matthew Kingsley. From third grade all the way through junior high, Christy was hopelessly gone over Matthew Kingsley.

George Washington Elementary School and Matthew Kingsley. What a rush of childhood memories were connected with those two names.

Ever since her family had moved to California, the Kingsleys had sent a family photo with their Christmas card. Every year Christy looked closely at Matthew in the photo. He was a high school graduate now, just like Christy. And he still lived in Brightwater.

Before they drove another block, Christy had to ask, "Mom, do you think we'll see any of our old friends while we're here?"

"Yes. Who did you have in mind?"

"Oh, no one in particular." Christy couldn't bring herself to ask about Matthew Kingsley. The last thing she needed was to arm her brother with ammunition he could use all weekend to tease her. The Todd un-look-alike incident was bad enough.

No, if Christy was going to see Matthew Kingsley this weekend, it would just have to be a nice surprise. Or as Katie always said, "a God thing." And what was it that Katie had said about mystery, romance, and adventure finding Christy when she least expected it?

Christy leaned back and smiled. She was ready for anything.

Chapter 3

Dad pulled into Christy's grandparents' driveway. After climbing out of the car and looping her backpack over her shoulder, Christy stood for a moment, drinking in the sight of her grandparents' two-story house. It was yellow. It had always been yellow. Yellow with white trim. The second story had two dormer windows that Christy had always imagined were the house's eyes. Those two upstairs bedrooms had belonged to Christy's mom and aunt Marti while they were growing up. Mom's room had been the one on the left.

Grandma's bright red geranium bushes were in full bloom along the front of the house. A handmade wooden birdhouse hung from the apple tree, which spread its welcoming shade over the right side of the small front yard. A modest porch fronted the house. Christy had eaten many a summer meal with her grandparents on the enclosed porch, which her grandpa always boasted was the "coolest and most bug-free spot in the house on a summer's eve'n."

Grandpa had worked at the hardware store in town for more than forty years, which was a good thing because his hobby was fixing things. Or, more accurately, improving things. Christy noticed the strips of safety tape on the three steps that led up to the front porch, obviously one of Grandpa's touches intended to prevent falls.

As Christy watched, her mom rang the front doorbell. Christy thought that was kind of strange. When her family had lived nearby, they used to just knock and walk right in. *Will I ring the doorbell when I come home to visit my parents in the future?*

Grandma, wearing a flowered apron over her skirt and white blouse, flung open the door. She spoke in a voice made high with delight when she saw them. Welcoming them inside with hugs and kisses, she tried to take one of the suitcases from Christy's dad.

Christy drew in a deep breath. What was that familiar scent? Grandma's house always smelled the same. It wasn't a sweet smell like cinnamon, and it wasn't yucky like mothballs. It smelled old. Like a cedar chest filled with old books and yellowing papers. The smell comforted Christy. Even if she had changed, Grandma's house hadn't changed a bit.

"Look at you two kids!" Grandma kissed Christy soundly on the cheek. "You've grown so much!"

Christy was amazed by how much her mom and grandma looked alike. She hadn't noticed the resemblance so clearly before. They were both short, with round faces and wavy hair. Grandma's hair was all white now, whereas Christy's mom's hair was turning gray around her face. Christy was taller than both of them were.

Grandpa appeared in the entryway with a socket wrench in his hand. Christy had to smile. Seeing Grandpa as "Mr. Fix-It" was a common sight.

"Well, come here, now," he said. "Let me have a look-see at you two." His quick, dark eyes resembled Aunt Marti's as he gave Christy and David a visual examination. As always, his evaluation was positive, with one suggestion for improvement. That was also a trait Aunt Marti seemed to have inherited from him—an eye for ways others could improve.

"Yessiree, you two are turning out just dandy. Of course,

David, you might want to get a haircut before the reception to-morrow. And you won't be wearing shorts, now, will you, Chris-tina?''

"No, Grandpa," Christy said warmly, "I brought a dress for tomorrow."

"Good, good." Grandpa motioned with his socket wrench for them to follow him into the kitchen. He never had been an especially affectionate man, so Christy wasn't surprised he didn't greet them with hugs and kisses the way Grandma had. She knew he was happy to see them, even though he acted as if he saw them every day.

Grandma suggested they leave the luggage in the living room.

Christy liked the kitchen best of all the house's rooms. It hadn't changed since Christy was a child. The kitchen table, covered with a red-checkered cloth, took up most of the space in the center of the room. Its chairs were silver chrome with vinyl cushioned seats. As a matter of fact, the '50s table was so old it was back in style. Christy had nibbled many a homemade cookie at that table. Dozens of her grade-school works of art had covered the front of the white refrigerator. She knew where the glasses were in the cupboard and where the "secret" jar of M&M's was kept in the pantry. But when Christy saw the chicken and rooster salt and pepper shakers on the stovetop, she knew for sure she was at Grandma's house.

"What do you think?" Grandpa asked, looking at Dad and pointing to a new faucet on the kitchen sink. "The old one leaked like a bucket with a hole in it."

"Looks nice," Mom said.

The others nodded in agreement as Grandpa stood there, eyebrows raised, challenging one of them to try his new faucet. From experience, Christy had learned not to be the first one to try anything Grandpa had just "fixed."

"Go ahead," Grandpa said, his eyes still on Christy's dad.

Dad stepped forward and lifted the faucet's handle. The water came out effortlessly.

"Cold is to the right," Grandpa instructed. "Hot, of course, is to your left."

Dad obliged, turning the handle first to the right and then to the left before pushing it down to turn off the flow.

"How about that?" Grandpa said, pleased with his handi-work.

Christy praised him and thought to herself, *I guess when you're seventy-three, you deserve to receive a little praise.*

The group gravitated to the kitchen table, as it always did, and Grandma offered lemonade and cookies. It wasn't very hot for a summer afternoon so they stayed in the kitchen. Other-wise, Christy was sure they would have been shooed out to the front porch.

David slurped his lemonade and gobbled up three cookies before he excused himself to go out in the backyard. The rest of them sat for an hour or so, chatting about relatives and neighbors.

"Oh, that reminds me," Grandma said. "The Kingsley boy called here this morning and wanted to know when you would be coming."

Christy felt her face turn warm. "Matthew?"

"Yes," Grandma said.

"I called Jane last week," Mom explained. "She said Mat-thew would definitely want to see you when we came."

"She did? I mean, he does?" Christy felt funny with her par-ents and grandparents watching her every expression. "What did you tell him, Grandma?"

"I told him to call back this evening." Grandma sounded pleased with herself, as if she had done Christy a favor. For all Christy knew, maybe she had.

After the conversation switched to the new warehouse hard-ware store that had gone in ten miles up the road and had taken all the business away from the Brightwater Hardware Store,

Christy excused herself and wandered out to the front porch. A refreshing late-afternoon breeze wafted in from the right side of the porch, welcoming Christy to sit in the padded chaise lounge and enjoy the coolness. It was a good place to contemplate what would happen when Matthew Kingsley called.

He had never shown much interest in Christy, or in any girl, for that matter. Matthew's first love was sports, especially baseball and soccer. In second grade he brought his sports equipment to class every time it was his turn for show-and-tell. Once he gave Andrew Preston a black eye when Matthew tried to throw Andrew out at third base during recess. Everyone felt sorry for Andrew except Christy. She saw how apologetic Matthew was and how his eyes teared up. That's when Christy decided she was in puppy love with Matthew Kingsley.

Unfortunately, Matthew had apparently never experienced such a deciding moment with Christy. He always acted as if she was just one of the girls. And not a very interesting one because Christy wasn't athletically inclined. Jennifer Morrisey was the sports queen, and all the guys chose Jennifer to be on their team. Christy was never the first pick for any sporting event.

So why in the world would Matthew Kingsley have called her grandmother and asked about Christy? Before she could come up with possible reasons, she heard a car pull into the driveway. Leaning forward, Christy saw a white pickup truck stop behind their rental car. She knew her wealthy uncle Bob and aunt Marti wouldn't be arriving in a pickup truck. Besides, they were staying at a motel in town.

Stretching her neck to see through the screen door's mesh, Christy caught sight of the visitor making his way toward her with long strides. What she saw made her hold her breath.

Chapter 4

"Matthew Kingsley," Christy whispered. The timid side of her personality urged her to jump up and run into the house to hide. Another part of her felt flattered that Matthew had come to see her.

She hadn't looked in a mirror since early this morning, so she had no idea how she looked, but she knew it couldn't be her best. On impulse she stood up before Matthew reached the screen door and quickly ran her fingers through her hair, flipping it back over her shoulder. Her heart pounded as she swallowed and reached for the handle before Matthew had a chance to knock. With a cautious pull, she opened the door to greet Matthew with an embarrassed smile.

"Hi," she said.

"Hi, yourself," Matthew said, obviously startled. His light brown hair was short and much thicker than it had been in grade school. He probably shaved every day now. For the first time in their lives, he was now taller than she was. In every way, little Matthew Kingsley had grown up.

Matthew seemed to be taking a casual visual survey of Christy. They both looked each other in the eye, and Christy laughed nervously.

"Hi," she said again.

"Hi, yourself," Matthew said again. His eyebrows were thicker than they had been when he was a kid. But his warm brown eyes were as tender as they had been the day he gave Andrew Preston the black eye.

"I heard you were coming," he said.

"Yes," Christy said awkwardly. "I'm here."

"You're here," Matthew said, nodding. He was still standing on the top step, and Christy was holding open the screen door.

"Do you want to come in?" Christy asked. "I'm probably letting in all the mosquitoes."

"They haven't been bad yet this year," Matthew said. "It hasn't been real hot."

"Oh," Christy said, nodding. She thought it comical that they were discussing the weather. She repeated her question. "Would you like to come in?"

"Oh, sure. Okay." Matthew stepped into the porch and stood there, just inside the door.

Christy smiled and tried to remind herself that she was nearly eighteen years old. She had experienced a few dating relationships. She should know how to act around a guy without being so self-conscious. But this wasn't any guy. This was Matthew Kingsley.

"How's California?" Matthew asked after a pause.

"Good. I like it there."

"It's probably a lot better than here," Matthew said.

"No, it's nice, but it's nice here, too. I mean, every place has good points and bad points. Sometimes I wish I still lived here so I could see my grandparents more and just be around all this familiar stuff. It's comforting, you know?"

Matthew gave her a look of disbelief. "Comforting?"

Christy felt her cheeks turn red. "I'm just saying I like it here, too, and I'm glad we could come visit."

"Do you want to go do something with me?" Matthew asked.

Christy waited for a little more information, expressing with her eyes that she wanted Matthew to expand his question before she answered.

"I thought we could drive around and get something to eat," Matthew said.

"I'll have to ask my parents."

"Okay."

"Okay," Christy said. This was all too bizarre. For seven long years—from third grade to ninth grade—she had waited for Matthew Kingsley to even look in her direction, let alone speak to her privately. Now he was standing a few feet away, ever so casually asking her if she wanted to "go do something." Catching herself staring at Matthew, Christy looked away and said, "Okay, I'll go ask them." She turned to open the door to the house and then stopped to say, "Would you like to come in?"

"Okay. Sure." Matthew casually stepped forward and followed Christy into the kitchen.

"Mom, Dad, do you remember Matthew Kingsley?" Christy said.

Dad rose from his chair and held out his hand to shake with Matthew. "How are your parents doing?"

"Fine, sir," Matthew said. "They're the same as always. I guess my mom has been making plans with you, Mrs. Miller, about the Fourth of July at the Dells."

"Yes, we thought we would meet there for a picnic like we used to when you kids were young."

This was the first time Christy had heard about the picnic plans. Why didn't anyone ever tell her anything? She could have at least had a little more time to prepare herself for all these encounters with Matthew.

"It's nothing like it used to be at the Dells," Grandpa piped up. "All commercialized now. You kids have no idea what it used to be like to take a canoe out on those waters and peacefully view the sandstone cliffs. Used to be a person felt he was exploring one of the wonders of the world, before all the tour boats started to clog up the waterways. That's the only way to explore the Dells, you know—by canoe. That's how the Indians did it. I can't rightly stand to see all the money-making businesses that have spoiled the place."

Grandma reached over and patted Grandpa on the arm as a signal for him to stop the tirade. "Plenty of places on the Wisconsin River and in the Wisconsin Dells area are still remote and undeveloped, dear."

"Well, it's a crying shame, that's what it is," Grandpa said. "I read in the paper just last week that over three million people come to the Dells each year. You tell me someone isn't making a pretty penny on God's natural wonder."

Grandma patted Grandpa's arm again.

"Only four places in the world where a person can see such unusual sandstone formations. Did you know that?"

"It's good to see you," Mom said to Matthew, taking the focus off of Grandpa.

"Switzerland is one," Grandpa said. "And New York and here. And Germany, too. I'll bet you they don't have any blasted helicopter tours in Switzerland. Or in Germany, either."

Grandma shot a stern look at Grandpa. He shook his head, still disgusted, but he kept quiet.

Dad sat back down and gave Matthew a wave, as if he were dismissing him. "Tell your folks hi, and we'll see them on the Fourth."

Matthew shot a look of "help" to Christy.

"Matthew and I were wondering if we could go do something," Christy said.

"Oh?" Mom said.

"What kind of plans did you have in mind?" Christy's dad asked.

"Nothing big," Matthew said, addressing Christy's dad with his shoulders back a little farther than they had been when Christy and Matthew entered the kitchen. "I thought we'd drive around and maybe get something to eat.''

Christy's dad looked at her mom. Mom smiled and nodded her approval.

Grandma stepped in before Grandpa had a chance to lecture them on how courting was handled in his day. "If you two want to go to the movies, I think it's still half price at the Bijou. But you have to arrive before six o'clock. Or maybe it's seven o'clock. You haven't much time if it's six o'clock, but you're welcome to call from here, if you'd like."

"That's okay," Christy said. The last thing she wanted was for her parents and grandparents to give their input on which movie they should see when all they wanted to do was hang out. If they didn't hurry up and get out of there, Uncle Bob and Aunt Marti might show up, and then Christy and Matthew would have even more input about what they should do.

"You two just go and have a good time," Mom said. Then, patting Dad on the arm the same way Grandma had patted Grandpa, Mom asked, "What time would you like her back here, Norm?"

"Ten o'clock," he said, trying to sound gruff.

"Okay," Christy said. "Ten o'clock."

"Or ten-thirty," Dad said with a softer edge to his voice. "Call us if you have any problems."

"Okay," Christy said. "Let me grab a sweat shirt, Matthew. I'll meet you out front." She left Matthew alone with the parental units while she went to freshen up.

Her hair had gone straight in the humidity. It would have helped if she had washed her hair that morning, but she hadn't had time. The tiny bit of mascara she had brushed on her eyelashes earlier was long gone. Her teeth needed a scrubbing, but since she hadn't unpacked yet, she borrowed some toothpaste and used her finger.

Grabbing her backpack and checking to make sure her sweat shirt and wallet were in it, Christy called out a good-bye to her parents and stepped lightheartedly out the front door, through the screened-in porch, and down the three steps lined with Grandpa's safety tape.

Perhaps some things, like Grandma's house and her dad's inquisitions, would never change. But Christy smiled at the unknown possibilities of the evening as she made her way down the driveway.

Chapter 5

"Sorry about all the questions in there from my parents," Christy said as she settled into the passenger's seat in Matthew's truck. "I hope it didn't bother you too much."

"No," Matthew said. "My parents are the same way, especially with my sisters. Sara turned fifteen last month, and they still won't let her go out even though she tells them she's the only girl in the whole school who's not allowed to date."

Matthew backed the truck out of the driveway and said, "You hungry? I thought maybe we would go by the Dairy Queen first."

Christy didn't answer right away. She was hungry, all right, but her old best friend, Paula, used to work at Dairy Queen. Christy didn't know if Paula still worked there. As a matter of fact, Christy had no idea what was going on in Paula's life since neither of them had kept track of the other during the past year or so. Several times she had thought about calling Paula to let her know about the trip to Brightwater, but Christy never quite made it to the phone.

"Or we can do something else," Matthew said when Christy didn't answer him.

"No, Dairy Queen is fine. I was just thinking." Christy

knew if she walked into Dairy Queen and Paula was working, she would be mad Christy hadn't called. The problem was, Brightwater was a small town. Paula would find out eventually that Christy was here—Paula might know already. After all, Matthew knew Christy was coming.

"You sure it's okay?" Matthew kept looking over at her as he drove.

"Sure," Christy said quickly. "I just feel a little strange being here and seeing all these places and people I haven't seen for so long."

Matthew smiled. He had a crooked tooth on the top right side. It wasn't noticeable when he spoke, only when he smiled. Christy hadn't remembered that about him. But in junior high she had rarely gotten this close to Matthew and certainly not this close when he smiled.

"Was it strange for you to see me?" Matthew asked, still smiling.

"Yes," Christy said. She was trying to adjust to this manly version of Matthew Kingsley. He was good-looking in a rugged, northern woodsman sort of way. She hadn't remembered his voice being this deep in ninth grade. Yes, Matthew Kingsley had turned out nicely. Did he think the same about her?

Matthew pulled into the parking lot at Dairy Queen and turned off the engine. He opened his door and got out.

Christy opened her door and found Matthew waiting for her at the back of the truck. She couldn't help but compare Matthew to Doug, the guy she had been spending time with lately. Doug also drove a truck, although it was a newer model. He often opened the door for Christy and sometimes even offered her his hand to help her out. Doug was a nice guy.

Christy hadn't experienced any twinges of romantic feelings toward Doug, but she knew she needed to be patient with herself. She had liked Todd for a long time.

And you liked Matthew for even longer. Christy grabbed her backpack and brushed the subconscious thought away. Right now she didn't need to think about Todd, Doug, or even Matthew. She needed to be ready to face Paula.

As soon as they entered the air-conditioned fast-food restaurant, Christy scanned the employees. When she didn't see Paula, she breathed a little easier.

She and Matthew ordered hamburgers, and Christy asked for a small frosty cone in a cup. As they sat at a corner booth, Christy was flooded once again with memories of all the times she had come here with her family when she was a kid.

"I can't believe I'm here," she said. "This is really strange for me. In some ways, nothing has changed."

"I've changed," Matthew said, giving Christy an engaging smile.

"Yes," she agreed, "you have."

"And you've changed," Matthew said.

"Yes, I have," Christy agreed again.

"I heard from Melissa that you became a strong Christian," Matthew said.

Christy was surprised. What he said was true, but why would Melissa have told him? Then she remembered that Melissa was a close friend of Paula's. Christy had shared with Paula about surrendering her life to Christ after Christy had moved to California. Paula apparently had told Melissa.

"When I lived here," Christy explained, leaning in and feeling a little funny talking about this with Matthew Kingsley, of all people, and in Dairy Queen, of all places, "you know how our families all went to the same church?"

Matthew nodded.

"Well, after meeting some friends in California who were really open about being committed to the Lord, I realized that being a Christian was a lot more than just going to church. I wanted a deeper commitment, too. I wanted God to be the center of my life and not just off to the side."

Matthew smiled. "I know what you're saying. I went to a

church camp with my cousins last summer, and I made a commitment to Christ, too."

"You did?" Christy smiled. "That's great, Matthew!"

"It is, but it's kind of hard because not very many people our age around here are really into God and studying the Bible and everything. A few of us started a Christian club at school this year, but we were definitely a small group."

"The group I hang out with is small, too," Christy said. "My friend Doug calls us the 'God Lovers.' "

"I know. I heard about the group from Paula."

As soon as he mentioned Paula's name, Christy knew she had to ask. "Do you see Paula much? Is she around this summer?"

"No, she went to Chicago. She has a friend who lives there. I think she found a job and is taking some classes in summer school."

Christy felt relieved. It wasn't that she didn't want to see Paula, but the last time they had tried to spend time together, it hadn't gone so well. That was two summers ago, when Paula had come to California to visit Christy for a few weeks. They had ended up traveling to Maui with Christy's wealthy aunt Marti. By the end of the trip, they were still friends, but the two weeks had been full of misunderstandings and disagreements.

"You and Paula used to be together all the time," Matthew said. "I remember that one year for the harvest party you dressed like identical twins and everyone kept asking if the two of you knew you had on the same outfit."

The memory brought a smile to Christy's lips. "Everyone thought we hadn't checked with each other ahead of time, and we had ended up in the same outfit by accident."

Christy pushed aside the last few bites of her ice cream cup and folded her arms on the table. *Should I tell Matthew what I'm really feeling?* She decided she didn't have much to lose. She had known Matthew practically her whole life. They had both grown up with Paula. Matthew had just told Christy about his decision to turn his life over to Christ. Maybe she should trust him and open up the way she used to open up to Todd.

"Paula and I haven't kept in touch much these past few years," Christy said. "We seem to have gone down two different paths."

Matthew nodded. "Paula was pretty upset when you moved to California. She said you didn't need any of us anymore because you had found God and a surfer boyfriend."

Why does Matthew know all this? Did Paula go around talking about me all the time? What else did she tell Matthew and the rest of the school? Christy squirmed uncomfortably. She had thought about Matthew maybe half a dozen times in the past few years, yet he had a full rundown on her life.

"What's your boyfriend's name? Todd?"

With a tightness in her throat, Christy answered, "Yes, Todd. But we're not together anymore."

Matthew looked surprised. "According to Paula, you should be engaged by now. Or maybe it was Melissa who said you were probably going to get married as soon as you graduated from high school."

Christy shook her head. "Todd had an opportunity to go on a long-term missions assignment, which is something he had wanted to do for a long time. He's overseas somewhere."

"You don't know where he is?"

"No. When we broke up, I knew he needed to be able to go without any strings attached. If you had ever met Todd, you would understand. He needed to just go and not look back or feel connected to me or to anything else at home."

"Wow," Matthew said, leaning back in the booth and resting his arm across the top. "That must have been pretty hard to do."

"It was," Christy said in a low voice, looking down. She picked up the spoon in her cup and stirred the melted vanilla ice cream. After a moment, Christy looked up and forced a smile. "So if you see Paula before I do, you can give her the update for me. Or you can tell Melissa, and she can tell Paula."

Matthew looked over the top of Christy's head and waved at someone who apparently had just walked in the door. "Why don't you tell her yourself?" he said. "Melissa just walked in."

Chapter 6

"I thought that was your truck. What are you doing here?" Melissa asked Matthew.

"Entertaining company," Matthew said.

Slowly, Christy turned to face Melissa and smiled at the girl who had taken her place as Paula's best friend after Christy had moved. "Hi," Christy said.

Melissa stared at Christy with her mouth open. "Christy Miller? What are you doing here?" Melissa had on a Dairy Queen uniform and wore her dark hair pulled up in a clip. She was short and thin. Christy noticed the row of earrings Melissa wore in each ear and the three silver necklaces around her neck.

"My family flew in this afternoon for my grandparents' fiftieth wedding anniversary party. It's tomorrow night. We're going home Sunday."

"Oh," Melissa said, still scrutinizing Christy. She looked at Matthew and then back at Christy. "What are you guys doing?"

Christy could tell that Melissa liked Matthew. Christy couldn't explain how she knew, she just knew. Obviously, Melissa felt Christy was invading her space. Maybe Melissa thought Christy was trying to take Matthew away from her.

"Matthew was just taking me around town," Christy said.

"Matthew?" Melissa repeated with a mocking tone. "You call him Matthew?"

Christy realized she always had thought of him as Matthew Kingsley, as if they were back in grade school and they had to make the distinction between Matthew Kingsley and Matt Flandenberg.

"Everybody calls me Matt now. Flandenberg moved a couple of years ago." Matt was smiling at Christy. He didn't seem to be paying much attention to Melissa.

"I get off here at nine-thirty," Melissa said. "Do you want to do something afterward?"

Christy didn't think Melissa was asking her, but Matt acted as if the invitation had been extended to both of them. "Can't," Matt said. "We both have to be home by ten. Ten-thirty at the latest."

"What about tomorrow?" Melissa said. She looked back and forth from Matt to Christy. Christy couldn't tell if Melissa really was trying to make plans with Matt, or if she was more interested in finding out what plans Matt had with Christy.

"I work tomorrow," Matt said.

"I know you do. But what about tomorrow night?"

"I'm helping at the church," he said, smiling at Christy again. "I told my mom I'd help clean up after the anniversary party for Christy's grandparents."

"Okay," Melissa said. "Whatever."

For some reason, Christy felt as if she needed to apologize. "Sorry, Melissa. I'm not trying to take all of Matt's free time."

Melissa gave her a strange look. "Don't worry about it, Christy. It's a free country." The tone in her voice sounded exactly like Paula's when she was really mad. "You can do whatever you want. I hope you and *Matthew* have a great weekend together."

With that, Melissa turned and took her place behind the food counter, leaving Matt and Christy alone. Matt didn't say anything at first, so Christy stepped in. "Are you guys going out?"

"Melissa and me?"

"Yes, Melissa and you." Christy wondered if she had been too bold.

Matt hesitated a moment, then he rose and motioned for Christy to get her backpack. "Come on. Let's go for a drive."

Once they were in the truck and out of the parking lot, Matt asked, "How much do you want to know?"

"How much do you want to tell me?" Then Christy added, "It seems you've kept up with my love life pretty well these past few years. I think it's only fair that you bring me up to the present with yours."

"Oh, you do, do you?" Matt seemed humored by her comment.

Christy rolled down the window and stuck out her arm. She liked this feeling of driving around with Matt and having him be the one on the spot. It was nice not always being the embarrassed one, like she was earlier today with the Todd look-alike at the airport.

As soon as she thought that, Christy felt compassion for Matt. It wasn't fun being the one on the spot. It wasn't fun being embarrassed, either.

"I take that all back," Christy said. She reached over and gave Matt a comforting pat on the shoulder. *Oh no! I hope I'm not patting Matt the way my grandmother pats my grandfather!* "You don't have to tell me anything," Christy said, pulling back her hand. "I hope I didn't make you feel uncomfortable."

"It's okay," Matt said. He kept quiet as he drove.

Christy had a nervous feeling that she had squelched the budding relationship Matt had initiated by coming over to see her. She decided that quick and snappy comments didn't fit her personality.

Matt kept quiet another block. Then he pulled up in front of George Washington Elementary School. He parked the truck and turned to Christy with a hopeful grin.

Looking out the window at the familiar brick building, Christy asked, "What are we doing here?"

"I thought you might like to take a walk through your past. You know, remember where you came from."

Christy gave him a puzzled look.

Matt reached for his baseball cap on the seat and put it on as he opened the door. "When I heard you were coming, I tried to think of what I'd want to do if I were you and I'd been gone so long. This is the best I could come up with."

Christy smiled broadly and joined Matt as they walked up to the front of the school, now closed for the summer. "This is so sweet of you, Matt. Thank you."

"Tell my mom that, will you? She said I was being sappy."

"Sappy?"

Matt nodded.

"I'll tell her I like sappy. I like being here." Then, before Christy could think about what she was saying, she added, "I like seeing you again."

Chapter 7

Matt didn't seem to take Christy's comment as anything more than friendly encouragement. At least he didn't act as if she had just opened some previously closed door in their relationship.

The two of them walked through the silent corridor of their elementary school campus, and Christy said three times in a row, "It's so much smaller than I remember."

And three times in a row Matt answered, "You were smaller."

"Do you remember Mrs. Elmadore, and the way she used to tuck a handkerchief up the sleeve of her blouse? I thought she was trying to perform some kind of magic trick every time she pulled it out to blow her nose." Christy peered into the window of their fourth-grade classroom.

Matt stood beside her, peering inside, too. "She used to write our names on the board in those big, flowery letters whenever we got in trouble."

"I wouldn't know," Christy said, playfully flipping her hair over her shoulder. "I never got in trouble in Mrs. Elmadore's class."

"Right, but you were always in trouble in sixth-grade band,"

Matt reminded her. "Why was Mr. Beaman always yelling at you?"

Christy followed Matt to their old band room. "I don't know. He didn't like Paula, either. He probably didn't like that she and I were always talking during class. We both took clarinet so we could practice together, and we both were horrible at it. And besides that, we only practiced together once or twice that I remember. Mr. Beaman was always splitting us up in class."

"Do you remember the year when it snowed so hard we had to stay at school until they could clear the roads, and we didn't leave until midnight?" Matt asked. "What year was that?"

"That was second grade. Miss Kaltzer's class. That was scary."

"All I remember is that we ate popcorn, and she kept giving us art projects to do."

Christy laughed. "I remember the popcorn, too."

They walked to the truck, and Matt drove to their junior high as they continued to reminisce.

"I didn't like junior high very much," Christy confessed. "I was so self-conscious all the time."

"Everybody is self-conscious in junior high," Matt said. "All I remember is playing baseball in seventh grade and our city league won the play-offs."

"Do you still play baseball?"

"Every chance I get."

"Let's go to the park," Christy suggested, cutting their visit to the junior high short. "I want to see where you play ball."

Matt drove, talking all the way about his long list of sports accomplishments. Christy took it all in, recognizing the names of a lot of the other players Matt talked about. It was almost as if he were catching her up on an era of life she had missed out on when she moved. And to hear him tell it, Christy actually felt sorry she hadn't been there for some of the hometown events. The blizzards, the class picnics, the parades, and the football games all sounded so appealing. Nothing like that had been part of her high school years in Escondido.

Matt conducted a tour of the baseball field and the new soccer field before driving her to the back side of the high school. He parked the truck and challenged her to a race to the top of the bleachers that overlooked the football field. Matt won.

Christy reached the top, laughing and yelling, "No fair! You had a head start in the parking lot. And you've probably done this before, right?" She stood in front of him with her hands on her hips, trying to catch her breath.

"A time or two," Matt said, only slightly out of breath.

Christy turned to survey the football field. "I suppose you have some great stories about victories you've won on this field in the past few years."

"No," Matt said. "I spent most of my time warming the bench. We had some really good players this year. Do you remember Kevin Johnson? He won a scholarship to Michigan State."

"You're kidding. That's awesome." As soon as Christy said "awesome," she thought of Doug. "Awesome" was Doug's favorite word. Why did she feel funny thinking about him when she was with Matt? Wasn't it normal, even a good thing, to have lots of guys as friends?

If she had been alone, Christy would have sat down on the bleachers in the coolness of the early July evening in peaceful Brightwater. She would have drawn in the familiar fragrances in the air: the cut grass, the hint of a dairy farm to the south, and the faint scent of the metal bleachers cooling after baking all day in the summer sunshine.

It would have been a perfect opportunity for her to do some soul-searching and to discover why she had spent the last few years experiencing such yo-yo emotions over guys, especially Todd. She knew she didn't want to go with Doug simply because Todd was gone, but she didn't have a plan. Her responses to guys always had been based on what came to her at the moment. Christy realized she had never determined ahead of time what she wanted in her relationships.

And how did she feel about Matt? How did he feel about her? Why had he sought her out? He seemed to have bounced back from the comment she had made earlier about how he should tell her the details of his dating life since he knew hers. But he hadn't answered her question about Melissa, which led Christy to believe they had gone together in the past.

Unfortunately, that was all the soul-searching she was able to do as she stood at the top of the bleachers because she wasn't alone. Matt already was heading back to the truck, promising her one more surprise on his tour.

He drove through Brightwater, heading north until he came to Ollie's Peewee Golf, where he pulled into the parking lot and stopped the truck. With a smile he turned to Christy and said, "Does this bring back any memories?"

Christy held her hand to her forehead and lowered her head. "I've been trying to forget," she said with a laugh.

"Your birthday party," Matt prompted her.

Christy looked up and shook her head. "That was in fifth grade. My aunt Marti came for my birthday that July and insisted I invite everyone from my class so it would be my first boy-girl party. How can you still remember that?"

"Easy," Matthew said, opening his door and getting out. "That was the first time Paula told me you liked me."

Chapter 8

As soon as his declaration was made, he shut the door, leaving Christy to open her own door. Her heart pounded as she squeezed the door handle. *Now what do I say?*

Christy hesitated before joining Matt at the gate that led to the miniature golf course. He was pulling some money from his pocket and paying the girl at the front ticket booth.

"Are we actually going to play miniature golf?" Christy asked.

"Sure. Or don't you do that anymore?" He didn't appear interested in discussing his last statement about Paula. At least not now.

Christy wasn't sure what to say.

"Come on," Matt said, handing her a golf club and a bright blue golf ball. "It'll be fun."

Matt was right. Playing golf at Ollie's was fun. She sunk a hole in one at the windmill and burst out laughing, holding her club high in the air as a victory salute.

The other miniature golfers watched Christy and Matt as they broke into a pretend argument in which Matt accused her of cheating.

"There is no way I could have cheated!" Christy exclaimed.

"You saw the whole thing. I lined it up, just like you've been telling me, I hit it through the windmill, and it rolled right into the hole. You're just worried because I might catch up with your score."

"I've never seen anyone get a hole in one on the windmill," Matt said. "And I'm not worried about your catching up. You would have to score a hole in one on the remaining five for that to happen."

"Oh yeah?" Christy said playfully, pushing up her sweat shirt's sleeves. "Then watch me."

Matt followed her to the next green, where she put down her blue ball and carefully lined herself up with the zigzag obstacle course. She took extra time evaluating the direction her ball would most likely go.

"Anytime now," Matt said.

Christy turned and glared at him. "Do you mind? I'm concentrating."

Matt held up his hands and took two steps back, giving Christy her space and silence. With great flare she whacked her ball. It flew over the obstacles, past the hole, and onto the cement sidewalk that lined the course. She slowly turned to see Matt's reaction. He had his hand over his mouth, but his brown eyes were laughing at her.

"Okay, okay," she said. "That might have been a little too hard. I think I should get to do it over."

"Nope," Matt said, stepping up to the green. "You have to play the ball where it lands."

"Oh, come on! This is peewee golf! Have you no mercy?"

"Not much. Would you mind stepping aside?"

Christy went after her ball, hoping she hadn't had an audience for that last hit the way she had at the windmill. Glancing around, she noticed that she and Matt were the only high school, college-age students there. Aside from a few parents playing with younger children, the crowd was mostly grade school kids.

She smiled, remembering her eleventh birthday and how Aunt Marti had tried, with little success, to organize all twenty-three kids who showed up. Christy remembered clearly the moment Paula came up to Christy by the volcano on the fourth hole and whispered in her ear, "I told Matthew Kingsley that you like him and you want him to give you a birthday kiss."

Christy remembered feeling paralyzed by Paula's announcement yet thrilled enough to catch her breath and ask, "And what did he say?"

Paula's response had been, "He's such a brat. He said he would rather kiss a toad."

Christy could remember feeling as if a grenade had landed in a previously undisturbed corner of her heart, the corner where she hid her secret wishes and dreams. That corner was secluded, hidden from view so she could go deep within herself when she wanted to be alone. If she lingered there a moment or an hour, she always emerged with her lips turned up and her cheeks rosy with hope.

That fateful July 27, seven years ago, was the first time someone had broken through the wall of that secluded corner and destroyed one of her private dreams. And to think that someone had been Matthew Kingsley, with his merciless I'd-rather-kiss-a-toad statement.

Christy returned to the green with a scowl on her face and a strong feeling that she wanted to punch Matt in the stomach and see how he liked it. She played the last four holes with him quietly, smiling politely when he did a little dance at the last hole to celebrate his overwhelming victory. But inside she was simmering. Why couldn't boys be taught to be nice to girls? Why did she go on liking him all those years after he said that?

As they turned in their clubs, Matt asked if she would like to get something else to eat.

"I don't know what time it is," Christy said. "I should probably get back."

"You're right," Matt said. "It's probably close to ten."

He drove to her grandparents' home, his silence matching hers. When they pulled into the driveway, Matt asked, "Are you okay, Christy? You turned kind of quiet."

Oh, so now you're Mr. Sensitivity, and you suddenly realize that girls have feelings?

She didn't think she wanted to open up to him now, even if he might be understanding. After all, he was the reason the cloud of gloom had come over her—or rather, a much younger version of Matt was the one responsible for her problem. How fair was it to blame this Matt for that Matthew?

"I don't know," Christy finally said. "I have to think about a lot of stuff from the past and . . ." She didn't know how to finish her thought.

Matt looked concerned. "Was it too much? Did I overdo the whole journey into the past?"

"No, it wasn't you. I mean, it wasn't that. It was . . ." Drawing in a breath, she decided to be honest. "It was at the peewee golf place. I was thinking back to my birthday party and when Paula told me that you said you would rather kiss a toad than kiss me."

Matt looked shocked. The windows of his truck were open, and in the awkward silence all they heard was the loud symphony of night crickets.

"I was ten," Matt said weakly in his defense. "Eleven, maybe."

"I know," Christy said.

"Are you still holding that against me?"

Christy looked down at her hands in her lap and felt foolish for bringing it up. "No, I guess not."

"If it helps at all," Matt said, reaching over and placing his hand on Christy's shoulder, "I would never say that now. I'd rather kiss you than a frog any day."

Christy felt her heart start to pound. *I wasn't hinting that I wanted him to kiss me! Or was I? Oh no! I can guess what he's think-*

ing. Should I pull away? Run inside? I don't want to kiss him . . . or do I?

Matt gave her shoulder a little squeeze. He appeared as nervous at this moment as Christy felt. They both sat there, neither making the next move.

Chapter 9

Before Christy or Matt had a chance to say anything more, the porch's screen door squeaked open and then slammed shut. Matt pulled away his hand from Christy's shoulder, and they both looked through the windshield to see Christy's uncle coming toward them.

"My aunt and uncle are here," Christy said.

"I better let you go," Matt said. "I'll be at the reception for your grandparents tomorrow. My parents are going early, I think. I'm coming after work so I'll probably be late."

"That's okay," Christy said, glancing at Matt and then at her uncle, who was headed for his rental car. She turned back to Matt, and with a more relaxed smile she said, "I really had a fun time, Matt. Thanks so much. I'm glad you're coming tomorrow. I'll see you then."

"Okay," Matt said.

Christy couldn't tell if he looked nervous or relieved that she was getting out of the truck. She waved as he started up the engine, and she called out, "Thanks again!"

"How's my favorite girl?" Uncle Bob asked, walking toward Christy with a smile.

"Good! How are you guys? How was your flight?"

"Not the best. A little bumpy coming into O'Hare. Marti has a headache so I'm getting her travel bag." Motioning over his shoulder in the direction Matt's truck had just turned, Uncle Bob added, "I hope I didn't cut into anything important for you."

Christy avoided the question. "That was Matt Kingsley. His mom is good friends with my mom."

"Sure," Bob said, reaching in the backseat of the luxury rental car and pulling out Aunt Marti's small suitcase. "Jane Kingsley. I've met her. Nice folks."

Bob had a casual, easygoing manner that Christy appreciated. He and Marti lived in a beautiful house at Newport Beach and had welcomed Christy and her family to California with open arms. Standing here in the heart of Wisconsin, wearing his knit polo shirt and khaki slacks, Uncle Bob seemed out of place to Christy. She could guess this visit was less than comfortable for Aunt Marti, who liked things always to go her way. She came off as sophisticated and stylish, and she didn't like people knowing that she came from such a small Midwestern community.

Christy's hunch about Marti was right, she discovered, when she entered the house with Bob and found Marti at the kitchen table, holding a cold cloth on her forehead.

"Oh, Christy dear," she cooed. "You will forgive me if I don't get up. I'm afraid I have one of my migraines."

"I didn't know you got migraines," Christy said. Her mother gave her a look that communicated to Christy, "Don't get her started."

"Did you have a good time?" Mom asked.

"You'll never guess what we did," Christy said, pulling off her sweat shirt and leaning against the kitchen counter. "Matt took me on a little tour of my past. We visited the Dairy Queen and all the schools, and then we went miniature golfing at Ollie's Peewee Golf."

"No fair," David moaned. "I wanted to go."

Christy ignored his comment and turned to Aunt Marti. "Do you remember my eleventh birthday when you came here and the party was at Ollie's?"

"Oh yes," Marti said without looking up. "That beautiful, big birthday cake I ordered nearly melted, it was so hot."

Christy didn't remember a thing about the birthday cake melting.

"Perhaps we should go to the hotel, Robert. I'll be better once I get some sleep. And I'm sure the air conditioning will help, as well."

"Did you want to take one of these before we go?" Bob asked, handing Marti a bottle of pills.

"Would you like a glass of water?" Christy asked. She was standing by the sink and thought it was the least she could do for her aunt.

"Oh yes, thank you. And add some ice, will you? The humidity here is awful," Marti moaned.

Christy hadn't noticed the humidity. The climate was certainly different from that at the beach in southern California, but it wasn't uncomfortable in Christy's estimation. Besides, Marti had grown up in this house. Was it so hard for her to accept things the way they were here?

Christy dropped two ice cubes into Marti's glass and then slipped it under the shiny, new kitchen faucet. Christy lifted the handy-dandy handle Grandpa had installed and turned it to the right for cold water. Suddenly the handle came off in her hand and a spray of water shot straight up like a fountain, soaking Marti and herself.

"What did you do to it?" Grandpa kept yelling.

"Nothing!" Christy tried to keep a straight face, but she burst out laughing. "I didn't do anything!" All she could do was stand there, using her hands as a shield from the jubilant spray of water.

"Turn off the water underneath," Dad barked.

"I'll get my tools," Grandpa shouted above all the yelling

and laughing. Marti was the one doing the yelling. Or perhaps shrieking was more like it. Christy was certain that if her aunt didn't truly have a migraine before, she certainly had one now.

Christy moved aside and took the hand towel Grandma offered her. The broken handle was still in her hand. "Honest," Christy said, looking to her mom for support. "All I did was turn the handle, and it came off."

Grandpa appeared with some tools, which he handed to Dad, who was now on his back on the floor with his head under the sink.

As quickly as it had begun, the shooting water show was over, and all was quiet. Christy looked at her grandfather sheepishly and held out the broken handle. "Honest," she said, "all I did was—"

"I know, I know," Grandpa said. "I'll fix it." He mumbled something about how they don't make hardware like they used to and wiped his wet face with his sleeve.

Christy turned to apologize to Aunt Marti, who was sopping wet. Christy's mom and grandma were still chuckling softly at the mishap as they handed Marti dish towels and tried to comfort her. Marti, however, would not be consoled.

"I'm so sorry, Aunt Marti."

"It was an accident!" Marti kept shrieking, as if she were trying to convince herself more than excuse Christy. Marti rose from the table with her husband's assistance, and the two of them left for their hotel.

Chapter 10

"You and David should get to bed, too," Mom said. "You're both upstairs in the bedroom on the left."

Christy hid her disappointment. She had hoped she could be by herself wherever she ended up sleeping tonight. She had a lot of thinking to do and wanted to have a few things settled within herself before she saw Matt again the next day.

Once they were in their room, David convinced Christy to play a game of Monopoly with him. She wasn't sure why she agreed. It could have been because she went miniature golfing and he didn't. Or because, as the oldest, Christy often was allowed to go more places and do more things than David, and she was taking pity on him and realizing this was his vacation, too.

Whatever the reason, they set up the old, well-worn board on her bed and began to divide up the crumpled play money. They kept their voices low and used a big flashlight David had found in the top dresser drawer instead of turning on the light. Neither of them felt tired. They argued only a little and played until after one in the morning. In the end David won, which made him gloat as if he were king of the world.

Christy fell asleep with a grin, realizing she and her brother had just spent several hours together, and they both had had fun. That happened so rarely Christy couldn't help but feel as if she deserved a pat on the back for being such a terrific big sister.

However, when Grandpa knocked on their door at six-thirty in the morning, calling them to breakfast, Christy felt she deserved a thump on the head instead of a pat on the back. Why did she think staying up half the night was such a good idea?

Dragging themselves out of bed, Christy and David went downstairs in their pajamas and sat down to Grandma's pancakes and warm maple syrup.

"Don't you two look like something the cat dragged in!" Grandpa exclaimed.

David and Christy looked at each other and exchanged subtle nods and knowing grins. They shared a secret. It wasn't a rich enough reward to make up for the lack of sleep, but it was fun.

"Maybe you two should go back to bed," Mom suggested. "I didn't think the time change would be this hard for you to adjust to."

"Would it be okay if we slept for another hour or so?" Christy asked.

"Fine with me," Grandma said. "Eat first, if you like. It will give you a nice full stomach to dream on."

"I'll wake you at nine-thirty," Mom said. "Do you think half an hour is enough time to get dressed? I'd like both of you to help at the church. I'm meeting Jane there to decorate the fellowship hall at ten o'clock."

"Sure," Christy said, pushing away her half-eaten stack of pancakes. "Wake me at nine-thirty. And, Grandma, these are great, but I'm full. Can you save them for later?"

"Certainly, dear. Sweet dreams!"

Christy shuffled back upstairs with David not far behind her. She dropped right off to sleep and felt much better when Mom came in and woke her at nine-thirty. David was already up. It turned out he wasn't able to fall back asleep so he had dressed and joined Grandpa in the garage, which is where Christy and her mom found them at ten. Dad was with them, and they were all working on some kind of contraption Grandpa had spread out across his worktable.

"We're ready to go," Mom said.

"Christina, are you going out with your hair dripping wet like that?" Grandpa asked.

"It'll dry on the way," Christy told him. She had taken a long shower and didn't want to hold up everyone else while she dried her hair. "It's a hot day." Christy noticed how true her statement was. It was hotter now than she remembered it being all afternoon and evening the day before. She wondered how Marti would deal with the heat.

When they arrived at the church and entered the fellowship hall, Christy noticed that Marti wasn't there to help. Christy decided it would be better not to ask why.

Mrs. Kingsley greeted them with hugs, and with a twinkle in her eye she said, "Matt had such a nice time with you, Christy. He said you were a real good sport about the journey to all your old schools."

"I liked it," Christy said. "It was a lot of fun. I thought he was very creative to think of it and go out of his way like that." Christy was surprised to find that she had a sweet, warm feeling inside when she talked about Matt and that she was looking forward to seeing him that evening.

"Did he tell you about his big decision?" Mrs. Kingsley asked.

"Yes, he told me how he became a Christian last summer. I was really happy to hear that."

Mrs. Kingsley looked surprised. "I meant his decision about which college to attend. He's been offered two scholarships."

"Oh," Christy said. "No, he didn't tell me."

"That boy," Mrs. Kingsley said, putting her hand on her hip. She turned to Christy's mom and said, "One of the offers is from a college in southern California. Rancho Corona. Have you heard of it?"

Mom shook her head. "Where is it?"

"I'm not exactly sure. Matt knows."

"It's not far from Lake Elsinore," Christy said. "I have some friends who are thinking about going there. I haven't been there, but I hear it's a good school."

"The other scholarship is for a college in South Carolina. Or is it North Carolina?" Mrs. Kingsley said. "Anyway, he needs to decide quickly. I thought he was meeting with you, Christy, so he could ask if you had any friends at Rancho Corona and to see if you had any information about it. He received the notices a week ago, and we've been so busy we haven't been able to spend much time researching either school."

Christy's imagination was running ahead of her. Rancho Corona was less than an hour from Escondido, where she lived. She started to imagine what it would be like if Matthew Kingsley came to California in the fall and went to college less than an hour away.

"I'll be sure to tell him what I know about the school when I see him tonight," Christy said.

"Good," Mrs. Kingsley said. "Now, let's put up these decorations. I have to pick up the flowers, but I thought I'd wait until a little later so they would stay fresh. It's going to be a hot one today. I asked that they bring all the church fans into the fellowship hall for us, but as you can see, we only have two. When I run out for the flowers later, I'll stop by home and get our box fans."

For the next three hours, Christy worked alongside her mom stringing crepe paper streamers while Dad and David set up all nineteen round tables. Then they all worked at covering the tables with white tablecloths. Mrs. Kingsley returned with the fans and a carful of flowers. Each table was supposed to have a fresh flower centerpiece, which Christy and Mom assembled on the stage in front of one of the fans. Dad and David went to find the rest of the chairs in various other rooms.

"I had no idea there would be so much to do," Christy said. "I hope we finish in time."

"We should be okay," Mom said. "I'm a little concerned about how hot it will be in here when the reception begins at five."

"Would it be okay if I went to the church kitchen and found us something to drink?" Christy asked.

"That would be wonderful," Mrs. Kingsley said. "And if a pitcher of iced tea isn't already made up in the refrigerator, you go ahead and make one. Help yourself to whatever you find in there."

Christy knew the church's layout by heart. The original church building was nearly one hundred years old, but the kitchen and fellowship hall had been added in the last thirty years. Unfortunately, no one had seen the value of including air conditioning when they built the addition. Or else air conditioning seemed like a luxury thirty years ago.

Christy found six women in the kitchen and one man. They were all older, like her grandparents, and they were working like busy bees. The women wore church aprons, which Christy recognized. She was sure those were the same aprons worn by every person who ever helped in that kitchen from the day she was born.

"Hello," one of the women said, pulling a large cake pan from the oven. The yellow cake was just a tad too brown on top. The kitchen was very hot, and Christy noticed four fans were going, which accounted for the fans Mrs. Kingsley thought were missing.

"Hi," Christy said back. All of them turned to look at her. Some smiled, some seemed to scowl. Christy recognized nearly all of them as old-time, faithful churchgoers and her grandparents' friends.

One of the women recognized her and said, "Why, Christina Miller, how wonderful to see you! Look at you . . . so grown-up!"

The woman was Mrs. Abbott. She had been Christy's Sunday school teacher in fourth grade. A chorus of welcomes and exclamations followed along with lots of hugs. By the time Christy explained the purpose of her mission to the kitchen, her cheeks were smeared with lipstick and perspiration. The kitchen help offered Christy a pitcher of iced tea along with a stack of red plastic cups.

She thanked the group of cooks and left, glad that she was working in the fellowship hall and not in the kitchen. She couldn't help but wonder if more lipstick and perspiration would be in store for them later this evening. Perhaps she should be a nice big sister and prepare David for the onslaught, just so he didn't make a complete goof of himself when the white-haired ladies began to swarm around him.

Chapter 11

As predicted, the fellowship hall was sweltering hot at five that evening, and many sweet old people swarmed to hug and kiss Christy and David. She had warned her little brother and was glad to see he had taken her stern words to heart, accepting the affectionate greetings with a little smile.

Aunt Marti and Uncle Bob showed up late. Uncle Bob had come by the church that afternoon and brought sandwiches while the group was arranging flowers. Bob helped Dad set up chairs before going back to the hotel. That evening Uncle Bob arrived carrying two more standing fans, which Christy guessed he had bought on the way.

Christy watched with amazement as Aunt Marti turned into the life of the party. Marti kissed every one of the perspiring old ladies and charmed all the older men, who enjoyed telling her how they "remembered her when she was in pigtails." She always had been the one to set up parties for Christy, and Aunt Marti was strict about keeping her social obligations. Christy shouldn't have been surprised at the transformation from the evening before, but she was.

Christy's mom, on the other hand, busied herself serving everyone. Each time Christy saw her, Mom had another pitcher of lemonade in her hand or was directing Dad to find another chair for someone who had gone through the buffet line and returned to his table to find his chair taken.

Christy mingled some, visiting with distant relatives and familiar people she had grown up with at church. Mostly she watched the door, waiting for Matt to arrive. Not many teenagers were in the crowd, but several kids David's age were there. David was off having a good time with them, which relieved Christy because she didn't have her little brother following her around all evening.

She had to admit she was eager to see Matt again. He had said he would be late. How late? Should she keep glancing at the door, watching for him? Or should she try not to think about him and focus on something else?

Settling in at one of the tables situated farthest away from the hub of activity, Christy decided to go on a little journey to the secret corner of her heart. She hadn't had a chance to explore all her thoughts and feelings last night. As long as she kept her plastic fork in her hand and kept taking tiny bites of the chicken, rice, and broccoli casserole on her plate, none of the older people at her table would try to strike up a conversation with her.

The first thing Christy tried to figure out was what had happened between Matt and her last night. If Uncle Bob hadn't come out to the driveway when he did, would Matt have kissed her? Would she have let him? And more important, did she want him to? What would that kiss have meant?

Christy stared at the piece of broccoli she had just skewered with her fork. What if she hadn't moved to California? Would she and Matt have ended up together? How did she feel about him now? Was it different from what she had felt in elementary school? Of course it was. But what was it? Friendship? Comradeship? Intrigue? Interest? Still a little crush? And what about Melissa?

Why didn't Matt answer my question about whether he was going out with Melissa? Would I be stepping into the middle of a relationship if I let myself become interested in Matt? And why would I let myself think about liking Matt when I've already decided it's too soon after Todd to make any decisions about Doug? How do I feel about Doug? What about Matt? Am I really over Todd?

Christy pushed the broccoli to her plate's edge. This was all too much to figure out in a stuffy fellowship hall with the taste of broccoli lingering in her mouth. This kind of thinking would be much better at the beach, with the wind kissing her face.

The beach was where she had met Todd. And from that first day, she was attracted to him. As she got to know him, Christy found something deep and spiritual about him that made him even more attractive to her.

Over the years their relationship sometimes went up, sometimes down; yet she had learned one thing would never change: Todd would always love God. And Todd challenged her to love God with all her heart, soul, strength, and mind. Even if she never saw Todd again, she knew he always would be tucked in her heart because no guy had ever made her think, feel, or grow the way Todd had.

With a sigh, Christy looked around the room. Her eyes were misting over just thinking about Todd. She blinked quickly and checked the door to see if Matt had walked in yet.

See? I'm not really thinking about Todd. I'm thinking about Matt. I'm eager to see Matt again. That must mean something. If I didn't care about Matt, I wouldn't be eager to see him, would I?

Glancing at her grandparents, who were positioned beneath a banner that declared *50 Years*, Christy wondered how anyone in today's world could stay with the same person for fifty years unless they made a firm commitment and kept all their promises to remain faithful to that commitment.

Christy slowly mouthed the word *commitment*, as if it were the key to this puzzle she was trying to put together. It certainly was a main ingredient in any kind of relationship that was going to stand the test of time.

Her commitment to Todd had come to an end, and she wasn't ready to make a commitment to Doug. *What if Matt ends up going to school in California? Would he want to spend time with me? I think I'd like to spend time with him. But what kind of commitment would one childhood friend expect from another? Or are we already somehow committed simply because our lives were so connected in the past?*

Before Christy could dig herself any deeper in her trench of contemplation, she felt a hand on her shoulder, and a deep voice said, "Christy?"

Christy spun around to see Uncle Bob's smiling face. "Didn't you see me waving? I thought you were looking right at me, but you didn't respond."

"I was daydreaming," Christy said quietly.

"The photographer would like for the whole family to join your grandparents for pictures."

Christy pushed back her chair and followed her uncle. She noticed that everyone else was already standing under the *50 Years* banner, and she hoped the group hadn't been watching her stare dreamily into space.

The pictures took only a few minutes, and then it was time to cut the cake. Christy stood back, smiling at the cute way Grandma posed for the camera and grinned at Grandpa. Christy thought Grandma was acting as if she were a young girl again and this were her original wedding reception.

Grandpa seemed unaffected by this historic moment in their relationship. He stood there with a steady expression on his face, his hands folded in front of him. When Grandma held up the bite of cake for him to eat, he swallowed it in two bites. Then it was his turn to feed a bite of cake to Grandma. Before he offered it to her, he leaned over and whispered something in her ear.

As Grandpa whispered to Grandma, Christy could see her grandmother's face soften into the sweetest expression of love.

With Grandma's face glowing, she whispered something back to him.

The scene brought tears to Christy's eyes, to think that her grandparents shared such sweet intimacy after all these years. Christy silently added "intimacy" next to "commitment" in her mental list of requirements for a lasting, meaningful relationship. She realized that intimacy was so much more than the physical part of a relationship. To her, intimacy meant knowing the soul of the other person and having access to that individual's secret places in the heart.

These ideas were revelations to Christy. She never had thought through any of this so clearly before and wasn't sure why it was so important that she do so now. She liked to record these kinds of thoughts so she could go back and look at them later and think them through some more. Remembering that her diary was in the bottom of her suitcase at her grandparents' house, she promised herself that before she went to bed that night, she would write down all this information. Looking at it on paper would help her to understand how she truly felt and what was going on in her life, especially with Matt.

Turning to face the entrance to the fellowship hall, as she had fifty times that night, Christy realized she might have to decide how she felt about Matt before she had a chance to write out all her feelings. Matt had just entered and was heading her direction with deliberate strides.

And Melissa was right behind him.

Chapter 12

"What have we missed?" Matt said casually, pulling up a chair next to Christy. Melissa sat down beside him and politely ignored Christy, scanning the room to see who else was there.

"Hi. What are you guys doing?" Christy heard an edge to her voice when she asked the question but hoped Matt and Melissa hadn't noticed. She suddenly felt as if the situation had changed, and she was now the one asking the same kinds of questions Melissa had asked at the Dairy Queen.

"I want to go to the movies," Melissa said. "But Matt said he had to clean up here. I thought maybe the cleanup was almost done and we could go to a late show."

Melissa wasn't excluding Christy in her plans, but she wasn't including her, either.

"Looks like the cleanup hasn't begun yet," Matt said.

"No. And there's lots to do," Christy said.

"Guess I better stay," Matt said to Melissa. "You can stick around and help, too, if you want."

Melissa hesitated only a moment before saying, "I don't think so, but thanks anyway." She looked hurt.

"Hey, don't say I didn't offer," Matt said.

Christy caught the teasing tone in his voice. She guessed

that if he really wanted to, Matt could have gone to the movies and gotten out of his commitment to clean up. Christy liked to believe he was sticking around so he could be with her instead of with Melissa.

"I suppose you have big plans already for tomorrow, too," Melissa said to Matt while casting a quick glance at Christy.

"We're going to the Dells," Matt said.

Christy noticed that he didn't explain both families were going. It sounded as if just Matt and Christy had made plans to go to the Dells.

"I'm not doing anything," Melissa said with a sigh. "Ever since Paula left, I've been trying to find somebody to do stuff with, but everybody always has plans that don't include me."

Christy couldn't decide if she felt sorry for Melissa. Christy certainly knew what it was like to lose a best friend, and oddly enough, she and Melissa had both lost the same best friend.

Rather slowly Christy said, "Do you want to come tomorrow, Melissa?"

Melissa gave Christy a startled look. "Are you sure?" Melissa turned to Matt.

Matt nodded. "Sure. You're welcome to come. It's just a big family picnic like we do every year."

"What time?" Melissa asked casually.

"Around ten."

"Okay."

Christy didn't know if she should be pleased with herself for being kind and generous or mad at herself for including Melissa in her last day with Matt.

"I guess I'll see you tomorrow," Melissa said, rising to go.

Christy and Matt both said good-bye, then sat in silence for a few minutes. Christy wondered if Matt was upset that she had invited Melissa. It was hard to know since he hadn't volunteered any information on how he felt about either Melissa or Christy. Perhaps the interest Christy felt toward him was as one-sided as it always had been.

"It sure was hot today, wasn't it?" Matt finally said.

"Yes. It's cooler in here now than it was a few hours ago." Christy reached over to touch one of the daisies in the center-piece. "I'm surprised any of these flowers are still alive."

"It's supposed to be hot tomorrow, too," Matt said.

"Oh," Christy said. The last thing she wanted to talk about was the weather. "Hey!" Christy said, brightening. "Your mom said you were offered a scholarship to Rancho Corona. Why didn't you tell me? I have some friends who want to go there."

"Have you ever been there?" Matt asked.

"No, but it's only about an hour from my house."

Matt's expression lit up considerably. "Really? I didn't know Rancho was so close to where you lived. Where are you going to school in the fall?"

Christy plucked a sprig of baby's breath from the center-piece and twirled it between her fingers. "I'm going to live at home and take classes at Palomar, the local community college. It seemed the best route for my first year since it's the least ex-pensive way to get my general ed classes taken care of."

"I thought of doing that, too," Matt said, "until these full scholarships came in. They were both a surprise."

"What were the scholarships offered for?"

"Baseball," Matt said with a smile. "You didn't think they were for academic excellence, did you?"

Christy shrugged and smiled, looking down at the flowers in her hand. "Some people have a burst of A's their last few years of high school."

"Were you one of those people?"

"No," Christy answered with a laugh. "I earned every mea-sly A I got. And believe me, there wasn't a bumper crop of them, especially this past year."

"Remember when we did those science projects in second grade with the lima beans and yours was the only one in class that wouldn't sprout?" Matt leaned back and balanced on two legs of the folding chair.

Christy cringed. How could Matt remember that? She had pushed that painful experience far from her life. "Miss Kaltzer gave me a D. It was the lowest grade in the class because she said I watered mine too much and killed it. I watered my bean just as much as everyone else did! That bean was a dud, and I still think the whole thing was unfair. It was a conspiracy! I think the janitor came in every night and watered just my bean."

Matt laughed.

"I still hate lima beans. I refuse to eat them. As a matter of fact, I hate anything that resembles a lima bean." Christy suddenly wondered if that was why she hated nuts.

Matt was laughing so hard the folding chair began to buckle underneath him. Christy noticed it and said, "Matt, your chair!" When he didn't hear her, she reached over to grab his arm. Just as she did, the legs gave way and the chair went down, taking Matt to the floor with it.

Matt kept laughing. He was laughing even harder from the floor, which made it impossible not to join in. Christy chuckled as a crowd of concerned adults gathered around to see what all the noise was about. Matt took a moment before he gained his composure.

"Are you okay?" Christy asked, offering him a hand to help him.

Matt took her hand and pulled himself up. She noticed how rough his skin was. Her dad had rough hands like that, which Christy always had considered evidence of hard work.

"I think I can fix it," Matt said to one of the older church gentlemen, who was more concerned about the broken chair than he was about Matt.

"No, this one's ready for the junk heap," the man said, carting off the pieces.

Matt's mom and Christy's mom had made their way over to the group surrounding their table. "Glad you could make it," Matt's mom said.

"I told you I'd be here in time to take down the tables," Matt said.

"Well, I didn't think you'd start 'taking down' the chairs," his mom said with a light tone to her voice.

"Hey, I didn't do that on purpose," he spouted.

"I know, I know," Mrs. Kingsley said quickly. "Your father wants to see you. He's in the kitchen."

"You're in trouble now," Christy teased.

"I'll be back," Matt said, giving Christy's elbow a squeeze. Christy smiled and noticed that more than half the guests had left. Her grandparents were seated one table over, sipping ice-cold lemonade and saying good-bye to another couple who was leaving. Christy noticed Grandma and Grandpa were holding hands. It was so cute. She didn't remember ever seeing her grandparents hold hands before. She had seen them kiss and hug, but hand-holding seemed so sweet and innocent.

Christy slid into a chair next to her grandma and smiled at the loving couple.

"What was all the commotion?" Grandpa asked.

"It was Matthew Kingsley," Christy said. It surprised her that she used his full name, as if she were in grade school, tattling on him. "Matthew leaned back in one of the folding chairs, and it broke." Then, for good measure, to prove to herself she wasn't tattling, she added, "It wasn't his fault. Mr. Gundersen even said the chair was ready for the junk heap."

"That's how it is with us old relics. Comes a point when we're all ready for the junk heap."

"Not you, sweetheart," Grandma said to him with one of her charming smiles. "You're as strong as you were the day we met."

"When did you two meet?" Christy asked.

"Oh, you know the story," Grandma said. "It was at a church social in Baraboo. He came to my house the next week to see me and then kept coming around until I finally said I'd marry him."

"That's right," Grandpa said. "Her mother told me to hurry up and marry her so I'd stop eating them out of house and home. She said if we got married she would only have to feed me on holidays and occasional Sundays."

Christy smiled. She had heard some of these kidding lines before. "How did you know Grandpa was the right man for you and that you were ready to get married?"

"You're not thinking of getting married, are you?" Grandpa asked.

"No, of course not. I mean, eventually, yes. But not now."

"You're too young," Grandpa said.

"I'll be eighteen on the twenty-seventh of this month," Christy said with a wry smile. She knew her grandmother had barely turned nineteen when she and Grandpa were married.

"You have a lot of time," Grandpa said.

"I know. But when that time comes, how will I know if he's the right one? How did you know?" She noticed that her grandparents had done a nice job of avoiding her question.

"You tell her, dear," Grandpa said to Grandma. "I'd like to hear your answer." He seemed fairly serious.

"All right," Grandma said. She let go of Grandpa's hand and reached across the table to take both of Christy's hands in hers. Her new position caused her orchid corsage to bunch up on her shoulder and rest against her chin. Christy felt as if she was about to be told a great secret.

"It's a choice, you know," Grandma said, peering through her bifocal glasses and looking steadily at Christy. "You get to know someone and then you ask yourself, 'Would I like to spend the rest of my life with this person?' If the answer is yes, then you wait until you have a big argument. Or until something goes wrong, or he does something you don't like. And when things are at their lowest, you ask yourself again, 'Would I like to spend the rest of my life with this person?' If the answer is still yes, then you know you're in love."

"That's it?" Grandpa spouted. With a hoot he leaned back

71

in his chair and laughed heartily. If he had been heavier, he probably would have crashed to the floor the way Matt had.

"No," Grandma said defensively. "That's only the beginning. You make one big decision and follow it up with a lifetime of little decisions that support that first one."

Grandpa had stopped guffawing and was wagging his finger at Christy. "The real way you know if it's the right person is to evaluate his background. Do you come from the same place? Then you have a much better chance of making it through the hard times when they come. That's how you know if it's a match."

Grandma let out a low chuckle. "Oh really, dear. You and I both know plenty of couples with opposite backgrounds that have made it through lots of hard times." She gave Christy's hands a pat and said, "The real answer, Christina dear, is that when it's right, you'll know."

Chapter 13

Christy wrote as much as she could remember of her grand-parents' advice in her diary that night. The group had been at the church cleaning up until nearly midnight. Uncle Bob and Aunt Marti hung around until almost nine before Marti felt one of her headaches coming on, and they left.

Matt and Christy were assigned to kitchen duty, where they washed every pot, pan, cup, and dish the kitchen owned. First Christy washed, and Matt dried. Then, when she complained that her fingers were too wrinkled up, Matt washed, and she dried. Matt used way too much soap when he refilled the sink, and a rollicking soap bubble war broke out between the two of them.

Christy had dollops of foamy bubbles on the top of her head, and Matt's back was covered when his mom stepped into the kitchen. She scolded them as if they were six-year-olds and left the kitchen shaking her head.

Matt and Christy went back to their soapsuds war until they were both laughing so hard that they called a truce. Handing Christy a dry dish towel, Matt said, "So what else can you tell me about Rancho Corona? Do you think I'd like it there?"

They talked seriously about college and moving away from

home for the first time. Matt admitted he was a lot more interested in Rancho now that he knew it was close to Christy's home. "If I went there, do you think you would be willing to hang out with me sometimes on weekends?" Matt asked. "You could show me the sights. I've never been to California."

Christy gave him a rundown of some of her favorite spots and how she made the adjustment when her family moved to California. When Matt walked Christy to the car in the church parking lot, he said, "I wish it weren't so late. We could go somewhere and talk some more."

"We have tomorrow," Christy reminded him. Then she remembered she had invited Melissa to come along. She wished she were going to have him all to herself tomorrow.

Matt must have been feeling the same way because the last thing he said to her was, "Maybe we can have some time to talk tomorrow, just the two of us."

When Christy's family arrived at her grandparents', everyone headed right to bed. David tried to convince Christy to play another midnight round of Monopoly, but she turned him down. He decided to sleep on the enclosed porch since it was the coolest place in the house. Mom and Dad told him that was fine, and Christy was glad. That meant she had the bedroom to herself, and she could use the time to write in her diary.

After putting down her impressions of the evening, Christy chewed on the end of her pen and leaned back against the bed's pillows. The soft light from the lamp on the nightstand cast a buttery glow about the room. She felt content. Tomorrow she would see Matt again, and that would be nice. She didn't know for sure if there was something between them, but she didn't feel as if she had to decide that yet.

Then, remembering the thoughts she had had about love at the reception, Christy wrote,

Here are two words I want to think about when it comes to relationships: commitment and intimacy. I think commitment needs to

be the foundation for any lasting relationship—just like I didn't have a deep and growing relationship with Christ until I first made a commitment to Him. With intimacy it's about knowing the other person's heart in a special way so that you share and treasure the same things that are important to him.

A thought came to her. She wrote quickly before it slipped away.

I never realized it before, but I want that kind of intimacy more in my relationship with the Lord. I want to share and treasure the things that are important to Him. I want to know what's in His heart.

Suddenly Christy had such a clear thought that she held her breath. For one sacred moment, everything was still. If her guardian angel had even slightly fluttered one wing in that moment, Christy was certain she would have heard it.

God wants to have that kind of intimacy with me. He knows everything that I've tucked away in my heart, and He wants me to share it with Him.

She felt astounded that Almighty God had chosen to be committed and intimate in His relationship with her. Love was a choice, just like Grandma had said. And God chose to love her. Not just one time, but over and over again He made that choice, even when she did things He couldn't stand.

As Christy scribbled that last thought in her diary, her eyes misted with tears. She closed her diary, turned off the light, and slid between the cool sheets. Outside the open window the crickets performed their nightly symphony. In the upstairs hallway the grandfather clock *tick-tock*ed with unfailing rhythm, sounding its whole notes at the quarter hour.

Through the bedroom window came a welcome breeze. Christy turned her face toward the window and noticed the moonglow tiptoeing into her room. The summer moon spilled a filtered trail of thin, ivory light across the edge of her bed.

The beauty of the moment caused Christy to think of a verse in Psalm 68 that was a line in a song Doug had been teaching her. *Sing to the one who rides across the ancient heavens, his mighty voice thundering from the sky . . . For God is awesome in his sanctuary.*

As she watched the moon slowly shift its shimmering pathway toward the foot of her bed, Christy tried to remember the tune and hum it. God wasn't thundering from the sky in His mighty voice tonight. He was murmuring. Or maybe He was humming the way she was, humming contentedly as He rode across the ancient heavens.

Chapter 14

"We're ready to go, Christy! Dad said to tell you to hurry up," David called out, pounding on the closed bedroom door.

"I'm coming, I'm coming!" Christy hollered back. She couldn't believe they had let her sleep in while everyone else was preparing for the picnic. She didn't have time to shower or anything. In five minutes she pulled on her bathing suit, shorts, and T-shirt and frantically stuffed a few essentials in her backpack while trying to slip on her sandals at the same time. "Tell them I'll be right there!"

Like a whirlwind, Christy grabbed her sweat shirt, a brush, and a clip for her hair. She flew from the bedroom and bounded down the stairs only to find Aunt Marti standing at the entryway wearing one her expressions of disapproval.

"Really, Christy, you should try to be a little more ladylike. This is your grandmother's home, you know."

"I know," Christy muttered, not in the mood for any criticism this morning, especially from Aunt Marti. Christy slipped past her aunt and stalked out to the car, where Mom was loading the trunk.

"Why didn't anyone wake me?" Christy asked, jamming her bag into an open spot in the trunk.

"I suppose we all had a lot going on," Mom said, giving Christy a startled look. "What's wrong?"

"Well, I would have appreciated having a little time to take a shower and eat something. It didn't help that David kept coming up and hanging on the door while I was trying to dress."

"We're only going on a picnic," Dad said, entering into the conversation. He was lugging a big ice chest to the back of the car. "It would have been nice, Christy, if you would have gotten up and helped to make some of this food."

"I would have been glad to, but no one woke me!"

"Seems to me a girl who's almost eighteen years old can figure out how to set an alarm clock and get herself up in the morning," Dad said gruffly. He hoisted the heavy ice chest onto the trunk's edge, and with a bark in his voice he said, "You'll have to make more room than that, Margaret. I told you the ice chest needed to go in first. Whose bag is that?"

"Mine," Christy said, snatching her bag and sliding into the car's backseat with a huff. She held her bag on her lap and sat there fuming. *I can't believe I went to sleep with all those dreamy, spiritual thoughts. Then I woke up this morning ready to bite the next person I see!*

Christy's brother came over to her open door and said, "Scoot over. I want to sit on that side."

"You can sit on the other side. I'm already here."

"You always get to sit there."

"So?"

"So it's behind Mom's seat, and there's more leg room. Dad pushes his seat back so far it gives me leg cramps."

"Oh, David, you don't get leg cramps."

"I do, too!"

"Well, my legs are longer than yours, and I'm already sitting here, so you go sit on the other side. The drive's not that far anyway."

Their mom called from behind the car where she and Dad were still trying to fit everything in the trunk. "David and

Christy, stop your arguing. I'll sit in the backseat. You can sit in the front, David."

He gave Christy a smirk, which she thought was about the worst thing anyone could have done to her at the moment. Christy pursed her lips together, working very hard not to let the words she wanted to say slip out. She drew in a deep breath and tried to calm down. It took her a minute before she felt as if her rampaging emotions had subsided. She prayed silently. Then she murmured, "David, I'm sorry. I'll try to be nice."

He turned around in the seat and looked at her as if trying to make sure she was serious. "Me too," he mumbled after a moment.

Christy pulled her brush and hair clip from her bag and worked on her hair, getting it off her neck. The day was already hot. Too hot to be sitting in the car in the sunshine.

When her parents finally were settled in the car and her dad had backed the vehicle out of the driveway, it seemed to grow hotter before the air conditioning finally kicked in. At last, coolness could be felt in the backseat.

"What are we doing today?" David asked.

"We're going to the picnic grounds at the Dells," Mom told him. "We'll meet the Kingsleys there and spend the day relaxing."

Christy wondered if they would be able to relax much. She didn't like the way things had been going so far. And if Melissa started to act like she had dibs on Matt, Christy knew she would be upset. She wished she had never invited Melissa to come. If only she and Matt could have the whole day together, just the two of them.

When the family arrived at the picnic grounds, they had to park far away from the entrance, which meant carrying everything a farther distance. Christy helped her dad with the ice chest. They lugged the heavy beast onto the picnic grounds, then Dad suggested they set it down. "I'll go find the Kingsleys. You sit here and wait."

Christy sat on top of the ice chest, watching all the people who were gathering for their picnics. Smoke from barbecues laced the air with the scent of charcoal and lighter fluid. A football flew over her and was caught by a man wearing a baseball cap with a stuffed fabric fish jutting out the front of it. Twin girls on tricycles pedaled past her on the cement pathway while an older sister trotted behind them, giving instructions.

Mom and David joined Christy with their arms full of stuff. "Are we waiting here for your father?" Mom asked.

"Yes. He went to find the Kingsleys so we wouldn't have to haul this around."

Everywhere Christy looked she saw the colors red, white, and blue. Some groups had flags. Red, white, and blue banners flew from poles planted on their picnic tables. She noticed a woman walking past who carried a big, round watermelon in her arms. She wore a denim jumper with a white shirt and a red bandana around her neck. She had large, dangling red, white, and blue earrings and a big red, white, and blue bow in her hair.

What caught Christy's attention was that from the bow the woman had attached a row of sparklers spread out like the silver skeleton of a fan. It seemed to Christy that the woman was begging some little kid to come along and light those sparklers. Then what would the woman do?

Christy felt as if her emotions were sticking out today, too, just begging for a flying spark to set them off. "Avoid little boys with matches," Christy muttered to the woman as she passed. Christy knew the admonition should be for herself, as well. One "spark" from Matthew Kingsley, and she would be running around like a crazy spectacle with her heart on fire.

Christy's dad appeared through the crowd and directed them to head toward the water. He and Christy lugged the ice chest the rest of the way, and as they took the last few steps to join the Kingsleys, Christy told her emotions to duck the sparks that were about to fly in her direction. Only three feet away stood Melissa. She had both her arms around Matt's middle and was giving him a cuddly hug.

Chapter 15

Christy felt her heart pounding faster—and not just from carrying the bulky ice chest. *Does Melissa want to make me jealous? What is she trying to prove? Why did I ever invite her to come? Does Matt like her? What am I interrupting here?*

"Hello!" Mrs. Kingsley greeted them, and a round of hellos, hugs, and chattering took place. Christy overheard Matt's mom say something to her mom about Noah's Ark Waterpark, and immediately David said, "Can I go, too? That's my favorite place! Please?"

Christy noticed that none of Matt's sisters was around. She had hoped his youngest sister would keep David entertained so he wouldn't continually be bugging Christy.

"What do you think?" Mom said, turning to Christy. "Would you two like to go? The Kingsley girls are already there."

"Yes!" David answered for both of them.

Christy forced herself to smile at Matt and then at Melissa. The hug apparently had been a momentary expression because they were now standing a few feet away from each other, and neither of them was acting as if they were "together."

Was the hug merely a show for me to see when I walked up? Two can play that game, Melissa!

Christy stepped closer and was about to give Matthew Kingsley the first hug she had ever given him, when Melissa said, "I was just telling Matt good-bye."

"Oh?" Christy said, retreating from the planned "hug attack."

"I don't have the money to go to Noah's Ark. My brother and some of his friends are on the other side of the park, so I'm going to hang out with them."

Something in Melissa's expression made her look lost and sad. Christy hadn't seen Melissa's brother in a long time. But several years ago, when Paula was interested in him, he'd seemed like a hoodlum to Christy. Was that the best group for Melissa to hang out with?

Remembering the feeling of being left out, Christy found, once again, that she had compassion for Melissa. Before Christy could change her mind, she asked, "Would you like to come to the water park if we all pitched in to pay your way?"

Melissa gave Christy a long gaze. "No, but thanks anyway," she said. Before turning to go, she asked, "Why are you being so nice to me?"

Christy shrugged. "I care about you, Melissa." While that was true, Christy knew she didn't care that much. She wanted to defend the ground she had covered with Matt, and her main motivation for being nice was that she kept thinking about how her friends always included everyone so no one felt left out. Without realizing it, Christy had taken on that caring quality, and sometimes she acted on it even when she felt very differently.

"Thanks," Melissa said again. "You know, Paula said that in spite of all the things that bugged her about you and your 'God friends,' she really liked the way you guys tried to be nice to everyone. She was right. You and Matt both treat me different from any of my other friends."

Oh, Melissa, if you only knew what I was thinking a few minutes ago, you wouldn't say I was so nice!

Before Christy knew what was happening, Melissa gave Christy a warm hug and waved good-bye to everyone as she took off to join her brother and his group.

"Can we go now?" David asked impatiently.

It took the adults a few minutes to give all the instructions as to what time the three of them were to return for the fireworks display. Mom tried to give them sandwiches to take with them, but they opted to buy food at the water park.

That turned out to be a bad choice because David hadn't brought enough money to pay for his admission to the park. Christy was able to cover their entrance fees, but that only left them with eight dollars to spend on food. David started to plead for food right away, and Christy was hungry, too, since she hadn't had breakfast.

"I have to meet my sisters at the entrance to Paradise Lagoon," Matt said once they were inside the huge park. "How about if we all meet in half an hour at the Jungle Rapids water slide?"

David chattered nonstop as he and Christy waited in line to order some food. She knew her parents were expecting her to be with him every minute, but Christy tried to come up with a plan so David could go away and she could just be with Matt.

Christy and David ate quickly, and then Christy directed him to the entrance to Jungle Rapids. Matt was already there when they arrived, but his sisters weren't with him. When Christy asked about them, Matt said, "They're doing fine. We decided we would check in again in two hours at the Paradise Lagoon."

Two hours for you and me to baby-sit David. Great.

David coerced Matt and Christy to go on the Jungle Rapids water slide with him. "When we used to live here, I was too little to go on this ride," he said excitedly. "I always wanted to. This is going to be my favorite ride. I just know it."

Their wait in line was long and hot, as the summer sun rose directly above them and beat down on their shoulders. The happy shouts and squeals from those who had reached the top of the line and were now enjoying the cool refreshment of the winding water slide served only to torture them. This day certainly didn't seem to be going the way Christy had hoped. David even positioned himself between Matt and Christy, making sure he was the center of attention.

"You know," Matt said, after David finally stopped talking, "I appreciate what you did with Melissa, Christy."

"What did I do?"

"You did what that verse in John 13 says to do," Matt said.

Christy wasn't sure what verse he was referring to and told him she didn't understand.

"It's that verse that says, 'Your love for one another will prove to the world that you are my disciples.' I think it's verse 35. Our Bible study group is studying John 13 through 15 this summer, and that's the verse we were going over last week."

Christy still wasn't sure how that applied to Melissa. Perhaps Matt thought that by inviting Melissa to come along Christy had been showing love to her and that proved Christy was a disciple, or follower of Christ. She knew her motives weren't so pure, but maybe what mattered most was that she had tried and that deep down, her heart was in the right place.

They were at the top of the slide now, so any further discussion would have to wait. David had just taken off down the slide with a squeal of delight, and Christy was next.

Chapter 16

The afternoon turned out to be one great splash after another. Christy gave up trying to be alone with Matt and started having the time of her life, even with David tagging along. Matt tried to show off his athletic abilities with daring twists and turns on some of the slides. Christy took each of them nice and safe. She didn't have the "need for speed" that Matt and David kept joking about. She enjoyed each ride at her own pace and ignored the guys when they teased her.

"Where to next?" Matt asked after they met up with his sisters and the whole group was together for the first time. David and Matt's sisters all spoke at once, saying they wanted to go on the Slidewinders.

"What about you, Christy?" Matt asked, looking at her warmly.

"I'd really like to go for a nice, leisurely float down the Lazy River. Would it be okay if David went with you guys, and I met you somewhere afterward?"

"I'll go with you," Matt said.

Christy was thrilled.

"Sara, you guys keep an eye on David, and we'll meet all of you here in an hour, okay?"

David and the girls took off, and Christy suddenly felt shy around Matt. They walked side by side on the hot pavement through the park, and the scent of chlorine seemed to surround them. Christy was sure her skin had never been so "bleached" in pool water before, but with so many people, she knew the water needed to be extra clean. She guessed her hair would have a green tinge by the day's end. For all she knew, it already could be turning green. She wondered if Matt would notice such a thing as green hair.

"Are you having a good time?" Matt was looking at her closely.

"Yes, I'm having a great time. Are you?"

Matt nodded and motioned for her to go first into the Lazy River. He followed her into the water, and soon they were bobbing leisurely along in their big blue inner tubes.

Matt reached over and took hold of the handle on the side of Christy's inner tube.

"Don't tip me over!" Christy cried.

"I'm not going to," Matt said. He pulled his inner tube right next to Christy's and said, "Okay. Do you want to hear the whole story about Melissa?"

Christy felt her emotions nose-dive. Now that she was finally alone with Matt, she certainly didn't want to talk about Melissa. But she nodded politely and said, "Sure."

"I asked Melissa to go with me to Homecoming our junior year, and you would think it was the royal event of the decade. It was a much bigger deal to everyone than I think it should have been, and I didn't have a very good time."

"So you and Melissa used to go out?" Christy asked.

"Just that one time. That was it. Except ever since, she seems to think I owe her another dance or something." Matt leaned closer to Christy's inner tube and said, "Can I tell you something?"

Christy nodded and gave him an expression of sincere honesty. She wanted him to know he could trust her with his secrets.

"That's been my total dating experience. I've been interested in different girls now and then, but because of sports and work, I never had any time to develop a social life. Then, when I became a Christian, the selection of girls who believed the same way I did went down to zero."

"Can I ask you something?" Christy asked.

"Of course."

"Why did you go out with Melissa in the first place? I mean, did you both really like each other, or did you think it was going to be a one-time thing?"

"I didn't know what it was going to be. Paula told me Melissa liked me at the beginning of our junior year," Matt said. "Paula was the one who convinced me to ask Melissa to the Homecoming dance."

Christy didn't mean to, but she laughed.

"What?" Matt said. "What did I say?"

"I'm sorry, Matt. I was just thinking that if it hadn't been for Paula, how would you ever know any girls liked you?"

"I knew you liked me," he said. "Before Paula even told me, I knew."

"Oh? And just how did you know that?" Christy asked, playfully splashing the water with her toes.

"You used to chase me," Matt said.

"I used to chase you?"

"Yeah. Don't you remember? In third grade at first recess you used to chase me around the schoolyard. I'd come up to you and tag you on the shoulder, and then you would chase me."

"That's right," Christy said. "How could I have forgotten that? You used to always say, 'Einee meenie boo boo,' whatever that meant."

Matt laughed. "That's right. Where did I come up with that?"

They both laughed, and Christy said, "And that's how you knew I liked you?"

"Yep," Matt said.

"But you never liked me back," Christy said, watching Matt's expression for a response.

"I never said that." His eyes were fixed on hers, and his jaw was set. Matt let go of the handle on her inner tube and reached for Christy's hand. The gesture surprised Christy, but she didn't pull back. Under the warm summer sun, drenched with the scent of chlorine, Christy and Matt floated down the Lazy River, hand in hand.

Chapter 17

Christy felt as if her childhood dream was coming true. Only now it was ten years after she had first dreamed of holding hands with Matthew Kingsley while floating down some imaginary, lazy river. Christy didn't know what to say, or even if she should say anything.

"When I heard you were coming," Matt said after a moment, "I wanted to see you because I wondered how much you had changed."

"Have I changed a lot?" Christy heard a nervous twitch in her voice and wondered if Matt noticed it.

"In some ways you haven't changed at all. And in the ways you have changed, well, all those changes have been for the better." Then quickly Matt added, "You do know, don't you, that I have a crush on you, Christy Miller?"

Christy was so surprised at Matt's declaration that she scooped up a handful of water and splashed him, saying, "You do not, Matthew Kingsley!"

"How do you know?" he said. "You can't see inside me to know what I'm feeling."

The wounded expression on Matt's face made Christy bite her lip. How could she have discredited his feelings like that?

She knew exactly what it felt like to have a crush. She knew how painful it was to have your crush revealed and then to have that person dismiss it with rude carelessness. She would have hurt him less if she had blurted out that she would rather kiss a toad, the way he had dismissed her crush years ago. But what she had just done was worse. He had confessed his feelings to her, and she had invalidated them in one breath.

Matt let go of her hand as they approached the Lazy River's exit.

"I'm sorry," Christy said. She felt awful. Worse than awful. Terrible. No, horrible. She felt horrible. She exited the water and hurried to catch up with Matt. Her wet feet flapped against the hot pavement as she tried to keep up with his stride.

"Matt, will you stop a minute?"

He stopped.

"Can we sit down?"

"Where?"

"Over on that bench."

Matt still looked hurt.

"You're right," Christy began. "I don't know what you're feeling. I know what I felt for you from third grade all the way through junior high. I know what a crush feels like. Crushes are real. I know they are. And the truth is, I don't know but that I still have a crush on you, Matthew Kingsley."

He looked over at her with his head down but with his face turned toward hers, looking expectant. "Really?"

"I think so," Christy said.

Matt sat up straight and looked at her. "What do we do about that?"

A nice, logical answer came to her mind. The right way to approach any such relationship would be to pray about it, develop a friendship, make the proper commitments at the proper times, and know that each choice was a follow-up to the first decision that strengthened it.

She had no idea where this thinking came from. She certainly hadn't seen things that clearly when she was so crazy about Todd.

"I don't know what we can do about our feelings," Christy told Matt. "Admitting them to each other is probably a good place to start."

"I suppose," Matt said.

"Maybe for now, it's just good that we both admit what we feel," Christy said. "It's more than we were able to do in elementary school."

Matt was about to say something when David came running up with the girls and started to ramble on about the Wave Pool and how they had to go there next.

Christy and Matt followed the others, walking next to each other. She was sorry that their serious conversation had been interrupted. What would have happened if they had kept talking, exploring their feelings? Would sparks have flown from Matt's words and ignited all her emotions?

The group went to the Wave Pool, and Matt and Christy, as a couple, were swallowed up in the brother-and-sister interactions among all of them.

Once Christy could relax again, she had a great time bobbing on her inner tube. Then the ride's alarm sounded, and the mighty, man-made wave rose and pushed them to the cement shore. It was nothing like the real experience of riding waves in California, but it was still fun.

As usual, Christy picked apart all her thoughts and feelings. She was glad that she and Matt had been able to talk so openly, but she still didn't know what to do about their confessions.

Matt splashed her to get her attention as she was drifting in her thoughts. "We need to head back to the picnic grounds. We told them we would be back by 7:00 for the barbecue. If we hurry, we might get there by about 7:15. I don't want our parents to worry."

David moaned about having to leave, but he perked up at the mention of food.

Matt's estimate was close. They joined their parents at 7:10. The picnic area was even more crowded than it had been that morning. Curls of smoke from lit charcoal briquettes mixed with the burnt smell of prematurely lit sparklers. Christy wondered if the woman she had seen earlier in the day still had those sparklers in her hair or if someone had lit them for her. Christy had to wonder if any of her emotional sparklers had been lit, and even more important, did she want to leave them so accessible?

The food was ready when they arrived. Two hot dogs, a mound of potato salad, three pickles, and a slice of watermelon later, Christy joined her dad and David in a round of Frisbee. Matt joined them and spun a couple of impressive throws in her direction, none of which she caught.

"You never were much for sports, were you?" Matt teased when they disbanded the game because it was growing dark.

"Nope. My best friend, Katie, says I'm 'athletically impaired,' which is a nice way of saying I'm a klutz."

"You're not a klutz," Matt said.

"I don't seem to ever recall hearing you say the words, 'Red Rover, Red Rover, send Christy right over.' "

"Maybe not," Matt said. "But if I remember correctly, you were pretty good on the ice at our eighth-grade winter party."

"That's right," Christy said, remembering how good it felt to skate around the rink without falling. She liked being with someone who had known her for so many years he could remind her of past victories.

"Come with me to get some more blankets," Matt said. "They're in the van."

Christy knew this would be their chance to finish their heart-to-heart conversation. In the last few hours, Christy's mind had spun wildly with the possible directions things could go with Matt. She imagined everything from saying good-bye to him tonight and never seeing him for the rest of her life, all the way to standing with him under an anniversary banner in the same church fellowship hall fifty years from now. Only the church would definitely be air-conditioned by then.

None of her scenarios seemed sure or clear. The future was as vast and unsearchable as the summer sky that spread over them like a deep periwinkle picnic blanket. Perhaps what she felt now was part of the mystery that always seemed to come along with the "romance" and "adventure" Katie had talked about.

Chapter 18

Matt handed her a blanket, and he held the other. They lingered a moment behind the van while he tried to lock the door.

"There," he said when he was satisfied the key had worked.

Suddenly a burst of bright color soared across the sky. Christy hugged the blanket, her chin pointed to the heavens as the two of them watched the beginning of the fireworks display. Matt stood beside her.

"Where are they coming from?" Christy asked.

"The parking lot of the municipal pool."

The second brilliant stream of glittering color burst in the sky, and Christy gave an appropriate, "Ohh! Ahh!"

"Ohh! Ahh!" Matt repeated teasingly when the next spray of vibrant lights dotted the sky.

"Sing to the one who rides across the ancient heavens," Christy said, casually resting her head against Matt's shoulder. "God is awesome in his sanctuary."

Another spray of fireworks splashed across the sky, and Matt asked, "Did you just make that up?"

"No, it's in the Bible. Psalm 68. A friend of mine is writing some music to go with the words."

Matt let his chin brush the top of her head. "Do you think we can go back, Christy?"

"Back to the picnic area?"

"No, you goof," he said, stepping away from her and leaning against the back of the van so he could face her. "Do you think we can go back to being whatever we were before I told you I had a crush on you?"

"No," Christy said, shaking her head. "I don't think we can."

Matt looked worried.

"I think we just go on from here. We don't have to change anything. Look at it this way: I had a crush on you for seven years. Did that change anything?"

Matt laughed. "I guess not. But I didn't have my driver's license then."

Christy smiled. "What does that have to do with it?"

"I guess it's symbolic. I can pretty much do what I want now, you know?"

Christy did know what he meant. It was that wonderful and terrible realization that they were on the brink of being adults and being responsible for making their own catastrophes from there on out.

"Yeah, I know," Christy said. She turned her head to see the next blast of fireworks. In the dim light, she noticed that Grandpa's canoe was still strapped to the roof of Uncle Bob's rental car. Grandpa had insisted the canoe accompany them for the day because he was sure the kids would want to go canoeing. But when they all left for the water park, obviously none of the adults could be persuaded to go out in the old thing. Christy's dad had said years ago that that canoe should be hanging in a museum because it was older than Grandpa, but Grandpa insisted it was still seaworthy. That claim hadn't been tried today.

As they watched the fireworks, Christy wondered if her old crush on Matt was still "seaworthy." It might be, but she wasn't going to unstrap it from where she had hung it on a wall of her heart. That "canoe" of old feelings would also go untried this day.

"I had a wonderful time being around you this weekend," Christy said, turning to face Matt. "I'm content to let everything be what it was and what it is and not try to push it any further. Is that okay with you?"

Matt paused. "You know what I think?" He reached over with a closed fist and gave Christy a playful punch across the jaw. "You're a good friend, but I think, without knowing it, I was practicing on you this weekend."

"Practicing on me?" Christy didn't know if she should feel insulted.

"I told you about my limited dating experience." Matt paused, as if trying hard not to be embarrassed. "I can't believe I'm telling you this, but I felt safe with you. I guess I thought I could practice my dating skills on you because you had a boyfriend. Then, when you said you and Todd had broken up, I started to wonder, 'What if?' "

Christy nodded. "I call it 'The Land of If Only.' It's an okay place to visit but a dangerous place to live."

"Yeah," Matt said. "That's what it was. A little journey to the Land of If Only. With us living so far apart, it's not very realistic to think about a relationship, is it?"

Christy shook her head. She reached over, took Matt's rough hand in hers, and gave it a squeeze. "I'm honored I was your practice date. I'd give you an A in all areas."

Matt squeezed her hand back. "No 'needs to improve' on my report card?"

"Well, maybe one," Christy said, letting go of his hand. "You could occasionally open the door for a girl. Or at least go around and stand by her side of the car after you get out so she doesn't feel abandoned."

"Okay," Matt said seriously, as if he were taking notes. "Anything else?"

Christy thought a moment. "No, just keep being your wonderful self, Matthew Kingsley. Girls will continue to adore you for who you are. I know I always have."

Matt stood, looking at her, smiling slightly. "I wish they all could be California girls."

Christy laughed. "I think I'm still a Midwest farmer's daughter. You come to Rancho Corona, and I'll introduce you to some real California girls."

"Who knows," Matt said, his grin broadening, "I just might do that."

The two of them turned their faces toward the ancient heavens, observing one more blast of dazzling brilliance.

"Come on," Matt said, motioning with his head toward the picnic area. "Let's go back."

"No," Christy said with a smile, "let's go on."

Matt and Christy walked side by side across the grass. A melancholy contentment hung over Christy. Was it possible to do the right thing, make the right decision, and say the right words yet still feel sad about it afterward?

Matt tagged her on the shoulder and said, "Einee meenie boo boo" and took off running.

Christy laughed and started to run after him, even though she knew this was the last time she would ever chase Matthew Kingsley.

Please Pick Up the White Courtesy Phone

A COOPER ELLIS NOVELLA

WENDY LEE NENTWIG

Chapter 1

"Cooper, missing our plane is not my idea of a good way to start a trip," Mrs. Ellis chided her perennially late daughter.

"We have plenty of time," Cooper countered while attempting to stuff more clothes into her already full duffel bag. She was almost done packing, but she was convinced she would need two more shirts on her trip. So while she carefully avoided her mother's disapproving gaze, Cooper wadded each shirt into a compact ball and crammed them in the corners of the black canvas duffel bag before zipping it closed with some difficulty. Cooper smiled triumphantly up at her mother from her spot on the floor, but her victory was short-lived.

"You're aware that none of that is going to be wearable by the time we get to Seattle, aren't you?"

"I guess it's a good thing, then, that you and Mrs. Hughes will be at that interior design show the whole weekend so you won't have to endure the pain of seeing your terribly wrinkled daughter," Cooper replied.

"Yes, but I'll still know you're out there, wandering around," her mother explained, her lips barely hiding a smile. "And the other tourists will be looking at you and thinking,

'Who raised that child? Didn't her mother teach her how to use an iron?' "

"I'm sure they'll be too busy looking at the Space Needle or the fish market to care what I look like."

"And what about Penny?" Mrs. Ellis persisted.

"Aunt Penny doesn't care about stuff like that," Cooper replied, dismissing the argument with a wave of her hand. "You got all the neat genes and all the worry genes, so by the time Grandma had Penny, I don't think any were left."

"Your aunt Penny could do with a few worry genes," Mrs. Ellis said in her most motherly tone. "She's far too unconcerned about important things like her future, her career, and life in general."

"I think it's called being laid-back," Cooper teased.

"Sometimes it's called being irresponsible."

Cooper knew her mom and her aunt frequently didn't see eye-to-eye, but Cooper was determined not to let that tension creep in and ruin her weekend. It was a good thing, then, that she and her best friend, Claire, would be staying at Aunt Penny's while their moms would be staying several miles away at the downtown hotel where the convention they were attending was being held.

Cooper couldn't wait. She always had felt a special bond with Aunt Penny, who, at age twenty-seven, was sort of like the big sister Cooper never had. They had so much in common. They shared a casual approach to life as well as a passion for quirky clothes, watching old cartoons in their pajamas, and consuming anything chocolate. And now they would have a whole weekend together. It was going to be perfect—if her mom ever quit picking on her packing techniques and they finally got to Seattle, that is.

"Ellen and Claire are probably waiting down in the lobby," Mrs. Ellis said, but her remarks were cut short by the phone's ringing. Of course, she used that to further illustrate her point.

"You see? That's probably them right now, calling to see what's holding us up."

"Tell them I'm just running to grab my backpack, and we'll be right there," Cooper instructed before dashing down the hall to her disorderly bedroom. Once there, she flipped the shiny black pack with white racing stripes upside down and emptied its contents onto the bed. She surveyed the mess for only a second before stuffing back in the bag her wallet, sunglasses, and key to their apartment. Then came the important stuff: an Empire State Building pen with King Kong floating up and down inside, a small note pad with a cover made from a recycled box of Lucky Charms cereal, half-chewed packs of both wintergreen and raspberry gum (one for fresh breath, the other for blowing bubbles when bored), a roll of cherry LifeSavers, two mini-containers of Play-Doh, and her little blue Bible with the cover that snapped closed so the pages didn't get mangled. She also remembered to grab from her bedside table the Seattle guidebook she had been reading and rereading and dropped it into the black hole, as well.

With her bag repacked, she surveyed the rejects: five movie ticket stubs, three gum wrappers, four more pens, a Ziploc bag containing several crushed Oreos, her New York City Public Library card, and a crumpled brochure from the Museum of Television and Radio. Then she slung the backpack over her left shoulder. On her way out of the room, she took a quick peek in the mirror to adjust the clip holding her long, dark hair up off her neck, tucked a few errant strands behind her ears, and wiped a stray eyelash from beneath her smoky gray eyes before racing back down the hall. As she skidded to a stop on the entryway tile, she was relieved to find her mom still on the phone instead of impatiently tapping her foot.

Cooper was relieved, that is, until she realized who was on the other end of the line.

"Alex, she doesn't have time to talk right now. We're on our way out the door," Mrs. Ellis was explaining to Cooper's other best friend, the third part of an inseparable trio that had formed back in junior high. He didn't seem to be taking the news well.

"We'll be home Sunday night," Cooper's exasperated mom continued. "She and Claire can call you then. Surely the three of you can stand to be apart for less than four days!"

Cooper knew better than to even try to convince her mom to let her talk to Alex for just a second, as much as she wanted to. He had been so disappointed to find out that Claire and Cooper were taking this trip without him, and for the last several weeks the girls had been forced to endure his endless whining about sexual discrimination. Cooper had tried to explain that the girls' vacation had more to do with their moms being best friends and running Ellis-Hughes Interiors together than it did with any plot to discriminate against Alex for being a boy, but he didn't buy it. Cooper finally had given up trying to convince or console him.

"Alex, we may miss our plane if we don't leave immediately. The girls will send you a postcard from Seattle, and we'll see you soon," Mrs. Hughes promised before saying good-bye and returning the cordless phone to its base.

"You would think you and Claire were leaving for months the way Alex was carrying on," Mrs. Ellis said as she and Cooper waited for the elevator that would take them first to the Hugheses' apartment and then down to the lobby of their Upper West Side apartment building.

"We're his best friends," Cooper explained with a shrug. "I tried to tell him he could drag plenty of other people to those obscure films he likes or on adventures through Central Park, but he says he's used to us. He has us broken in to just the right degree of friendship and hanging out with anyone else requires too much 'back story.' "

"Back story?" her mother queried with a raised eyebrow as they boarded the elevator and pushed the button for the Hugheses' floor.

"It's one of his new screenwriting terms. He's been reading

up on his chosen profession again," Cooper said. "Anyway, he says when he spends time with anyone new he has to explain everything, and it's just too much trouble."

"You kids are fifteen years old! It's not as if he has some sordid past he's trying to hide!"

"I think he just has a hard time making friends," Cooper theorized as the large metal doors opened.

"I'll hold the elevator," Mrs. Ellis directed. "You run and let them know we're finally ready—if they haven't given up on us and headed downstairs."

Cooper hurried down the carpeted hallway and knocked on her best friend's door. Before she even had returned her arm to her side, the door flew open, and Claire and her mother were standing there with their bags in hand. Actually, Claire's Asian-inspired floral bag, a Chinatown find, was slung awkwardly over her shoulder, while Mrs. Hughes was wheeling her compact hunter green suitcase behind her.

"Let's get this show on the road!" Mrs. Hughes announced in that sweet but clichéd way moms seemed to make a habit of.

With that pronouncement, they were on their way. They greeted their building's doorman in the lobby, and he quickly hailed them a cab. Within a matter of minutes, New York City was flying past the taxi's grimy windows in a gray blur as they headed to LaGuardia Airport in Queens, about a twenty-minute drive from their Manhattan home if the traffic wasn't too heavy.

Cooper sat in the front seat since only three people could fit in the back, which meant unless she wanted to try to talk to Claire through the air holes in the thick plastic partition that divided the front seat from the back, she would have to wait until they were at the airport. Cooper did turn to give her best-friend-since-babyhood a sympathetic smile since she was sand-wiched in between their mothers, who were, as usual, embroiled in a boring discussion about some client or other. Claire just smiled back contentedly, causing her warm brown eyes to crinkle. Cooper wasn't surprised. Her friend was definitely the more tolerant of the two.

With nothing else to do, Cooper leaned her head back and closed her eyes. It wasn't that early—somewhere around nine—but she felt as if she had been up for hours. Had her father really only left for work sixty minutes ago, with a big hug and a "be good, shorty," his ironic nickname for his tall daughter, before heading out the door?

Her head was pounding, and Cooper knew she would never be a morning person, as much as her mother hoped to change her into one. At least she could count on sleeping in at Penny's, she told herself as she leaned her backpack against the window to use as a pillow and dreamed of the fun to come.

Chapter 2

Loud plane noises woke Cooper as the taxi pulled up to the Departures area, and she stretched awkwardly, trying not to touch either the cabdriver or the meter. Outside the cab she gathered her bag, which had by then been removed from the trunk, then noticed how the already-steamy New York weather made her feel as if she were about to wilt. Just in time, they hurried inside and were hit with a blast of air conditioning. It wasn't as strong as the icy blast found in department stores. Those were Cooper's favorite places to cool off and escape the midsummer humidity, but it would do, she thought, as she trudged along behind her mom.

"Now, girls, don't disappear anywhere. We need to check in right away, and they'll need to see ID from both of you, too," Mrs. Ellis explained.

"And just where would we go?" Cooper whispered to Claire, who shrugged in response.

"You both have your school IDs, don't you?" Mrs. Hughes asked, as if the horrible thought they might have left them behind had just occurred to her. "They won't let you on the plane without picture ID."

"My mom reminded me about ten times and even made me

show it to her in my wallet last night," Cooper replied, digging in her backpack now to find the item in question.

"I have mine, too," Claire said, examining the card closely for what was probably the first time since the school year ended.

Cooper examined her own mug shot and grimaced before announcing, "I'm not looking forward to school starting again, but I have to say, I can't wait to have a new picture taken. I look so horrible, and I'm all slouchy."

"You were just going through a growth spurt," Claire said kindly.

"My whole life is a growth spurt!" Cooper groaned, making reference to her almost 5'9" frame.

"You're really not that tall, and slouching in pictures doesn't make you look shorter," Claire countered.

Cooper already had moved on to her next complaint, though. "And why on earth did you let me cut my own bangs the night before picture day? What kind of friend are you?"

"They didn't look that bad," Claire said, peering over her friend's shoulder to take another look at the offending photo.

"That's easy for you to say. Your wavy brown layers always seem to fall perfectly to your shoulders."

"Oh, my hair has its own issues, and you know it. And the problem wasn't that you decided to cut your bangs, but that you cut them to just a fraction of an inch long!"

"We had to keep all sharp objects away from her for months after that little episode," Mrs. Ellis teased. "She wasn't allowed near a pair of scissors for ages, and we even made her cut her meat with a butter knife."

"Very funny," Cooper said in a tone that implied she thought it was anything but. It didn't stop her mother, though.

"I thought I didn't have to worry about that sort of thing once I got you through the preschool years. That's traditionally when kids give themselves bad haircuts. Who knew you would wait until you were a high school freshman to try it?"

"What can I say? I'm a late bloomer," Cooper replied before rolling her eyes in her mother's direction.

"At least they're all grown out now," Claire reminded Cooper as the group made its way to the now-available ticket agent, who was waiting not very patiently.

After studying everyone's ID, querying them about accepting packages from strangers, and stamping and stapling a variety of documents, the ticket agent finally announced, "You're all set. Your bags are checked through to Seattle. To reach your gate, you're going to turn right just past this counter."

At the metal detector, the buckles from Cooper's overall shorts set off the alarm, but they figured this out only after she had taken off her silver watch, four silver rings, her favorite silver daisy earrings, and the matching necklace made from a bunch of silver daisies strung together. She even had to take the metal clip out of her hair. When she was jewelry-free and still set off the alarm, she was asked to step aside, and a security guard waved some weird wand in front of her. Every time it got near a buckle or button it beeped. The metal shoelace rings on her heavy black boots set it off as well, and Cooper felt as if she had been caught doing something wrong. The female guard then patted her down, checking for Cooper wasn't sure what beneath her faded, baggy overall shorts and red T-shirt. Finally she was pronounced "okay" and was free to put herself back together. She felt silly accessorizing in the middle of the busy airport, and her cheeks were still bright pink by the time she joined Claire and their moms where they stood waiting off to the side.

"If I ever considered a life of crime, that changed my mind," Cooper said as she approached. "How humiliating!"

"I warned you not to wear those big, ugly boots," Mrs. Ellis said.

"No, you asked me not to wear them because you think they're hideous, but you didn't warn me I was going to be detained by the fashion police. Anyway, my overalls set off the alarm, too."

"Good! Maybe now I finally can persuade you to get rid of those. I'd be willing to buy you a new pair that actually fits."

"They're supposed to be loose," Cooper argued, then turned to her friend for support. "Claire, you're the fashion expert. Tell her, will you?"

"Everyone wears them like that," Claire agreed.

"You don't," Mrs. Ellis pointed out, taking in Claire's fitted Capri pants, retro top, and sandals, which made her look sort of like Audrey Hepburn. "And I bet when you start to study fashion design, you're not going to have anything like that in your collections."

"No, but I also wouldn't wear most of what I see on the runway."

"Okay, I give up!" Mrs. Ellis said. "Cooper and I are never going to agree on clothes."

"At last, you've seen the light! Hallelujah!" Cooper cried. "Maybe now I can have some peace."

"I wouldn't count on it. There's still that messy room of yours and your habit of oversleeping, so we have plenty to disagree about," her mother promised.

"Well, can you disagree with Mrs. Hughes for a while instead so Claire and I can go to the newsstand and look at magazines?" Cooper asked as they arrived at their gate.

She was already tugging on her friend's arm to follow her when her mom said, "Our plane is scheduled to leave in thirty minutes. Why don't you girls just stay close-by?"

"We'll be close-by. The newsstand is just over there," Cooper answered, pointing to the shop about fifty yards away from where they were standing.

"We have a two-hour layover in Minneapolis. Why don't you wait, and then you can go off and have a snack or look at magazines or whatever you want?" Mrs. Ellis bargained.

"But we'll have nothing to do on the flight to Minneapolis," Cooper argued.

"You should have thought of that earlier and planned ahead," her mother countered.

"I did plan ahead," a frustrated Cooper explained. "I planned to pick up something to read once we got to the airport."

"But I don't want to have to come find you once our plane is boarding."

"You won't," Cooper promised, fighting to stay calm. "We'll be close enough to hear the announcement."

"I'd really rather you wait until our next stop," Mrs. Ellis said with finality and then sat down to retrieve a nail file from her annoyingly orderly purse. By the way her legs were crossed and her attention was given to reshaping the fingernail on the left index finger, Cooper knew her mother had decided the discussion was over. Her mom's calm dismissal of what Cooper thought was a reasonable request made her want to scream. Her mother could be so unreasonable. Cooper knew it wouldn't do any good to keep arguing, though, so she plopped down into a seat a few feet away and sighed loudly instead.

"Why don't you show me that place you found in your Seattle book that you want to visit?" Claire gently suggested. "It sounded really cool."

"I might as well," Cooper said, digging in her full backpack for several seconds before finally producing the travel tome.

"Look at all the pages you've marked already," Claire observed. "You've folded down the corners of half the book!"

"I want to do and see a lot of things on this trip," Cooper explained simply, the anger at her mother fading just a little as she focused on their destination.

"Well, narrow it down a bit for me. Where's the really good stuff?"

"Okay, here's the café that's also a Laundromat I was telling you about. I definitely want to go there, and—"

111

Cooper's words were cut short as she heard her name announced over the intercom system. "Cooper Ellis, please pick up the nearest white courtesy phone. Cooper Ellis to a white courtesy phone."

Her heart jumped into her throat, and she automatically looked to her mom for answers. The slight look of concern she found on her mother's face did nothing to relieve the pounding Cooper felt in her chest. Instead, it set off her imagination, which had no trouble conjuring up a variety of scenarios, each one worse than the last. What if they had decided she was a security threat after she set off the alarm so many times? What if they wouldn't let her board the plane? What if something horrible had happened to Aunt Penny? Or her dad? There seemed to be a million possibilities, but none of them were good.

She was so caught up in her imagining she almost forgot the call was waiting. Before she drifted away completely, though, Claire brought her back to the present. "Cooper, you better go find out who it is before they hang up."

Cooper turned to her mom as she stood. "Is it okay for me to answer the phone, or is that off limits, too?"

"Don't be ridiculous!" her mother replied. "It's probably just your father with a last-minute message. Although I don't know why he would page you rather than me."

That thought eased Cooper's mind, and she was happy to be released from her mother's watchful gaze for at least a few minutes. But she still grabbed Claire's hand and dragged her along. She didn't know why she was being such a chicken, but calls on the airport courtesy phone seemed to rate right up there with calls in the middle of the night. The news was always bad.

Once at the phone, Cooper summoned all her courage, whispered a quick prayer to God that everyone she loved was all right, and finally offered a tentative "Hello?" into the mouthpiece.

"It's about time you answered the phone! I've been waiting forever."

"Alex!" Cooper practically screamed out in relief. "What are you doing calling me here?"

"Your mom wouldn't let me talk to you before you left this morning, so I thought I'd track you down at the airport," he explained, sounding very proud of his ingenuity.

"You're crazy, you know that?" Cooper told him, before turning to Claire and unnecessarily announcing who was on the line.

"That's why you love me," Alex replied. "So how's the trip so far? Let me in on all the details so I can feel like I'm right there with you guys."

"Well, I was running late as usual. I packed too much. I had to ride in the front seat of the cab. I set off the metal detector several times and had to practically undress in front of the security guard. My mom still hates my wardrobe—no big surprise there. Our magazine-browsing privileges have been revoked until Minneapolis, and now one of my best friends just scared me half to death by paging me over the airport intercom system," Cooper finished breathlessly before adding, "And how's your morning been?"

"I think I have you beat," Alex said. "My two best friends are leaving to spend a fun-filled weekend in scenic Seattle while I'm stuck in this swamp that is New York City in July, babysitting my younger brother—without financial compensation, I might add. Oh, and our Fourth of July plans so far consist of watching professional wrestling and arguing over whether it's fake or not."

"Sorry," Cooper replied. "Your dad ended up going out of town after all, huh?"

"You got it. It's still not too late to take me along, you know. I could be at the airport in under thirty minutes."

"You can't leave your brother home alone, and our plane leaves in about twenty minutes. So I think you're going to have to settle for a souvenir. Is there anything in particular you want?"

"Besides for you to rescue me from my dreary existence?" Alex asked.

"Yes, besides that. That's too big a job for me, anyway. I was thinking more along the lines of a tacky T-shirt or a pen or a set of erasers with various Seattle tourist attractions printed on them. Now, wouldn't they be fun to take back to school with you?" Cooper prodded. "All the senior girls wouldn't be able to stay away from you then."

"Very funny. Actually, I didn't call to ask you to bring me something, although that's a wonderful idea. I wanted to remind you of a few places you need to be sure to visit. There's the marina where Tom Hanks and Meg Ryan first see each other in *Sleepless in Seattle*, and there's a coffee shop where Matt Dillon and his pretend band hang out in a movie called *Singles*. One sec, I have the name written down. I'm sure it will be easy to find."

Cooper could still hear Alex rummaging around when they announced her plane was boarding. She looked over at her mother, who was motioning impatiently for her to hurry.

"Alex, I have to go. Our plane is boarding . . . Al-ex!" Cooper called into the phone, but to no avail.

Finally, just as Cooper was contemplating hanging up on her friend, he came back on the line. "I know I have that name written down somewhere," he said, oblivious to the rush Cooper was in.

She didn't waste any time clueing him in. "My plane is boarding, and my mom is waiting so I have to go right now. E-mail it to me if you find it, and I'll try to check my email at Aunt Penny's. I'll talk to you later. Good-bye!" Claire was adding her good-bye even as Cooper was hanging up the phone, and then the girls ran over to join their moms in the line to board.

"What on earth was that all about?" Mrs. Ellis asked as

soon as Cooper was within hearing distance.

"It was Alex," she said, knowing those three words were explanation enough. As proof that Cooper was right, her mother merely nodded knowingly before hurrying her daughter ahead.

The trip was finally underway.

Chapter 3

Claire and Cooper were happy to find they were sitting in the row behind their mothers, which meant at least a little freedom. They even found, if they concentrated really hard, they could convince themselves they were traveling alone, off on an adventure without adult supervision.

"Here, you want some Play-Doh?" Cooper offered, handing Claire a tiny yellow tub with a neon orange lid. "It's not a magazine, but it's better than nothing." She popped open her own container of neon green and set about making little clay flowers until the flight attendant came by and asked them to put up their tray tables. Cooper and Claire carefully moved their creations to their laps and continued to mold.

A few cans of Coke and a dozen or so Play-Doh flowers later, they were in Minneapolis, where Cooper practically bounded off the plane, eager to stretch her long legs.

"Wait for me!" Claire called, chasing Cooper into the airport.

"Okay, you've caught up. Now let's go explore!"

"One second, young lady," Mrs. Ellis said, in an authoritative tone that let Cooper know her mother meant business.

"Don't you even want to know where your connecting flight is or where to meet us?"

"Oh, that," Cooper joked. "I guess it would be helpful. What's the number?"

"Why don't you walk over there with us so you'll know where it is, and you can keep track of how far away from it you've wandered," Mrs. Ellis suggested. "You have about an hour and a half, but you need to be sure you don't lose track of time. That's all we need for you girls to cause us all to miss our plane."

"I can't believe you would even think such a thing," Cooper answered, feigning indignation. "As if I would ever be late to anything!"

The words were barely out of her mouth before Claire started to choke back laughter.

"It wasn't that funny," Cooper told her friend and then fell in line behind her mother as she led the way to their future meeting point.

"I don't know why you can't just give us the gate number," Cooper complained while following grudgingly but obediently. "We're perfectly capable of finding an airport gate."

"It doesn't hurt to play it safe," her mother admonished. "One of these days you're going to get yourself in trouble by thinking you're too capable, and you're going to wish you had learned to exercise more caution."

"I don't know about that," Cooper replied skeptically.

"Anyway, don't get lost," Mrs. Ellis warned. "And stay in the terminal."

"And don't be late," Mrs. Hughes added.

Cooper nodded absently as she took the twenty-dollar bill her mother offered her. "That's for magazines and a snack," her mom directed, "and I'll expect some change."

"I don't know—airport food is expensive," Cooper shot back with a mischievous smile.

"Change," her mom repeated, raising her eyebrows for effect.

"Okay, okay. Are we excused now?" Cooper queried.

"I guess, just remember—" Mrs. Ellis began, but Cooper cut her off mid-sentence.

"We know already! We won't talk to strangers, we won't lose our tickets, we won't be late, we'll remember our gate number, and we will not only bring back change but also receipts for tax purposes. Now, pleeeeeeease, can we go?"

Her mom was still nodding her head when Cooper leaned down and gave her mother a quick kiss on the cheek before racing off in the direction of the airport's shops.

"We're finally free!" she said, squeezing Claire's hand as they rounded the corner that would lead them to the airport bookstore.

"I know! I thought they would never let us out of their sight," Claire agreed.

"And warning us not to leave the terminal? I'm surprised she didn't tell us not to play in traffic! Sometimes I think they forget we're not twelve anymore."

"I think it's more like seven or eight," Claire countered. "Not that they don't have their moments—like letting us tag along on this trip—but I don't think they'll ever let us grow up."

"I guess it's a good thing that parental permission isn't required, and we'll keep getting older whether they choose to acknowledge the passage of time or not," Cooper replied. "Unless, of course, my mother warns me to death, and I die while still in my teens."

"Death by overparenting," Claire joked. "I can see the headlines now."

After that the girls turned to the headlines shouting at them from the magazine racks. Only after reading a good portion of several magazines while standing there did they make their decisions.

"I'll run up to the counter and pay for these, and then let's get some food. I'm starved!" Cooper said, patting her stomach for effect.

"Me too. Those peanuts from the flight didn't go far."

"Okay, what are you in the mood for?" Cooper asked when she returned to Claire's side.

"I think some real restaurants are down there, but this little café would be fine, too," Claire answered, motioning to a sort of mini-coffeehouse with croissants and pastries on the menu board.

"This works for me," Cooper agreed. "Besides, we have less than an hour now, and a regular restaurant might take too long." Then, laughing, she added, "We wouldn't want to be late, you know."

After waiting in another line, they finally were seated with a ham and cheese croissant and a cream cheese croissant to share, plus two iced mochas.

"Isn't this great?" Cooper leaned over and whispered to Claire. "With a little imagination, we can pretend we're traveling alone, no overprotective parents in sight."

Just as she said the words, a boy tripped over her foot and bumped the back of her chair, knocking Cooper's backpack to the floor as the older girl with him mumbled a barely audible "Sorry."

"At least we don't have to travel with a little brother!" Cooper said, observing the girl with nutmeg brown hair that was swept up with a clip much like Cooper's hair. "And I thought New York was crowded!" Cooper added. "This place is busier than Times Square!"

"But it's cleaner," Claire pointed out.

"That's true," Cooper agreed, peeling off a bit of pastry, causing flaky crumbs to go flying everywhere. "At least it was cleaner until I got here," she said, smiling sheepishly.

When they were finished, the girls began to make their way back to the assigned gate with several minutes to spare. As they passed the bookstore again, Cooper stopped abruptly, causing Claire to bump into her.

"Look at that skirt!" she said, pointing to a girl with long blond hair near the shop's entrance. "That's what I want you to make me for back-to-school."

"It looks like it's just a bunch of neckties sewn together. It shouldn't be too hard. I assume I could do it," Claire agreed.

Cooper knew her friend was just being modest. She could make anything. From the time she was old enough to be trusted with a needle and thread, Claire had been fashioning clothes for their stuffed animals out of scraps. Now she made almost all of her own clothes and as much of Cooper's as Claire could be conned into.

"I'll start raiding my dad's closet as soon as we get home," Cooper vowed.

"I'm sure my dad would be willing to contribute a few ties, too, and maybe we can even find a few at some thrift stores in Seattle," Claire suggested.

"Oooh, I can barely wait! You're the best!" Cooper said, slinging her arm over her best friend's shoulder and giving her a little squeeze.

"Well, if it does for you what it seems to be doing for her, I might have to make myself one, too," Claire teased as she noticed the two good-looking older guys accompanying the girl whose skirt they were studying.

"As long as you finish mine first," Cooper agreed.

Their moms were sitting in the waiting area exactly where the girls had left them, each reading a book. Cooper's mom's diversion was a collection of short stories, while Claire's mom was busy with a novel Cooper remembered seeing in the airport bookstore on the bestseller shelf. It wasn't until the girls were directly in front of the women that they even noticed Cooper's and Claire's arrival.

"Oh, what time is it?" a startled Mrs. Ellis said when she

finally looked up. "They're not already boarding the plane, are they?"

Mrs. Hughes said nothing but instead consulted her watch.

"Relax," Cooper said. "We're early. They're not even pre-boarding yet. Thanks for just assuming we were late, though."

"We weren't assuming anything," Mrs. Ellis protested. "Not that we wouldn't have been justified, if history is any indication."

"Well, it's not," Cooper said, plopping down into the seat next to her mother. She didn't even have time to get comfortable before pre-boarding was announced for the flight to Seattle.

"Let's get in line so we're ready when they call our row," Mrs. Ellis suggested, rising from her seat and stowing her book in her sleek black carry-on bag.

"What's the hurry?" Cooper asked. "We have assigned seats. It's not like I'm going to have to race someone to get to 14-C first."

"I never said you were. It doesn't hurt to board early and get settled, though," her mom replied.

"Fine," Cooper grudgingly agreed, sighing as she followed her mother and Mrs. Hughes into formation near the plane's gate with Claire trailing behind her.

This time the girls were across the aisle from their moms, so it was a little harder to pretend they were traveling solo. Instead, they focused on their magazines, took a pretzel-and-Coke break when the flight attendants came around serving those, and eventually slept for a bit. Cooper had been up late the night before doing laundry and packing, so she was exhausted and drifted off as soon as she reclined her seat. The next thing she knew, she heard the announcement instructing passengers to put their seats and tray tables in their upright positions in preparation for landing in Seattle.

"You amaze me with your ability to sleep anywhere," Claire said after adjusting her seat.

"You just have to make it a priority," Cooper explained. "If you love sleep enough, you find ways to get it wherever you are."

"I like sleep," Claire said. "I just don't like the knees of the person behind me in my back."

"Just one of the challenges you need to learn to overcome."

"I'll keep that in mind," Claire promised just as the plane touched down on the runway.

"I hope Penny didn't forget about us," Mrs. Ellis was saying from across the aisle.

Cooper rolled her eyes. "Mom, don't be ridiculous. You talked to her last night. It's not like she's going to forget we're coming. We've been planning this trip for two months."

"She used to forget to feed her fish, and they were on the table next to her bed," Mrs. Ellis responded.

"That was years ago," Cooper said. "Besides, it's not like goldfish are known for living particularly long lives."

"Not without food, they aren't."

Cooper threw up her hands in surrender. "I give up! There's no convincing you that Aunt Penny is responsible, so I guess we'll just have to wait and see when we get off the plane."

"That sounds good to me," Mrs. Ellis agreed. "This is one instance in which I'd be happy to be wrong."

"And when you are, I think you'll owe Aunt Penny a big apology," Cooper said.

"*If* I am," Mrs. Ellis corrected, "but in my mind that's still a big if."

The passengers in front of them seemed to take forever to exit the plane, but finally Cooper was able to push past the throngs into the Seattle-Tacoma International Airport. Her eyes scanned the waiting area for her aunt's auburn hair and smiling face, but they were nowhere to be found. Then before Cooper knew it, her mother was standing behind her, searching the crowds, as well.

Mrs. Ellis gave Cooper one of her knowing looks and said, "It seems I'm not going to be the one apologizing this time."

Chapter 4

The foursome had made its way to baggage claim, waited for close to fifteen minutes before the luggage came circling around on the conveyor belt, and then stood outside looking at the gray Seattle afternoon and for any sign of Penny.

"I'm going to call her," Mrs. Ellis finally announced. "She's probably sitting at home and has just lost track of time."

Cooper started to defend her aunt but then decided against it. She would wait to see what her mom's phone call turned up. In the meantime, Cooper trained her eyes on the oncoming cars and willed one of them to be Penny's red Toyota.

"Still no sign of her?" Mrs. Ellis asked when she returned a few minutes later.

"No," Cooper sadly admitted.

"Well, I got her answering machine so there's no telling where she is. I think we're going to have to take a cab to the hotel, and you girls will have to come with us. Then, if Penny ever decides to surface, she can come and pick you up."

"Oh, Mom," Cooper protested, "can't we wait a few more minutes? It's silly to go all the way to your hotel when Aunt Penny will just have to turn around and come get us."

"It's sillier to stand here and get rained on when we could

be in our nice, dry hotel room. Besides, our plane landed almost an hour ago. If she were coming, she would be here by now."

Somberly, everyone gathered up their belongings and headed over to the taxi area. They were in line behind a youngish couple when they heard yelling. "Louise! Cooper! What are you doing in that line?"

Cooper turned to see Aunt Penny standing on the curb, waving frantically. She was so loud even the cabdrivers were turning to see what all the commotion was. Cooper took off running, calling to Claire to follow, and flung herself into her aunt's arms.

"Where have you been? Mom was just about to make us go to the hotel with her!"

"I'm sorry. There was a huge accident was on the 5, and it turned the freeway into a parking lot. Traffic was stopped completely. I left my house almost two hours ago and have been on the road all this time."

By now the moms had caught up and were hearing the tail end of Penny's explanation.

"You couldn't have pulled off the freeway and taken an alternate route?" Mrs. Ellis asked her younger sister.

"No, I was in the left lane. I couldn't get over, especially since no one was really moving."

Cooper knew her mom wasn't about to give up that easily.

"If you had a cell phone, you could have at least called and changed the message on your answering machine so when I phoned I would have known you were on your way and hadn't just forgotten us."

"But I don't have a cell phone, and how could I forget you? We talked last night!" Penny cried.

"That's what I told her," Cooper chimed in.

"It doesn't make sense to stand here arguing about it in the middle of the street," Mrs. Ellis finally declared. "We might as well get on the road. We're barely going to make it in time to register for the design show as it is."

"Well, I'm sorry I'm late," Penny continued calmly, although Cooper thought her voice sounded as if she was fighting to stay that way. "I really don't know how I could have foreseen a several-car pileup, though."

"It just seems these things always happen to you," Penny's big sister pointed out.

"Always? They always. . . ?" Penny began to sputter, then calmed down again. "Okay, whatever. I'm not even going to go there. Let's just get your luggage in the trunk."

"That sounds good to me," Mrs. Ellis agreed.

This time Cooper's mom rode in the front seat, and Cooper sat next to Claire in the back. They hadn't driven too far before the Space Needle came into view, and Cooper squeezed her friend's hand excitedly, whispering, "I can't believe we're finally here!" Claire smiled back with equal excitement shining in her eyes.

"We're just about to where the accident was," Penny said a few minutes later. "It was near the next underpass. I'm surprised traffic is moving in that direction at all."

Cooper noticed her mom remained silent until they were on the scene—the alleged scene, anyway. One car with a crumpled fender was on the road's shoulder, and some bits of broken plastic and glass were scattered across the highway. But traffic was moving normally, and not a police car was in sight.

"But it was there! It was a huge pileup. Really!" Penny protested in vain to her sister.

"They certainly cleaned it up fast" was all Mrs. Ellis said in return.

The car was silent for the rest of the ride to the hotel. Once there, though, Mrs. Ellis began to talk nonstop. "Ellen and I will be somewhere in the hotel most of the time. If you need anything, call and ask to have us paged," she instructed Cooper. "And, Penny, please don't let them stay up all night and don't feed them only junk food. At least one vegetable per meal—and neither French fries nor onion rings count."

"I'll guard them as if they were my very own," Penny vowed as she swung an arm over each girl's shoulder and drew them close to her.

"That's what I'm afraid of," Mrs. Ellis mumbled. She wasn't quiet enough, though.

"I heard that!" Penny said, shaking her head in mock disappointment.

"Anyway, you girls be careful. I don't want you out alone after dark, and while Penny's at work tomorrow, stick to the familiar tourist stuff, okay? No wandering off into the unknown."

"Okay, okay. We get the message," Cooper said, hopping impatiently from one foot to the other. "Are we free to go now? Please?"

"Yes. Give me a hug first, though."

Cooper obliged, and Claire hugged her mother, as well. Then, when that was over with, the girls couldn't climb into Penny's car fast enough.

As soon as they pulled out into traffic, Penny turned to the girls and said, "So we're finally free from parental control. What do you feel like doing? Shall I show you around the city?"

"Sounds good to me," Cooper replied. "It's been three years since I've been here, and Claire never has, so we want the grand tour."

"One complete tour package coming up. First, we're going to backtrack for a minute, but bear with me. It will be worth it," Penny promised.

After looping around several blocks, the first sight Penny pointed out was the Kingdome. "Before they built the new stadium, that was the home of our very own Mariners," Penny explained, listing off Seattle's other pro sports teams and sounding every bit the professional tour guide. "Now, down here on South Main is the Elliott Bay Book Company, the best bookstore in the world."

"Is that an opinion or a fact?" Cooper queried.

"Oh, I think it's a proven fact. You'll see if you stop in there," Penny said before continuing her running commentary. "As we continue down First Avenue, you'll see Pioneer Square on your right. The totem pole there is a copy of the one early settlers stole from the Native Americans, an ugly little episode in our history. And across the street is the Pioneer Building. You can get info there about underground tours, which are pretty cheesy but still interesting."

"Why would we want to go on a tour underground?" Claire asked.

"Before the fire in the late 1880s, the city used to be one level lower than it is today. It was too wet, though, so when they rebuilt, they raised the streets."

"I think Dad dragged me on that tour last time we were here," Cooper recalled. "You know what a history freak he is. He loves that kind of stuff."

"Now we're at Pike Place Market," Penny said as she turned left toward the water. "It's pretty touristy, but it's fun to watch the workers in the market throw fish, and some interesting craft booths are inside, too."

"Great, can we get out and take a look?" Cooper asked.

"I'm hunting for a parking space."

After circling several times, Penny maneuvered her car into a tight space on the street, directly in front of Starbucks Coffee.

"Another Seattle institution," Penny said, pointing to the small shop as she fed the hungry parking meter. "I know you have these in New York, too, but I still think Starbucks tastes better here. Maybe it's the water or something."

To test Penny's theory, the trio ventured inside and ordered a round of Frappuccinos to sip as they meandered. Then they made their way across the street to the market. Just as Penny had promised, fish were flying through the air. Anytime a customer placed an order, one of the guys would yell it out, and the appropriate items would be tossed his way. He caught them in a piece of white butcher paper and wrapped them up. Farther down, other stalls were set up. Pottery, jewelry, and colorful photos of the Seattle scenery were all on display. The girls tried on rings, tasted homemade jam, and inspected other various crafts before coming to the end of the line.

"Nothing you couldn't live without?" Penny asked as they exited the market.

"I definitely liked some stuff, but I've promised myself I won't buy any more rings," Cooper explained. "I have enough to wear three on every finger, and I keep looking at more. I think it's a sickness."

"Yeah, you had better watch it, or we'll have to send you away to a treatment program," Aunt Penny teased. "Jewelry Wearers Anonymous, here you come!"

"Very funny," Cooper shot back.

"I liked some of the photography," Claire said. "But I thought I'd wait to make sure I don't find anything I like better tomorrow. I don't want to spend all my money the first night."

"You girls are so much more reasonable than I was at fifteen."

"You seemed reasonable to me when you were that age," Cooper argued.

But Penny was quick to set her straight. "That's only because you weren't even in kindergarten yet. Anyone who didn't watch *Sesame Street* would have seemed mature to you."

"You have a point there," Cooper agreed as she got back in the car.

"Are you girls hungry yet?" Penny asked before continuing their magical mystery tour.

"A little," Cooper admitted.

"You should be," Penny said. "It's after nine in New York."

"Well, when you put it that way, we're starved!" Claire chimed in from the backseat.

"Good. Then let's head toward my place. I was going to take you over to the Fremont District. They have some cool little restaurants and cafés, but it will probably be crowded. Besides, I thought you might want to wait and explore that tomorrow. It's an artsy neighborhood with some funky retro boutiques I'm sure you'd love."

"You'll have to show us how to get there on the map," Cooper said.

"I can do better than that. I thought I could drop you off on my way to work," Penny said. "I don't go in until almost eleven, so you won't even have to get up early."

"Now that's my kind of job!" Cooper replied. "Maybe I've found my calling in social work. I never knew the hours were so good!"

"Don't forget I have to stay overnight at Harbor House two shifts per week," Penny reminded. "And as much as I love working at a group home, those kids and their problems can really wear you out."

"I guess it's back to the drawing board, then, in my search for a career that allows me to sleep in," Cooper said with a sigh.

"Sorry to burst your bubble."

After crossing over the freeway, Penny announced, "Welcome to my neighborhood, Capitol Hill. It's a little gritty, but no worse than SoHo in New York."

Cooper took in the surroundings as the car sped along. She looked up at a street sign and noticed they were on Broadway, a street lined with shops, cafés, and grungy-looking kids sitting against the storefronts.

"I thought we could eat at Johnny Rocket's up here on the right. It's a chain, but it's one of my favorite diners, and they have the best chili-cheese fries in the free world."

"That sounds fine with me," Cooper said while Claire added, "You can't go wrong with a diner."

"Johnny Rocket's it is, then."

Penny was right. The fries and burgers were delicious, and by the time they left, Cooper was so full she practically waddled to the car.

"I think I'm going to be sick," she mumbled happily.

"Please don't," Penny begged. "I don't want to have to explain it to your mom."

"It's not your fault," Cooper said. "Besides, I had lettuce on my hamburger so I fulfilled the vegetable requirement."

"I doubt that's what your mom had in mind," Claire pointed out. "Not that I ate any better."

"What's a vacation if you can't make yourself sick?" Cooper reasoned.

"I guess that's one way to look at it," Penny said, giving her niece a quizzical look.

"Oh, you know what I mean" was all Cooper said.

"Just so long as you don't leave a reminder of what a good time you're having in my car," Penny warned.

"Oh, I'm not sick like that," Cooper assured her aunt, stepping around a group of kids her age who looked as if they hadn't bathed in weeks and were sharing a cigarette Cooper guessed contained something a little stronger than tobacco.

"Keep it that way, and we'll get along just fine," Penny said.

Chapter 5

"It's so weird to think that if we didn't live in New York City, we would be learning to drive now," Cooper said to Claire as Penny started up the engine of her Corolla.

"Just because you live in the city doesn't mean you can't learn," Penny said.

"Our parents don't even have cars," Cooper said.

"So what? Your favorite aunt in the whole world does."

"You're my only aunt," Cooper pointed out unnecessarily.

"You know I'd be your favorite even if you had fifty aunts," Penny said confidently. "Especially if I taught you to drive."

"But I don't have a permit," Cooper said.

"Then we'll just stay in the parking lot."

"I don't know," Cooper hedged. "I've never operated any heavy machinery before."

"You'll do fine," Penny told her. "And this way, if you ever want to get your license, you'll be ready."

Before Cooper could protest any further, Penny pulled around behind Johnny Rocket's to a grocery store parking lot and started to explain which pedal was which. "Just remember, the gas is on the right and the brake is on the left," Penny coached before putting the car in park and getting out to trade places with Cooper.

"C'mon, you'll be fine," she urged when Cooper made no move toward the driver's seat.

Reluctantly, Cooper took her place behind the wheel.

"Start with your foot on the brake, and then take off the parking brake," Penny instructed.

Cooper did as she was told and then eased the gearshift into drive.

"That's it. Now take your foot off the brake, and give it a little gas," Penny said.

"How do you know how much is a little?" Cooper asked.

"You'll know," Penny said.

"That's a little vague," Cooper replied.

"Oh, just put your foot on the gas and push down until the car starts to move," an exasperated Penny told her.

Cooper did as she was told, and the car lurched forward, sending Claire's head bobbing into the space between the two front seats. The car continued to jerk until Cooper got the feel of the accelerator. By that time, she was at the end of the parking lot.

"Okay, now turn and go back to where we started."

"Can't I practice going straight for a while longer?" Cooper suggested meekly.

"If you want to run into that Dumpster you can," Penny replied.

"But I've gone too far. I don't think I have enough room to turn now," Cooper said, panicking just a little.

"That's what reverse is for," Penny explained.

Cooper was about to protest that she didn't think she was ready to switch gears since she was far from mastering the one she was in, but then she thought about going back and telling Alex she had learned how to drive. That bolstered her courage. Taking a deep breath, she repositioned the gearshift, and as Penny had instructed, Cooper looked back over her shoulder before carefully easing backward. When she had gone about ten feet, she smashed her foot down on the brake, bringing the car to an abrupt halt.

"You don't have to push quite that hard," Penny said as Cooper shifted back into drive and began to turn the wheel.

"Hey, look at me! I'm driving!" she cried. The car moved slowly but smoothly forward.

"See, I knew you could do it," Penny said, patting Cooper on the back.

Claire joined in with her congratulations, and Cooper felt elated. She could feel her mouth curl up into a big grin that she couldn't wipe off. She kept repeating to herself, "I'm driving. I'm really driving!"

"One more lap and then it's Claire's turn," Penny said, breaking into Cooper's inner monologue.

As she surrendered control of the car, Cooper couldn't believe how quickly she had learned to love driving. She enjoyed the feel of being in control and the freedom she felt as she decided where they would go next even if it was just choosing one side of the parking lot over another. She was certain she would never be content riding the subway again.

Claire caught on even more quickly than Cooper, and as Penny drove the few blocks to her rented house afterward, the girls couldn't stop thanking her for giving them their first taste of the open road—or in this case, the open parking lot.

"You're very welcome. And you can pay me back by cleaning my apartment tomorrow," Penny said.

"You're kidding, right?" Cooper cautiously asked.

"Of course," Penny said as she unlocked both deadbolts on her bright blue front door. "The place is already spotless. Do you think I'd let your mom come to town and not clean? You know she'll be reporting back to our mother about how I'm living, and Mom already bugs me enough about leaving Connecticut. I don't need to make it worse by giving her any reason to think I'm not doing fine out here on my own."

"Wow," Cooper said, "so even when you're grown-up they don't let you grow up."

"It's the curse of the youngest child," Penny replied. "In your mother's eyes I will always be twelve."

"That's so funny!" Claire chimed in. "Cooper was just saying today that our moms think we're still twelve."

"Well, in my house you can be any age you want to be," Penny said defiantly.

"I think we'll be eighteen for the weekend, then," Cooper declared, with Claire nodding agreeably behind her.

"I think that's a wonderful decision," Penny said. "Now, why don't I show you two adult women around your home base for the next few days."

The tour included Penny's tiny kitchen with red walls; her bedroom, furnished with a double bed covered in a bright coverlet Penny said came from India, a dresser, nightstand, and small table all painted coordinating wild colors right down to their multicolored knobs and trim; and then the living room. This was where the girls would sleep on the futon that folded out into a double bed. Across from it was another painted dresser, but on top of this one sat the TV. Along one entire wall of the living room, Penny had stacked mismatched wooden crates to create an eclectic bookshelf that housed several hundred volumes interspersed with various other knickknacks.

Just as the girls plopped down on the futon, Penny startled them by crying, "Oh, I forgot to show you the best part of the house! Hurry, get up!"

The girls staggered back to their feet. It was now almost midnight in New York, and the hour as well as the jet lag were beginning to catch up with them. They managed to follow Penny to a set of French doors that opened onto a quaint country garden that seemed out of place in the middle of the city. But that only made it more special. It was like a secret hideaway, filled with rusty but charming metal patio furniture, the kind Cooper imagined you would find in a Paris bistro.

"This is where we're going to barbecue on Saturday for the Fourth of July," Penny explained. "The design show is over that afternoon so your moms are coming, and I've invited a few friends, too. I thought you girls could help me do the shopping that morning. We'll have a big blowout before going to watch the fireworks in the harbor."

"You can count on us," Cooper said.

"Good, now let's get back inside. It's cold out here."

Once inside, Cooper and Claire busied themselves unfolding the futon and making it up with the sheets Penny had given them from an old steamer trunk that stood in the entryway to the house. "This place has almost no closets," she explained when Cooper questioned her unique linen storage. "But the hardwood floors more than make up for it, and my landlord lets me paint the walls any color I want."

"Maybe your landlord can talk to my landlord," Cooper suggested. "Mom insists we keep all our walls a boring, ugly white."

"Hang in there," Penny said sympathetically. "Grandma never let me paint, either, but you'll be out on your own soon enough."

"It doesn't seem soon to me," Cooper said.

"I know, but in just three short years you'll be off to college, and you can decorate your dorm room any way you want and not eat a single vegetable for a whole semester."

"Oh, great," Claire said. "So she'll be sick but independent and have a cool room."

"Okay, maybe you could eat a salad or a few carrot sticks every now and then just to keep from becoming completely vitamin-deficient," Penny amended her earlier statement.

"That's better," Claire agreed.

With that settled, the girls slipped into their pajamas, which for Claire meant a tank top and a pair of men's boxer shorts and for Cooper consisted of a pair of baggy flannel pajama pants and one of her dad's discarded T-shirts. Then they climbed into bed, armed with the remote control, Cooper's Seattle guide-book, and a map of the city. They were watching *Nick at Nite* and planning their day when Penny reemerged from the bedroom in gray sweat pants and an Old Navy tee.

"Are you girls hungry?" she asked as she headed into the kitchen. "Ice cream is in the freezer, and Cokes—regular and diet—are in the fridge."

"I'm still full from dinner," Cooper yelled to make sure her response traveled around the corner and into the kitchen.

"Well, if you get hungry later, help yourselves."

"We will," Cooper promised.

Then Cooper heard other voices coming from the kitchen and wondered whom Penny was talking to. At first, Cooper thought her aunt might be on the phone, but then she remembered she would only hear one side of the conversation. Unable to contain her curiosity, Cooper forced her weary body out of bed and peeked around the corner.

"I forgot to check the answering machine when we came in," Penny explained when she saw her niece's face in the door-way.

"Oh," Cooper replied, "I wondered who I heard talking."

"A girl from the group home phoned. She had a fight with one of the other girls and was calling to tell me her side before I got to work tomorrow," Penny explained just as a male voice filled the tiny room.

"Hey, Pen, I just got in. Those meetings ran really late. I guess you're still out with your niece. Anyway, I hope you're having a good time. Call me when you get in no matter how late it is. I missed hearing your voice today."

Cooper turned her questioning gaze on her aunt, but just as Penny was about to speak, another voice emerged from the little black box.

"Hi, Penny, this message is for Cooper. I just wanted to give her our room number in case she or Claire needed to contact us. We're in 316 and can be paged anywhere in the hotel if we don't answer here. Now, make sure they write this number down and take it with them when they go out tomorrow. Oh, and girls, be careful. You're in a strange city where you don't know your way around, so don't go wandering off anywhere that isn't well populated."

Cooper sighed in resignation. Apparently her mother didn't realize that while under Penny's roof, the girls were adults who were capable of taking care of themselves.

Chapter 6

It only took as long as the answering machine rewound for Cooper to forget her mother's overprotectiveness and turn her thoughts back to Aunt Penny's mystery man.

"Well?" she said, waiting expectantly to be filled in.

"Well what?" Penny teased.

"Who's the man on your answering machine? The one who can't wait to hear your voice?" Cooper asked, her voice infused with impatience.

"Oh that! Why didn't you say so?"

"I did!" Cooper cried. "Now, who is he? I want all the juicy details."

Just as Penny began to explain, Claire called from the other room, "Hey, what am I missing in there?"

"Aunt Penny was about to spill all the details about the mystery man on her answering machine," Cooper yelled back. "We'll come in there so you can hear, too. I think this is going to be a good one."

Once they were settled on the futon, with Aunt Penny in the middle and the volume on the TV turned down, she began to unfold her story.

"I met Brian about a month ago," Penny started. "My

friend Lori invited me to hear this new local band at a club downtown. I didn't want to go, and I was on call at work, but Lori was leaving for three weeks in Europe the next day so I finally caved."

"And Brian was in the band?" Cooper prodded.

"No!" Penny answered, giving her niece a playful swat. "He's not in a band."

"I just thought I'd give it a shot," Cooper said with a shrug.

"Why don't you let me finish my story and save your questions for the end?" Penny suggested.

"Okay," Cooper reluctantly agreed but not before adding, "even though it would be cool if he were a musician."

Penny rolled her eyes in response before continuing. "So I get there, and Lori has invited several other friends I've never met. Brian is one of them. I start to suspect she's trying to set us up, but Brian's so easy to talk to that I don't really mind. Just as I'm finding out a little bit about him, the band comes out, and conversation is impossible. Still, I figure we can continue where we left off between sets. Then, just as the band is about to take a break, my pager goes off."

"But you don't have a pager," Cooper corrected, causing Penny to remind her of their agreement to hold all questions until the end.

"Anyway, my pager, which I have to wear when I'm on call at work, goes off," Penny explained, "which means I have to leave."

"Couldn't you just ask Brian for his phone number or something?" Cooper asked.

"Ah, ah, ah!" Penny chastised, covering Cooper's mouth with her hand this time. "Don't make me apply the duct tape. It's been a long day for you guys, and I'd like to finish this before the sun comes up."

"Mmm-khay," Cooper mumbled through her aunt's tightly clamped fingers. Cooper then raised two fingers as if to further vow she would behave.

"That's better," Penny said approvingly. "Now, as I was saying, I had to leave, and to make it worse, I knew Lori was going out of town so I couldn't have her set up another little meeting anytime soon. I wasn't about to ask him for his phone number, and he made no move to ask for mine. So I said good-bye and tried to convince myself he wasn't right for me anyway. I told myself he probably lived at home in his parents' basement and that he no doubt was a huge Barry Manilow fan and that he spent every weekend glued to the TV watching football. By the time I reached Harbor House, he was a complete loser—in my mind."

"So what happened?" Cooper asked before realizing her slip and clamping her hand over her own mouth.

"I had resigned myself to not seeing him again when I ran into him in the church parking lot that Sunday. It turns out we go to the same church, but because it's so big we had never met before. Then he invited me out to lunch after church, and we went down by the waterfront, got clam chowder from a little stand there, and ate it as we walked along the Sound. We found out we both went to Seattle Pacific University. We think we may have even had a class together. We have several friends in common, and we probably passed each other on campus dozens of times without knowing it."

Cooper and Claire both sighed at the romantic story, then eagerly waited to hear more.

"After that he dropped me back at my car in the by-then deserted church parking lot, and he said he had a confession to make: He saw me with Lori at the movies a few weeks earlier and had asked her to introduce him, so the set-up at the club had been his idea, not hers. I was stunned, but since he was coming clean, I decided to tell him about my little game in which I tried to convince myself he wasn't worth getting to know better. Luckily, he laughed and then admitted that while he had his own place and his musical tastes were a little more alternative, he did watch his fair share of football on the weekends. I figured I could accept that and wasn't sorry when, on our first official date two nights later, he showed up with this." Penny retrieved something from one of her crate-shelves and flashed it at the girls.

"A Barry Manilow album?" Cooper said, breaking her vow of silence once more. "Where on earth did he find that?"

"He said he had to go to four used record stores to find it, and then had to endure the humiliation of having the nose ring–wearing clerk think he was buying it to actually listen to!"

"That is the most romantic story I've ever heard," Claire gushed when Penny was finished.

"Yeah," Cooper agreed. "Now, when do we get to meet him?"

"You may have to wait until the barbecue on Saturday," Penny replied. "He's just been assigned to a new project so he's been working really long hours, and I work until nine tomorrow night myself."

"What does he do that he has to work such long hours?" Cooper asked, then added, "Since we know he doesn't play in a band."

"He's a computer programmer," Penny explained, "which is why he works so much. It's a great job, but it's competitive— so he has to be willing to work when they need him. He may be able to get away to meet us for a late movie tomorrow night, if you girls are up for it, but I'll have to check with him then to see for sure."

"We're always up for a movie!" the girls chirped.

"We'll plan on that, then," Penny agreed. "Now, why don't you get some sleep? I'm going to call Brian back before he wonders what happened to me."

"Okay," Cooper said. "Tell him we said hello and can't wait to meet him."

"I'll be sure to do that."

"And don't wake us up too early," Cooper called after her aunt.

"Sleep!" was the only response Cooper got.

"If we were really eighteen and on our own, we wouldn't have anyone telling us to go to sleep," Cooper said to Claire with a hint of resignation in her voice. Then, for emphasis, she rolled over and punched her pillow.

"If we were really eighteen and on our own, we could meet a wonderful guy at a club and go out without having to check with anyone, and we could call him no matter how late it was without anyone monitoring our phone usage," Claire added.

"Penny doesn't know how great she has it. Her own place. A new boyfriend. No one telling her what to do, checking up on her, or making her write down phone numbers."

"At least we have no one telling us what to do for a whole day," Claire said, grabbing the guidebook from the foot of the bed, where it had been discarded when Penny began her fairytale-like bedtime story. "So we had better start to plan."

Thirty minutes later the girls had arrived at a solid list of activities, making notes on the inside of the book's cover of everywhere they wanted to visit. Then they turned off the TV, turned out the light, and drifted off. Tomorrow they would get another taste of Penny's perfect life, and they would need their sleep.

Chapter 7

Cooper was awakened the next morning by a loud "I knew it!" coming from the entryway. At least she thought it was the entryway, but since she wasn't used to her new surroundings and she still felt a little groggy, she couldn't be sure.

"I told your mother it was a big accident," Aunt Penny said as she perched herself next to Cooper on the futon. "See? Isn't this exactly what I described?"

Cooper rubbed her eyes before inspecting the front page of the *Seattle Times* that Penny was thrusting in Cooper's face. Sure enough, taking up most of the space above the fold was an article about a serious accident accompanied by a gruesome photo showing several mangled cars and rescue workers helping a woman who had blood running down her face.

" 'A five-car pileup brought traffic to a standstill on Interstate 5 yesterday, adding chaos to the traffic congestion a holiday weekend brings,' " Aunt Penny read triumphantly.

"I think the person you should be reading this to is my mom," Cooper gently pointed out. "I never questioned your story."

"Why bother? She would still find some way to make it my fault," Penny said, waving her hand dismissively. "Anyway, we have better things to spend our time thinking about—like breakfast.''

"Great! I'm starved," Claire said, popping her head out from under the covers.

"What are you making?" Cooper added, looking at her aunt expectantly.

"Nothing, unless you girls want Cheerios," Penny replied. "I was thinking more along the lines of picking up something. I know a place that makes great breakfast tacos, and it's on the fringes of the Fremont District where I'm dropping you off."

"We're up for that, aren't we, Claire?"

"Sure, as soon as I take a shower."

"Good. That's all settled, then," Penny said. "I'm going to read the paper and drink my coffee, so the shower's all yours. You don't need to rush, but we should leave here in a little over an hour, so plan accordingly."

Claire dug around in her bag and gathered up her things before padding down the hall toward the shower. At the same time, Cooper reached for the remote and sank back against her pillow. She located the Cartoon Network, which was airing an episode of *Scooby Doo*, then wandered into the kitchen in search of something to drink.

"What are you looking for?" Penny asked, peering over the top of the paper.

"I don't know," Cooper shrugged. "Some juice or something?"

"Some frozen concentrate might be in the freezer. You'll have to thaw it out by running hot water over it first."

"Could I just have a Coke?" Cooper suggested, waiting for the inevitable no that would follow.

"Sure, if that's what you want," Penny surprised her by saying. "It can't be any worse for you than my coffee habit is for me. Caffeine's caffeine, after all."

"That's what I'm always trying to tell my mom," Cooper said, "but she just rolls her eyes and hands me a glass of milk."

"Well, I didn't hear anything in her instructions yesterday that mentioned caffeine intake, so I think we're in the clear."

"I don't remember anything, either," Cooper agreed, sipping happily as she returned to the living room.

It was a little crazy with all three of them trying to get ready in one bathroom, but eventually they were set to head out the door—only after Cooper learned a neat little no-iron trick from her aunt. As Cooper's mom had promised, all of Cooper's clothes were wrinkled beyond wearability, but Penny showed her how she could tumble what she wanted to wear in the dryer for a few minutes, and it would be as good as new. What a revelation. This would save her tons of time during the school year, and she couldn't wait to impress her mom.

Due to the bathroom backlog, it had taken an hour and a half before everyone was ready, and as a result, they needed to hurry. But the breakfast tacos at Benny Lyle's were wonderful. Cooper ordered hers filled with bacon, eggs, and avocado. "You guys are my witnesses; I got my vegetables in!" she proclaimed and then devoured it in a matter of minutes.

As Penny dropped them off at Fremont Avenue, she asked Cooper, "You have the spare house key I gave you, right?"

Cooper was already out of the car and standing on the curb. "Yes, it's in my backpack on my keychain along with the Post-It note with your address."

"Okay, then. I don't want to sound like a mother, but I'd hate for you two to find yourselves locked out."

"We'll be fine," Cooper assured her.

"I'll see you tonight when I get off work, and we can check movie times then."

"Sounds good," the girls agreed, waving as they did so.

A second later Penny was speeding away, her car horn beeping a muted good-bye.

The girls needed no more incentive to get started. They strolled down the street until they reached a thrift store with a display that caught their eye. Inside they found racks of vintage cardigans, old prom dresses with faded crinoline and tulle drooping below their hems, and boxes full of little hats that reminded Cooper of something her grandmother or Jackie Kennedy would have worn. They didn't end up buying anything, but they had fun looking.

In the next store, their wallets didn't get off quite so easily. It was full of T-shirts with sixties and seventies cartoon characters on the front—Speed Racer, Johnny Quest, Josie and the Pussycats—or product logos like Tide detergent or Crest toothpaste. They also had games and candy Cooper remembered from her childhood.

"Look, Kerplunk!" she said to Claire, her voice laced with nostalgic excitement.

"And Mr. Potato Head," Claire added, holding up one of the plastic spuds.

"Oh, and they have those orange wax harmonicas!" Cooper continued, racing headlong down memory lane.

"I thought you could only get those on Halloween."

Before leaving the store, Cooper and Claire had loaded up on harmonicas, syrup-filled wax bottles, Pop Rocks, and Everlasting Gobstoppers. Once they felt they had enough sugar to keep them wired for the rest of the weekend, they moved on toward their next stop, a record store called Cellophane Square.

"Maybe we can find some more Barry Manilow albums for Penny," Cooper said with a laugh as they dug through the bins of used music. Sadly, they couldn't find anything suitably cheesy, so they crossed the street to continue looking for thrift store finds.

Eventually, Claire's persistence paid off in the form of a fifties-sytle full skirt complete with lemons, cherries, and blueberries dancing across it. "With a red tank top and a little cardigan, this will be perfect for the barbecue tomorrow."

"Cute and patriotic, too," Cooper said approvingly. "You always manage to find the best stuff. You're like one of those drug-sniffing dogs at the airport."

"Excuse me?" Claire said, feigning indignation. "Did you just compare your best friend in the whole world to a dog?"

"Only in the nicest possible way," Cooper assured her, but not before getting a hat thrown at her for her trouble.

"Okay, if that's the way you want to be," Claire said, continuing to pretend she was miffed. She sniffed haughtily and lifted her nose high into the air before moving through the rest of the racks. With her head held so high, though, Cooper wondered how Claire could see where she was walking. After only a few steps, Claire stumbled over something—then that *something* responded with a loud "yowl!" and scurried away.

Cooper nearly doubled over with laughter at her friend's misfortune, and while at first Claire tried to maintain at least a little of her composure, in a matter of seconds she was laughing hysterically, too. When the girls finally recovered, which took considerable time, they started to head for the exit until Cooper felt Claire grab her arm.

"I still have to pay for this skirt," Claire hissed to her friend. "But I can't face that cat."

Cooper almost started to laugh again until she noticed her friend looked genuinely pained. Instead, without comment, Cooper took the skirt from Claire and held out her other hand for the money it would cost.

"Thank you, thank you, thank you!" Claire chanted quietly, giving her friend a little squeeze. "You definitely are forgiven for comparing me to a dog."

"Not just any dog but a dog with a nose for fashion," Cooper corrected before making her way up to the counter.

As the garment was being rung up, the black cat that had caused the whole catastrophe started to rub up against Cooper's leg and purr contentedly. Apparently all had been forgiven, or her new feline friend didn't make the connection between Cooper and Claire. Whatever the case, Cooper leaned down and gave the kitty a quick pet as the girls exited.

"You're the best," Claire said as she took the bag and the change Cooper offered.

"I know," Cooper joked. "Just don't you forget it. What do we want to do next?"

"What's on the schedule?" Claire asked.

"Well, if we're hungry, we could try to find the Sit & Spin, or if we want to do more shopping, we could head toward Ruby Montana's. That's sort of near the bookstore Penny drove us by last night."

"I could go either way," Claire said in her usually agreeable manner.

"I'm getting hungry," Cooper admitted before consulting her watch to make sure her stomach clock and the real one were in sync. It was almost two, which seemed about right since they had eaten a late breakfast.

"So how do we get out of here?"

"Oh no!" Cooper cried, pausing by the curb and slapping her hand to her cheek. "We were running late, and Penny forgot to give me the bus schedule!"

"That's okay," Claire replied, refusing to get rattled. "Remember, we're very mature eighteen-year-olds exploring the city on our own. We don't need a bus schedule."

"Yeah," Cooper agreed, catching up to her friend. "We can always take a cab if we need to. This is no big deal."

"Exactly. It will cost a bit more, but we'll get there faster so we'll be able to squeeze more into our day, which will make it more than worth the money."

"Now, which direction should we walk to find a cab?" Cooper asked.

"It looks really busy down there," Claire suggested, pointing toward a crowded area just up ahead.

As the girls walked closer to the crowd, music began to waft toward them, and they realized the street was filled with delicious smells neither recognized.

"Look." Cooper pointed to a banner that hung from one

side of the street to the other. "There's a Greek festival going on; that's why it looked so crowded."

"And the street's blocked off for the next several blocks. I doubt any cabs are coming through here," Claire added.

"What do we do now, sophisticated world travelers that we are?"

"I guess we can head back in the direction we came from," Claire suggested.

Before Cooper could answer, a breeze blew the scent of some spiced meat their way and made up her mind for her. "I say we revise the plan to include eating lunch here."

"Fine by me," Claire agreed.

Within minutes the girls had each purchased a roll of tickets and joined the line for gyros. Cooper's mouth started to water as she watched a man expertly cut thin slices of seasoned lamb and pile them on a sort of pita bread before dousing it with yogurt sauce and rolling it up.

"First we had breakfast tacos and now Greek tacos," Cooper said as she took a bite that caused juice to drip down her chin.

They ate as they walked, taking in all the sights and sounds around them.

"Look at those dancers," Claire said, pointing to a group that had formed a circle to the left of the stage where the musicians played.

"It reminds me a little of the dancers in that Off-Off-Broadway production of *Fiddler on the Roof* we saw last year. The guys in that were amazing," Cooper remarked.

"These guys are almost as good, and I bet they aren't even professionals," Claire concluded.

"You're probably right. Too bad I'm such a klutz. I'd love to learn how to do something like that."

"You're not such a klutz," Claire loyally argued.

"Our ballet teacher suggested I take up kickboxing instead!"

"She was only joking."

"I don't think so," Cooper said.

"Even if she were serious, that doesn't mean you wouldn't be good at any other kind of dance."

"I don't plan to find out. Now, how about some baklava?"

"Mmm!" Claire said by way of response.

The girls used the rest of their tickets to purchase pieces of the dense, sticky Greek pastry, which they quickly devoured. They were watching the dancers one last time and licking the sugar from their fingers when a guy with long-ish, wavy brown hair shyly approached Cooper. His gold eyes met her gray ones, and instead of saying anything, he raised his eyebrows questioningly and motioned toward the crowd now dancing in the street.

"Oh, I don't think so," Cooper said as soon as she understood what he was asking. "I really don't dance."

Then he smiled at her and looked sort of sheepish, and Cooper's heart began to melt. Before she could decide what to do, Claire leaned over and whispered in Cooper's ear, "Maybe the eighteen-year-old, very independent Cooper is a wonderful dancer."

Without consciously deciding to give it a try, Cooper found herself in the middle of the street holding hands with a boy whose name she didn't know. This was definitely something she wouldn't do at home in New York.

Chapter 8

Cooper couldn't believe she had agreed to join this nameless boy when, as if reading her mind, he leaned in and said, "Hi, I'm Noah."

Cooper introduced herself as best she could while following the circle first one way and then the other. Thankfully, the tempo slowed after a minute, and the steps to the next part of the dance were easier to pick up. Cooper was so busy staring at her feet, she practically forgot her partner. When she did look up again, she was startled to find him studying her. She could feel her cheeks turn red, which only made her more embarrassed, but her new friend just smiled, unfazed.

"Where do you go to school?" he asked over the music.

"Hudson High in Manhattan," Cooper answered, knowing it wasn't what her dance partner expected to hear.

"Manhattan, as in New York City, Manhattan?"

"Yeah. I'm just out here for the weekend visiting my aunt."

Noah's face fell a little at that news, and Cooper couldn't help but feel a thrill rush through her. *He's disappointed I don't live around here!*

Without warning, her partner broke away from the group, taking her with him. They were dancing all on their own, and even though Cooper knew people were watching, she didn't feel self-conscious. After all, if the cute guy she was dancing with didn't seem concerned about her lack of coordination, why should she be?

Then, all too soon, the music ended.

"I'm just on my lunch break, and I have to get back or my boss will go ballistic," Noah explained.

Cooper wracked her brain for something meaningful to say in response, but all she could do was nod her head in understanding.

"My friend's band is playing later tonight, though. If you're not doing anything, maybe you could stop by? You could bring your friend, too. There's no cover charge if you get there before eight."

Cooper felt so stupid, and for some reason she still couldn't make her mouth move. Instead she just continued to nod as if she had been struck mute.

"So is that a yes, you'll be there?" Noah asked, his expression hopeful.

"I'll try," Cooper finally managed to blurt out, never before so thankful for the gift of speech.

"Great! It's downtown at a place called. . ." But Noah's directions were drowned out by the music starting up again. Cooper heard enough to get them there, if Claire agreed to go. It was at Rockin' D-something. She figured she could look it up in the phone book at their next stop, and then she wouldn't have to feel foolish asking Noah to repeat himself. How many clubs could there be in the downtown area that started with the word *Rockin'*?

Again, Cooper nodded her head. This time it wasn't because she couldn't speak, but so she didn't have to yell over the music. With one more quick smile, Noah disappeared into the crowd, and Cooper went off in search of Claire.

"And you said you couldn't dance!" Claire said as soon as Cooper was within hearing range. "I told you, you just needed to find the right kind of dancing. Or was it finding the right partner that made the difference?"

At that Cooper could feel herself blush for the second time in a matter of minutes. When she regained her composure, she couldn't help but ask her friend, "He was really cute, wasn't he?"

"Definitely," Claire agreed. "Where did he run off to?"

"Apparently he works somewhere around here. He said he had to get back, but he invited us to hear his friend's band tonight at some place downtown."

"Did you tell him we would come?" Claire asked.

"I told him we would try."

"That's going to be tricky since we promised we would be in before dark and Penny gets home at nine."

"But, Claire, he was so sweet, and did you see those eyes? Besides, it doesn't get dark until nine, so we don't have to be home until Penny does. We can catch a cab at 8:30, and we'll arrive before we turn back into pumpkins."

"Unless something goes wrong," Claire pointed out in her annoyingly practical way.

"Just promise me you'll consider it. We don't have to decide until tonight."

"Okay, I'll consider away all afternoon. Now, let's get moving. It's past two, and this neighborhood is the only one we've explored so far."

"Ruby Montana's, here we come!" Cooper shouted before charging full speed down the street. She had only gone a few steps when Claire interrupted.

"Uh, Cooper? The water is over there, which means downtown is that way," Claire explained, pointing in the opposite direction of the one her friend was heading.

Once they were turned around, they had no trouble finding a cab that took them where they wanted to go, a shop that the guidebook classified as vintage-retro.

The new neighborhood was far more buttoned up than the

previous one, and everyone Cooper saw in the few seconds before entering the shop was dressed in some variation of the tra-
ditional business suit.

"They all look like our dads," Cooper whispered to Claire,
who was also taking in the local scenery.

"I know what you mean. I hope the guidebook didn't mis-
lead us."

When they stepped inside, though, the girls knew the de-
scription was right on the money. Fifties dinette sets greeted
them, and display cases were full of antique toys. The furniture
looked as if it belonged at Graceland, and in one corner was the
biggest display of salt and pepper shakers Cooper had ever seen.

"It's like a warped Disneyland, isn't it?" Cooper asked
Claire as they continued to peruse the kitschy ceramics.

"Definitely," Claire agreed, "but are you going to buy anything?"

"Oh, I think I have to get something, if only to remember
the place by. I was thinking of these salt and pepper shakers,"
Cooper said, holding up a toaster with two slices of bread boast-
ing teeny holes in the tops of their crusts.

"What on earth would you do with them? Your mom would
never let you put those on the kitchen table."

"I'm going to put powder in them," Cooper announced,
proud of her resourcefulness. "You know, that kind I have with
the little sparkles in it."

"That's a great idea!" Claire replied, warming up to the
plan.

"Did you find anything?"

"Nothing for me, but I think I have the perfect souvenir for
Alex. Look, it's a floaty pen that honors Ruby Montana's an-
nual Spam Carving Contest. Can you believe it?"

"Spam, as in the meat that comes in a can?" Cooper asked,
trying not to sound too disgusted.

"The one and only."

That was all Cooper needed to hear before pronouncing her friend's find perfect indeed.

After making their purchases and bidding a fond farewell to Ruby's, the girls decided to walk the few blocks to Elliott Bay Book Company. The day was unusually sunny, and the drier Pacific Northwest weather was a nice change from New York's steamy humidity that often made the city in midsummer seem like a sauna.

Elliott Bay was as wonderful as Penny had promised, and the girls had no trouble passing almost an hour there as they browsed through the shelves before wandering downstairs to use the bathroom, the first one they had come across all day. A restaurant was on the lower level, but Cooper still had her heart set on tracking down the Sit & Spin, so when they finished up, they went back outside to search for a cab. They caught one across the street from the bookstore, in front of a little flower shop, and were soon off again.

The Sit & Spin's neighborhood wasn't nearly as populated or as clean as the one they had been in. In fact, the Laundromat-café seemed to be the only business open, but inside it was lively.

"I think I'll just have an Italian soda," Cooper said. "I'm still full from lunch."

"I think I'll have that, too," Claire agreed, patting her own full stomach.

As they waited for their orders, Cooper peered into the adjoining Laundromat. It wasn't terribly thrilling, but the bright colors made it look different from the stark laundry room at home.

"For some reason everything's more exciting when you do it on your own," Cooper surmised.

"I don't know if I'd call doing laundry exciting, but I think I see what you mean."

Once they were settled in a shiny vinyl booth that looked like something out of *Grease*, Cooper renewed her pitch to track down Noah. "I looked up the club in the phone book while you were in the bathroom at Elliott Bay, and it was right there in the white pages, Rockin' Eddie's. I copied down the address and can look it up on the map so we can at least see how far it is," Cooper pleaded, putting on her best pouty face for her friend.

"I guess it wouldn't hurt to at least see where it is," Claire agreed. "It has nothing to do with that overdone puppy dog look you were giving me, though. That wouldn't convince any-one to do anything."

"I don't care why you agreed, as long as you did," Cooper said happily. "Now, let's see if I can find this street."

A few seconds later Cooper had the map spread across the table and was busily trying to find F–5.

"Can you at least leave me a little corner for my drink?" Claire protested when the map hid her colorful Italian soda from view. "You're going to spill it in my lap, and then we're going to have reason to find out if that Laundromat is as fun as it looks."

"Picky, picky," Cooper chided before giving in to her friend's request. "I found the general area so I can fold it up a bit. It should be somewhere right around here," she continued, talking to herself more than to Claire.

"What's that spot you already have circled?" Claire asked after giving the map a cursory glance.

"Good question," Cooper replied, leaning in to look closer.

"Isn't that where we are right now?"

"You know," Cooper said, "I think it is. Claire, my friend, you are a topographical genius! You ought to consider giving up your dreams of fashion design to become a map reader full-time."

"Thanks but no thanks."

"Suit yourself," Cooper replied with a shrug. "If you want to turn your back on your calling, I suppose I can't do anything about it. But now, on a more superficial note, you do know what your discovery means, don't you?"

"That I've found where we should put the 'you are here' arrow?" Claire asked.

"No, silly! That the club I've been trying so hard to find is only . . . wait, let me count . . . five, six, seven, eight, no, nine blocks from this very spot! Can you believe it?"

"That is pretty coincidental," Claire agreed.

"So does that mean you're in as far as the club outing goes?" Cooper asked.

"Well, I was hoping to look in some of those shops on Broadway that we didn't check out last night," Claire stalled.

Cooper clasped her hands together and began chanting, "Pretty please, oh, pretty please."

Claire shook her head at her obstinate friend. "Oh, all right. I guess it's the least I could do since you saved me this morning from the cat that was out to get me."

"Have I mentioned lately that you are the best possible friend a girl could ever have?" Cooper said.

"Yes, but you can't say something like that often enough," Claire teased.

Then Cooper remembered her other best friend and whispered up a quick prayer. *God, thank you for this wonderful weekend and for giving me Claire and Aunt Penny to make it so special. And one more thing, if it's not too much trouble. Can you make the music tonight not so loud that I can't hear what Noah's saying? Thanks in advance. Amen.*

And with that, the evening was officially underway.

Chapter 9

"According to the map, we should go right and then walk four blocks before turning left and going five more blocks. It seems pretty simple," Cooper said.

"Just so long as you know where we're going," Claire replied.

"I do."

"And it's not farther than nine blocks."

"It isn't."

"And we get home before your aunt," Claire finished.

"Any other stipulations you would like to put on the evening's plans?" Cooper asked, her voice tinged with sarcasm.

"No, I think those are all my conditions," Claire said, pretending not to notice her friend's tone.

"Good. Then let's start walking. It's already after seven, and if we're only going to stay until quarter past eight, I want to get there as soon as we can."

"A little eager to see your new friend Noah again, eh?" Claire teased.

"What makes you say that?" Cooper asked, trying to play it cool. Walking at twice her usual pace gave her away, though. She finally decided she might as well give up trying to hide her excitement, and instead she looped her arm through Claire's and began to skip down the next block.

"Here's where we should turn left," Cooper said, then added, "only five more blocks to Noah!"

"This club must be in some sort of warehouse," Claire said once they made the turn.

"A lot of clubs are in warehouses. I'm sure it will be fine," Cooper replied.

"I don't mean to be the voice of doom, but if a club is out here, shouldn't we see some cars or at least some people?" Claire asked a few blocks later.

"I bet the entrance is around the corner or something. When we get up to the next block and look down the street, we'll see wall-to-wall people," Cooper assured her friend. But even as she said the words, her confidence was fading.

At the next block there were no crowds, no music, and least of all, no cars.

"Are you sure you have the address right?" Claire asked.

"Yes, I'm sure, but it's still early. Maybe no one's here yet?" Cooper suggested.

"Not even the band?"

"Maybe you're right. I might have messed up the address somehow. What if I switched two of the numbers around, and instead of its being at 1924, it's at 1294?"

"Or maybe we're on the south end of the street, and the numbers repeat again on the north side?" Claire suggested helpfully.

"Exactly!" Cooper cried. "Which means if we just keep walking this way, we're bound to run into 1294 and the north end of the street."

Twelve blocks later the girls weren't so hopeful. It had been blocks since they had seen any traffic, and the neighborhood was more deserted, not less. In fact, Cooper couldn't believe she hadn't noticed before how run-down everything was and how quiet.

"How long do we keep walking?" Claire finally asked.

"I was just wondering that myself," Cooper replied.

"I mean, I don't want to ruin your plans or anything, but I have the feeling you're not going to see Noah tonight."

"I'd settle for seeing something I recognized!"

"Me too," Claire agreed. "It's sort of creepy around here."

"I think this definitely counts as wandering away from the standard tourist attractions," Cooper said. "It's a good thing my mother can't see me now."

"You wouldn't be allowed out of the house unchaperoned until you were thirty!"

"Thanks for that cheerful mental image."

"You're welcome. Now, can we find a taxi and get out of here?" Claire asked.

"Sure. Let's head up this street. It should intersect at some point with that main street we were on to begin with. Then we should have no trouble hailing a cab."

The girls walked out of the neighborhood much more somberly than they had walked in. After continuing in silence for several blocks, Claire finally broke the ice. "You know, I wasn't trying to rain on your little Noah parade back there. I really would have been happy for you if we could have tracked him down."

"I know. I'm just disappointed is all." Then, as if the clouds were taking their cue from Claire, the sky opened up, and rain came down at warp speed.

Cooper's khakis and short-sleeved denim shirt were soaked immediately. Even the lace-trimmed tank she wore underneath was wet. But at least she had on her heavy boots, which kept her feet relatively dry. Claire, on the other hand, was wearing a floral dress made of the thinnest possible cotton and delicate sandals. The only protection she had from the deluge was the pale pink beaded cardigan she pulled close around her.

"So much for catching a cab," Claire said. "They'll be full of people trying to escape the weather."

"Still, let's hurry. At least on a busier street we have a better chance of finding a restaurant to duck into or an awning to hide under."

"You're right there," Claire agreed, and the girls sprinted in the direction they had come from originally. Of course, that seemed like hours ago now. Eventually, they did reach a main street. Not the one they thought they were heading toward, but one with cars and people, which was no small answer to prayer. They weren't home yet, but at least they didn't have to be quite as worried that they were going to end up on an upcoming episode of *Unsolved Mysteries*. The victory was short-lived, though.

"Now what do we do?" Claire asked her dripping friend.

"I guess we see if we can still read our soggy map and use it to lead us in the direction of a tourist attraction. We'll probably have the best luck catching a cab some place like that."

"And if we don't catch a cab?"

"I'd rather not think about that," Cooper said.

"Maybe we have to," Claire gently suggested. "We could always call our moms and have them come pick us up. I'm sure cabs are in front of their hotel at all hours."

"I'd rather die first," Cooper declared a bit melodramatically. She knew she was being stubborn, but she wasn't going to spend the evening listening to a lecture from her mom. There had to be another way. No sooner had she thought that, than it hit her. "We can call for a cab! It didn't even occur to me because plenty of them are around in New York, but I'm sure if we call a cab company, they would be happy to dispatch a driver over here."

"Let's find a pay phone right now," Claire said, her pace picking up for the first time in blocks.

Several blocks later, they found a phone, and Cooper dialed as fast as her fingers could manage. She was put on hold, though, and when an actual person did come back on the line, Cooper was told she would have to wait more than an hour before a cab could come. "Thanks. I guess I'll just have to try another company," a dejected Cooper said.

"You're welcome to try, but on a rainy Friday night, and a holiday weekend to boot, you're going to hear the same song and dance from everyone you call. The best you can hope for is that the rain will let up, but I wouldn't count on that. This is Seattle, after all."

"Great, you've been a big help," Cooper said before returning the receiver to its cradle. Then she turned to her friend and said, "It looks as if we had better keep on walking."

By now it was 8:30, and the chances of beating Penny or the impending darkness home were looking slim. Then, just when all hope was lost, a cab turned the corner and pulled up almost in front of the girls. A couple got out and entered the building the girls were standing next to, a sort of nondescript apartment high-rise, and Cooper and Claire couldn't scramble into the back of the cab fast enough.

"You know, I was about to go on a break," the cabdriver said, and Cooper felt her stomach drop to her knees.

"Is there anyway you could postpone it for ten minutes? We're stranded here," Cooper half-asked, half-whined.

"Well, I might be persuaded, if the price were right."

"Fine. We'll pay you double what the meter reads when we get to our destination," Cooper grudgingly agreed.

"Technically, I can't charge you more than what the meter reads, but I certainly wouldn't turn down a generous tip," the driver explained.

"We'll call it a tip, then," Cooper said. "Anything to get this cab moving."

"We would be happy to call it a tip," Claire agreed, giving her friend a nudge that Cooper knew meant "Can't you be a little nicer to this man who holds our lives in his hands?"

"You've got yourself a ride, then," the driver finally agreed.

"Great. We're heading in the direction of Capitol Hill. Just give me a minute, and I'll dig out the actual address."

"No hurry. We're not even across the freeway yet," the

driver said, suddenly becoming Mr. Amiable.

Cooper began to doubt he had even been planning to take a break. Oh, well, she couldn't do anything about it now. At least they would be home soon. She would never see Noah again, but she would be dry, warm, and safe. Not a wonderful trade-off, but it was the best she could do. Besides, she had to dig in her backpack and come up with Penny's address before this con artist drove them all around town to run up the meter.

"Aha!" Cooper said when she finally retrieved the key and the Post-It note from the depths of her backpack. "128 Olive Street, please. And we would like the most direct route," Cooper added, meeting the driver's gaze in the rearview mirror. He may have had them over a barrel, but she wanted him to know, now that they were en route, that she was no pushover.

A few minutes later the houses began to look familiar, one in particular. "This is it, the white cottage on the left," Cooper directed when Penny's house came into view. Once the cab was curbside, the girls pooled their money and paid the fare along with the agreed upon generous tip and then bounded up to the front door.

"I've never been so happy to see a building in my life," Claire said as she sagged against the front door. "I don't care if we see another inch of Seattle!"

Cooper had to agree with her. Being independent women of the world was more exhausting than it looked.

Chapter 10

"Sorry for leading you on a wild-goose chase," Cooper replied once they were safely inside. "You were a good sport to go along with me."

"I didn't know I had a choice!"

"At least we made it home in one piece, and while it's hard to tell if there's any sun up there with all this cloud cover, I think it's still technically daylight," Cooper ruled. "And we even beat Penny home."

"Well, if we're early, maybe we should go back out. I'm sure there's somewhere in the city we haven't walked today," Claire joked.

"Very funny. The only place I want to go is to bed."

"But what about the movie Penny talked about?"

"Oh, I completely forgot about that!" Cooper said. "I guess I won't be getting into my pajamas right away after all."

"Not unless you know something I don't about the dress code at Seattle movie theaters," Claire said.

Cooper emerged from the bathroom a few minutes later a new woman. She was wearing her favorite jeans, the pair that was a little loose and could be cuffed up once at the bottom— a rarity for someone as tall as she was—and an old white dress shirt of her dad's knotted at the waist. Her hair was still damp, but at least it hung smoothly down her back, and the mascara smudges were gone from under her eyes. Claire was looking much better, too, having slipped on her overalls and a long-sleeved T-shirt. The girls were stretched out on the futon happily sipping Cokes and watching *The Mary Tyler Moore Show* when Penny walked in.

"So did you girls have fun braving Seattle today?" she asked first thing.

"I don't know if fun is exactly the word I'd use," Claire replied.

"What do you mean? Did you have trouble getting around?"

"Define trouble," Cooper challenged.

"Difficulty? As in the opposite of easy?" Penny shot back.

"Then, yes, I think it's fair to say we encountered a small bit of difficulty in our travels today," Cooper admitted.

"Whoa. Back up. I think we need to start from the beginning," Penny said before suggesting, "Why don't you tell me everything that happened since I last saw you."

"It could take a while," Cooper hedged.

"Don't we have a movie to catch?" Claire added.

"So we'll rent a video instead. Now start talking."

"Well, first off, you were soooo right about the Fremont District," Cooper said. "The shops were wonderful."

"And I found a skirt," Claire added, holding up the soggy bag containing her purchase.

"Then things got even better when I met this gorgeous guy at a Greek Festival near where you dropped us."

"You should have seen them dancing together," Claire chimed in. "They looked so cute."

"You really think so?" Cooper asked, interrupting her own story. "I wasn't towering over him like I do with most guys our age?"

"Not at all. He had to be at least a full inch taller than you."

"Yoo-hoo! Girls? Excuse me, but I'm still waiting for the difficulty part, and I was just wondering if we were going to be getting there any time soon?"

"Sure," Cooper replied. "Why didn't you say so? I'll speed things up for you. We ate, we went to Ruby Montana's. I bought salt shakers—they're toast in a toaster. Remind me to show you later. Then we went to Elliott Bay, where they have very clean rest rooms, by the way. Then to the Sit & Spin, where we had Italian sodas before going in search of some club Noah's friend's band was playing at, getting an eensy bit lost, then stuck in the rain, ripped off by a heartless cabdriver, and now here we are, safe and sound. The end. See, it's really not that interesting a story after all."

"No, nothing much to tell here," Claire agreed.

"Why don't you let me be the judge of that. I was with you all the way until the part about Noah and the club. Run that by me again, if you don't mind, and start by telling me exactly who Noah is."

"He's the guy from the Greek Festival. We go way back, all the way to lunchtime. He invited us to come hear his friend's band at some club called Rockin' Eddie's, but we had a little trouble finding the place."

"So let me get this straight: You went wandering around the streets of Seattle into neighborhoods you had no idea were safe in search of some guy you met at a Greek Festival?"

"Did I mention he was really cute?" Cooper joked.

Penny's response was not what Cooper expected. Suddenly her cool aunt turned into a carbon copy of her mother. "This is not funny. You can't just pick up strange men at street fairs and then arrange to meet them at clubs," she lectured.

"He wasn't strange," Cooper protested. "And we never found the club."

"Not for lack of trying, it sounds like."

"I'm nothing if not tenacious," Cooper said, smiling. She was still expecting Penny to turn back into herself at any moment and be proud of them for surviving their little adventure. It didn't happen, though.

"I wouldn't brag about that if I were you," Penny warned. "And I've never even heard of a place called Rockin' Eddie's. How do you know this guy wasn't just trying to lure you to some deserted area or something?"

"You're starting to sound like McGruff the crime dog," Cooper said. "Anyway, I think I just misunderstood Noah when he told me the place's name. Loud music was playing, and I think I missed a few syllables."

"By any chance could he have said Rock Candy?" an exasperated-sounding Penny asked.

"It's certainly possible," Cooper answered. "Why? Is that a club?"

"Yes, it's spelled weird, but it's pronounced Rock Candy, and it's just across the freeway. I think some alternative band owns it or is a partner in it or something."

"That must be it!" Claire cried, as if a huge mystery had been solved. "We were supposed to go to Rock Candy, but since it's spelled weird you couldn't find it in the phone book."

"I'm glad I've been able to help you girls put all the pieces of the puzzle together, but that doesn't change the fact that you were out wandering the streets in neighborhoods your mother told you to stay out of *and* making plans to meet up with guys you didn't even know in clubs you're not old enough to get into."

"How is that last part possibly my fault?" Cooper asked. "I told Noah very clearly I was in high school. So how was I supposed to know we weren't old enough to get in? And how come it's okay for you to meet your new boyfriend in a club, but when I do it, I'm in danger of being stalked by a serial killer?"

"Oh, please! You can't even compare the situations," Penny said. "First off, I went to the club with a friend. I didn't even know Brian was going to be there. Second, I knew where I was going and that it was a safe location. Third, I'm not fifteen years old and in a city where I don't know my way around."

"I bet when you were fifteen you would have done the same thing we did," Cooper challenged.

"Maybe I would have," Penny admitted, "but that doesn't mean I can't expect you to be smarter than I was at your age."

"But that's not fair! It's a double standard!"

"I bet your mom won't think it's fair, either, that she trusted you to use common sense, and you threw it all out the window for some guy you barely knew."

"You're not going to tell my mother, are you?" Cooper said, horrified at the thought.

"I'm certainly not going to lie to her," Penny replied.

"But I trusted you! I wouldn't have told you all this if I had known you were going to turn me in!"

"Me either," Claire added.

"Well, I trusted you, too, but that didn't seem to matter a lot to you. Your mother would strangle me if she knew I let you chase some guy around the streets of Seattle."

"But it wasn't your fault," Cooper protested.

"No, it wasn't, but I'm sure your mother will find some way to blame me."

"Then why do you need to tell her?" Cooper asked. "Everything turned out okay in the end. We found our way back here, and we're safe and sound. We were even in before dark."

"I'm sure that was a happy accident," Penny said. "Your mom—both of your moms—trusted me to look out for you two, and it wouldn't be right not to let them know what happened."

"But I still say there's no reason to worry them since everything turned out all right," Cooper countered.

"So what's to keep you from doing this again?"

"What if we gave you our word we wouldn't?" Cooper said, desperate to change her aunt's mind.

"I don't know. . . ." Penny replied, although she obviously was wavering.

"Couldn't you at least agree to think about it overnight before making a final decision?" Cooper begged.

"Okay. I agree to sleep on it, but I'm not making any promises."

"That's all we ask. Right, Claire?" Cooper prodded.

"Right," her friend agreed.

"I guess I'll see you two in the morning," Penny said.

"Okay. See you in the morning," the girls echoed.

Only after Penny disappeared down the hall did Claire say, "I guess this means no movie, huh?"

"And very little sleep while we worry all night," Cooper said.

"What was that we were saying last night about Penny being so cool?" Claire asked.

"I know," Cooper agreed. "It's like she morphed into an adult right before our eyes. I guess she's one of them after all. She was just hiding it well."

"Let's hope she has a change of heart by morning, or I don't think either of us will be living to see our own adulthood."

"You can say that again!"

Chapter 11

Cooper was awake when Penny emerged from her bedroom the next morning, and even though Cooper tried to study her aunt's expression for signs of a decision, she came up empty. She was trying to think of some other way to find out what conclusions her aunt had reached overnight when Penny surprised her by blurting out, "I've decided I'm not going to say anything about your little escapade yesterday." She continued to scoop coffee into the pot's filter-lined basket and spoke without looking up.

Cooper was still breathing a sigh of relief when her aunt added the condition that always seemed to accompany decisions like this. "I think you girls should tell your moms yourselves."

"If we don't, are you going to force us to?" Cooper asked, unclear now as to whether Penny had changed her mind or merely her strategy.

"No, I'm leaving it up to you. I do want to say, though, that being mature is more about making wise decisions and owning up to the unwise ones than it is about acting older than you really are," Penny said, causing Cooper to squirm.

"So you're going to guilt us into confessing," Cooper summed up.

"No," Penny protested. "I'm telling you what I think is the right thing to do, and then I'm backing off and letting you make your own decision. That's how I'd want to be treated; so that's how I'm treating you."

"Gee, thanks," Cooper said, giving her aunt a spontaneous hug. "I don't know what to say except I knew you would come through."

"And I know you'll come through for me, too," Penny said. "Eventually anyway."

Cooper wasn't sure what her aunt meant, but it felt good to be off the hook. So good, in fact, that she decided to go back to bed and make up for some of the sleep she had lost the night before as she tossed and turned, wondering what her fate would be come morning.

When Cooper woke up again two hours later, Penny was bustling about the house making preparations for the barbecue later that day. Cooper, wanting to show her appreciation, immediately offered to pitch in.

"What can I do to help?" she asked, appearing in the kitchen doorway.

"I'm almost done with my list, and then I'm off to the grocery store, if you and Claire want to tag along."

"Sounds good to me," Cooper answered agreeably.

"Great. Let's plan to leave in an hour. Can you be showered and ready by then?"

"Sure."

Not wanting to do anything to aggravate her aunt, Cooper was ready fifteen minutes early. Then, during their shopping, she insisted on pushing the cart, carried the groceries in when they got home, and even helped put them away.

She was trying to find a place in the fridge big enough for the watermelon when Penny interrupted her good works. "You know, Cooper, I appreciate all this help, but if you're doing it to keep me from changing my mind, it's a waste of time. I gave you my word, and I won't go back on it."

"I know. I'm just trying to let you know how grateful I am," Cooper explained.

"Good. Now that we have that straightened out, why don't you and Claire show your gratitude by making the fruit salad. I'll marinate the chicken and start the potatoes for the potato salad."

"Aye-aye, Captain," Cooper said while giving Penny a mock salute. It felt good to have things almost back to normal. Cooper was in such a good mood she even broke down and put on a dress just to make her mom's day. It was a plaid sundress in shades of melon and turquoise that she wore with her white tennis shoes. Cooper knew her mom thought it would look "just darling" with a pair of matching sandals, but she had her fashion limits. Claire wore her new skirt, which matched so well with the fruit salad, Penny kept threatening to make her part of the dish.

Before they knew it the doorbell chimed, and Cooper ran to answer it. She was surprised to note that the clock near the door showed it was almost four o'clock.

"Hi, I'm Brian," the sandy-haired man at the door said. He was wearing denim shorts, a faded red T-shirt, and Birkenstocks. Not exactly what Cooper expected a computer programmer to wear, but she had to admit she was pleasantly surprised. Also, she noted, he looked more like a jock than a techno-nerd. Suddenly, her aunt's attraction to him became much clearer. "And you must be the niece I've been hearing so much about."

"That's me," said Cooper self-consciously before extending her hand to be shook.

She barely had a moment to chat with Brian before the bell rang again. This time she found two women on the front porch.

"You must be Cooper," the one with the curly red hair said before adding, "Your aunt talks about you all the time." She was inside before she realized she hadn't introduced herself yet.

"Oh, I'm Lori, and this is my roommate, Jennifer."

Cooper escorted them in, then went to tell Penny they were here.

"That just leaves Matt and your moms," Penny said to Cooper and Claire, who was busy spreading garlic butter on loaves of sourdough bread.

Then, as if on cue, the doorbell chimed a third time, and the three missing guests were on the porch.

"How has your time with Aunt Penny been?" her mom asked as soon as she was through the door. "Have you been behaving yourself?"

Cooper felt a pang of guilt as she answered in the affirmative, but then she reminded herself that if Penny had come to the conclusion she wasn't going to say anything, then neither would Cooper. Instead, she set about enjoying herself. Penny appointed her music monitor, and Cooper took the task seriously, making sure music was wafting through the house and out into the backyard. She was working her way through Penny's Motown collection because she thought it was funny to see her mom and Mrs. Hughes singing along to songs like "Respect" and "Tears of a Clown."

"It looks like everything's turning out just fine," Claire said as she joined Cooper in the kitchen. "Even your mom and your aunt seem to be getting along great. Penny has your mom doing the hand motions to 'Stop! In the Name of Love,' and she's cracking everyone up."

"Wow, that's a miracle," Cooper said, popping the bread under the broiler. "Who would have thought that was possible?"

As the afternoon melted into evening, the mood mellowed, and Cooper sat lazily in a lawn chair staring at her aunt's flowers. She couldn't believe that by tomorrow at this time she would be back in New York. She wasn't ready to return to her ordinary life.

"Hey, come inside and watch the fireworks on TV," Brian

called to her, snapping her out of her reverie. She didn't understand why they needed to watch the festivities on the small screen when in an hour or so they would head to the waterfront to watch the real thing. Not wanting to create waves, she headed inside.

"Look, honey, it's the Statue of Liberty and New York harbor," her mother said excitedly as soon as Cooper was within earshot, as if she couldn't recognize those familiar landmarks on her own. She settled onto the floor since the futon was full and watched with feigned interest.

"I love that skirt, Claire. Is it new?" Cooper's mom asked.

"I bought it yesterday," Claire replied, not volunteering any more information.

"Was that before or after your little detour through the warehouse district?" Brian asked, laughing as he said it.

Cooper's eyes searched out Penny's, and as they met, they both seemed to see what was coming but were powerless to stop it. Her aunt obviously had talked to Brian since hearing of their adventure, and he had misunderstood the part about her deciding not to relate it back to her big sister. It was too late to clue him in now.

"What detour?" Mrs. Ellis asked. "And what is the warehouse district?"

"It was nothing; we got a little lost," Claire attempted to explain.

"How lost, and what were you doing there in the first place?" Mrs. Ellis continued. "I thought you girls were going to stick to tourist attractions and easy-to-find landmarks?"

"It was no big deal," Penny said, jumping in to do some damage control. "The girls were invited to a concert, and they weren't familiar with the area."

"No big deal to you, maybe, but this is my daughter we're talking about, and I don't treat her safety as casually as you do. This is just the sort of irresponsible behavior I expect from you."

"It wasn't exactly a concert," Cooper blurted out, trying to shift the focus away from Penny. She knew there would be no peace until her mother had the whole story, so Cooper swallowed the lump in her throat and prepared to tell her tale once again—this time to an even less appreciative audience than her last one. It was particularly painful after seeing her usually calm aunt's reaction the night before.

When Cooper had finished, her mother looked as if she were one of those cartoon characters who becomes so angry steam pours out of its ears. She didn't yell or scream like Cooper expected her to. Instead, Mrs. Ellis calmly said, "Girls, get your things. We're going back to the hotel. Now."

Chapter 12

Penny protested and tried to get her sister to listen to reason, but Cooper could tell her mom had made up her mind. What was even worse was that her anger wasn't directed at Cooper, where it rightfully belonged, but instead it was heaped on Penny, who had only been protecting her niece.

The cab ride back to the hotel was silent, and for once Cooper was glad to be riding up near the driver.

Once they were settled at the hotel—or as settled as the four of them could be in one room—Mrs. Ellis instructed Cooper to stay put. "We're going downstairs to arrange for a shuttle to the airport tomorrow since your aunt Penny won't be taking us." Then she added another dig. "At least we know we'll be on time this way."

With their moms gone, Cooper and Claire had a few minutes to debrief. They went out on the balcony, where they could watch the sun dip into the ocean, something you can't see on the East Coast.

"Your mom sure is mad." Claire stated what both girls knew.

"That doesn't bother me so much as that she's mad at the wrong person," Cooper said.

With nothing else to say, Claire nodded sympathetically.

Then both girls resumed staring silently out at the horizon. The sun was still sliding into the water when the phone jarred Cooper from her moping. She ran in to answer it, figuring it was either her dad or Claire's. Either way, she didn't know how to explain what she was doing in her mother's room when she was supposed to be with her aunt. She toyed with not answering it at all, but in the end her curiosity won out.

"Hello, Cooper speaking," she said so there would be no confusion. Nothing was more embarrassing than to have her dad mistake her for her mom and call her "baby" or some other romantic endearment.

"Oh, hi, Cooper. It's Penny. I was hoping to talk to your mom."

"She's down in the lobby arranging for a shuttle for tomorrow," Cooper explained.

"So she didn't calm down any on the ride back to the hotel, huh?"

"I'm afraid not. But, Penny, I hope you know I'm really sorry," Cooper said. "You were right. If I had told my mom about what had happened, this whole thing could have been avoided. I feel just awful. I'm the one she should be mad at, not you."

"Thanks, but you didn't get into this all by yourself. I was enjoying having you and Claire admire my life so much that I didn't bother to point out that along with all this freedom comes a lot of responsibility. I mean, I love my house, but the bills never stop. You don't realize how wonderful it is to have your phone, electricity, and water paid for by your parents each month. Do you know I even have to pay to have someone pick up my trash? It's insane!"

"Yes, spending money on garbage is not my idea of fun," Cooper agreed.

"Neither is fighting with my sister. Do you think I can convince her to talk to me?" Penny asked, her voice cautious but hopeful.

Cooper hated to burst her aunt's bubble, but if she were to be honest, she would have to say she doubted it.

"What about a surprise attack then?" Penny suggested. "I know it's a little sneaky, but desperate times call for desperate measures."

"What did you have in mind?"

"I thought if you could get your mom down to breakfast, I could approach her there. I'm banking on her not being rude in a restaurant full of people."

"I hope for your sake you're right," Cooper said.

"So you'll help me?"

"It's the least I could do after getting you into this."

"Thanks, Cooper. I said you would come through for me eventually, and you are."

"How did you know I would?"

"Because you have a good heart and a conscience that knows to use the Bible as its guide—most of the time, anyway," Penny explained.

"Well, thanks for having faith in me," Cooper replied, choking back tears.

"You're welcome. Now, you had better get off this phone before your mom comes in. I'll see you downstairs for breakfast around nine o'clock tomorrow morning."

"Okay, I'll see you then," Cooper agreed.

The girls watched the fireworks from the room's balcony that night, and Cooper couldn't help but think that the very thing they were celebrating—freedom—was the thing that had caused her so much trouble during the past few days.

I was so anxious to rush ahead, God, and to break away from all my mom's annoying warnings that I grabbed a bit more freedom than I could hold, and it got me into trouble, Cooper told the night sky. *I promise I'll try to take it more slowly from now on. But I really blew it this time, and now Penny is paying. So could you please help me clear up this mess I created?*

She knew God well enough not to go looking for answers in

the sky. He would answer in His time, not hers. Still, she couldn't help wanting to rush Him just a bit. *In case I forgot to mention it, God, we're leaving tomorrow.*

Then, content that she had done all she could, Cooper slipped back into the room, where her mom and Claire's mom were sleeping soundly. After putting on her pajamas, Cooper slid between the sheets next to her best friend and drifted off to sleep, dreaming of Laundromats and warehouses.

The next day dawned sunny and clear, which Cooper took as a sign that everything was going to work out. She wasn't superstitious, but she chose to look at it sort of like her personal rainbow. If God could send that as a sign to His people after the great flood, why couldn't a single day's sunshine be a sign to her?

"My, you're up bright and early," Mrs. Ellis said when she saw her usually morning-hating daughter getting ready without being told several times.

"I thought maybe you and I could have breakfast together downstairs," Cooper suggested, trying to sound nonchalant.

"Ellen and I have been ordering room service in the mornings instead."

"Couldn't you do something different today? Besides, do you think those rates—look what it costs for a tiny box of cereal!—are a good use of your money?" Cooper hoped she wasn't laying it on too thick, but she was desperate. It was twenty minutes before nine, and she had to get her mother downstairs.

"Okay, I'll do it, but you choose the oddest times to think about watching finances, I must say."

"You're always telling me not to just learn it, but to apply it," Cooper replied. "Now, let's go. I'm starved."

"Okay, but I really don't see what the rush is."

"No rush. My stomach is just rumbling. Dinner was a long time ago," Cooper added, purposely bringing up a reminder of last night's fiasco to see how her mom reacted. The response was about as expected. Her mom winced slightly, then carried on as if nothing had been said.

Cooper continued to hurry her mother through the buffet, reasoning that if Mrs. Ellis had a full plate in front of her, she would be less likely to leave when she saw her sister. The stage was set for a confrontation and hopefully a reconciliation, but Cooper was having a hard time eating since her stomach felt like a Boy Scout had been using it to practice tying knots. Since she couldn't get anything down, she decided to break the ice.

"You know, Mom, I'm really sorry about yesterday," Cooper began.

"If you had been staying here with me it never would have happened," Mrs. Ellis said.

"Yes, it would have," Cooper argued tentatively. She didn't want to upset her mom further, but Cooper wanted to be sure she made her point. When she received no response, she decided to take the plunge so she blurted out, "It wasn't Penny's fault that I made a bad decision. It was my choice to look for that club, and I probably would have made the same choice if you had been around."

"Not if I could help it, you wouldn't."

"But you can't help it, Mom. That's what I'm trying to tell you. I'm fifteen!" Cooper's voice rose a bit. "You can't follow me around all day and make sure I don't pick up any germs from the counters in public rest rooms or talk to strangers or forget to take a jacket when it's cold out."

"But I can tell you not to wander off into deserted areas of strange cities and expect you to listen to me."

"You're right," Cooper agreed, "and I've already admitted that I made a mistake. But maybe if you weren't also reminding me to look both ways when I crossed the street and to eat my vegetables like I was still in preschool, I'd be able to hear the more important warnings a little better."

"Are you saying I treat you like a baby?"

"Just a smidge," Cooper said, pinching her thumb and fore-finger together for emphasis.

"If you want to be treated like a responsible near-adult, you'll have to start acting like someone who's responsible," Mrs. Ellis chided.

"I think I can handle that," Cooper replied. "And look, I'm off to a good start by taking responsibility for blowing it the other day, aren't I?"

"You're still not off the hook on that one."

"I have no doubt you'll come up with some devious punish-ment for me by the time we get home, but do you think, in the meantime, you could cut Aunt Penny some slack?" Cooper pleaded. "It really wasn't her fault."

Before her mom could answer, Penny appeared at the table carrying a breakfast tray of her own. "Is this seat taken?"

The silence was unbearable, and for a minute Cooper was sure her mother would say "Yes," but instead she motioned to the empty chair next to her. Only then did Cooper let out the breath she hadn't realized she had been holding.

"I'm sorry for not being more honest with you yesterday," Penny began. "You have every right to know what's going on with your own daughter."

"Cooper and I were just talking about that, and I guess it wasn't all your fault. She's responsible, too."

"That's all I was trying to do, to get her to take responsi-bility and tell you what happened herself."

"I thought maybe you were trying to cover for her," Mrs. Ellis said.

"If anything, I was trying to cover for me," Penny corrected. "I didn't want to give you another reason to think I'm irre-sponsible."

"I don't think you're irresponsible . . . not all the time."

"Or maybe you're a little too responsible," Penny suggested to her older sister. "You always have to be in control of every-thing, and that's not possible. Like with the pileup on the freeway the other day. You thought I should have found some way to fix that."

"I don't expect you to control the traffic," Mrs. Ellis clarified. "I'd just like to see you allow enough time to get somewhere so that a traffic jam won't completely control you and inconvenience those waiting for you. "

"I'd be on time to every appointment I have for a month if I could see you loosen up just once, maybe put on a pair of jeans, or go out with your hair messed up."

"I don't know about the hair, but I could probably wear jeans," Mrs. Ellis said thoughtfully.

"Without creases," Penny added.

"I'll do you one better. I won't even iron them," Mrs. Ellis said, then laughed at the shocked expressions on her daughter's and her sister's faces.

"We could go shopping for a pair right now," Penny suggested. "Your plane doesn't leave for several hours, and we haven't spent any real time together."

"I just have to stop by the front desk and cancel the shuttle I ordered on our way out."

"If you do, I promise I will deliver you to the airport a full hour before your plane is scheduled to leave," Penny vowed.

"Fifty minutes should be plenty of time," Mrs. Ellis said to her sister while smiling mischievously.

"So does this mean maybe you could start to loosen up a bit with me, too?" Cooper asked hopefully.

"Sure, sweetheart," her mom agreed much too quickly. Then, before Cooper could wonder what her mother was up to, she added, "Now, don't forget to clean your plate."

Departures

MONTANA

In the Event of a Water Landing

A SIERRA JENSEN NOVELLA

ROBIN JONES GUNN

Chapter 1

Sierra Jensen stuffed the last of a granola bar in her mouth and surveyed the airport waiting area that had become way too familiar during the past hour. She brushed back her long, wild blond hair and asked her friend Jana, "When do you think the guys will be back?"

"I don't know," Jana said, her brown eyes looking past Sierra's shoulder for the hundredth time. "Maybe the airline they went to check on doesn't have any openings on its flights to Montana."

"Then what do we do?" Sierra asked.

"Don't ask me," Jana said. "I've never been the victim of an airline strike before."

Sierra tapped her foot in time to the song that had been stuck in her head for several hours. "Why did they have to go on strike on a holiday weekend? There should be laws against that."

This was the first time fifteen-year-old Sierra had traveled anywhere without her parents or one of her five brothers and sisters. The plan had been a simple one. Jana's parents were driving to their family cabin on a lake near Glacier National Park to spend some time alone. A week later Jana, her older brother, Gregg, his friend Tim, and Sierra would fly up for the Fourth of July weekend.

None of them expected the connecting flight in Seattle to be rerouted to the central terminal in Minneapolis. Now the group was on its own, trying to find a flight to Montana.

"Isn't there a big mall in Minneapolis?" Sierra asked. "If we can't catch a flight, we could hang out at the mall."

Jana looked wary. Her short brown hair was tucked behind her ears and off her face, which meant her thoughts were easily read in her open expression. Jana was physically larger than Sierra and six months older. They had been friends for several years in their small northern California town of Pineville. Sierra and Jana were both top students in their class, and they both loved sports—although Jana often complained that Sierra had an unfair athletic advantage because she was thinner and faster. The friendly competition they shared was one of the foundation stones of their friendship.

Jana was the cautious one of the two, and she didn't seem to think the mall was such a great idea. "All I know is that we're supposed to wait here for Gregg and Tim, and when they come back, we're supposed to call my parents to tell them what we found out."

"Do you think it would be okay if I went to that café over there to buy something to drink?" Sierra asked. She ran her tongue over her back teeth, releasing bits of oats left over from the granola bar.

"I don't know if you should leave," Jana said.

"I'll only be gone for a few minutes, and you can run over and get me if the guys come back."

Jana looked around, as if calculating all the factors before nodding to Sierra.

"Do you want anything?" Sierra offered.

"Lemonade, if they have it. No sugar."

"What if the lemonade already has sugar in it?"

"That's okay. Just don't add any."

"Okay. I'll be right back." Sierra grabbed her backpack and took off mumbling to herself, "Like I would go around slipping sugar into her lemonade!" Sierra knew it wasn't fair to be critical of Jana's concern over calories just because Sierra had never had to concentrate on her weight.

Walking around relaxed Sierra. She decided to make a quick detour into the bookstore next to the café. An interesting magazine might help her friend relax a little, too. Who knew how long they might be stuck here.

The bookstore was small, and the space was so tight Sierra took off her backpack and balanced it at her feet. A tall, good-looking guy walked in and stood next to Sierra at the magazine rack. He had sun-bleached blond hair and was wearing a white T-shirt with a surfing logo on the back. While Sierra flipped through one of the magazines, she decided to conduct an experiment with this unsuspecting guy. She had tried this before but never with satisfying results; maybe today would be different.

The goal was to see if the guy would notice her without her trying to draw attention to herself. She felt ready to move beyond her image of a freckle-faced tomboy and to be noticed by guys the way her gorgeous older sister, Tawni, was. The tricky part was figuring out if guys thought she looked interesting enough to pay attention to her.

Sierra flipped through the magazine and tossed a subtle, sideways glance toward the guy. About two minutes into the experiment, the results were zilch.

Then Sierra heard a girl greet the guy. "Hello" was all she said.

Sierra kept her head facing the magazine while doing her best to see what was going on out of the corner of her eye. The guy didn't respond to the teenage girl's hello.

Then Sierra heard the girl say, "Hi," in a more decisive tone. Sierra couldn't see the girl's face, but she could see that the guy had turned to look at her. When he did, the girl broke into a string of stammering words. It appeared to be a case of mistaken identity.

Sierra had to look. She turned nonchalantly toward the guy just as the girl hurried away. The tall girl had long nutmeg brown hair, and a tag-along boy beside her was loudly giving her a hard time. The boy reminded Sierra of her two younger brothers and how they often acted around her.

She was glad that even though she was stuck at the airport, she was with her friend and not her younger brothers.

Just then the guy next to Sierra tried to move past her and said, "Excuse me."

Sierra stepped aside and kicked her backpack out of his way. *So does that mean he just noticed me? At least he was polite. I'd score this experiment as a three out of ten. Maybe a four. No, a two and a half. Yeah, a two and a half. I still have a long way to go before I catch a guy's attention—and not because I'm in his way.*

Sierra gave up on the magazine. Jana would have to come pick out what she wanted. As Sierra reached for her backpack, her bracelet caught on a thread in her skirt, and she had to stand there a minute trying to untangle it. Her mom had helped her make the skirt, but her sister thought it was dreadful, which was probably one of the reasons Sierra liked it so much. Made from a collection of her dad's old ties, the skirt was distinctive. Each of the wide ties was opened up and sewn together at the sides so that all the pointed ends came to just above her knee. Sierra liked being unique. But more than once her bracelet had caught on the worn-through part of a blue tie on the right side.

With her bracelet released, Sierra headed for the café. She had just stepped outside the bookstore when she heard her name called from across the open area. Looking up, she saw Gregg waving from the entrance of the waiting area where she had left Jana.

Gregg had dark hair like Jana's. His eyes and eyebrows were darker than hers were and more striking so the first thing a person noticed about him were his warm eyes. Even if his mouth was serious, his eyes made him look as if he were about to start laughing.

He was four years older than Jana, just like Sierra's brother, Wesley, was four years older than she was. It was another one of the similarities Sierra and Jana shared. Sierra thought Gregg was good-looking. She liked his quick wit and casual approach to life.

Gregg's buddy Tim was more serious and, according to Jana, more intelligent than Gregg was. He appeared easygoing because he dressed in loose shorts and old, beat-up sandals. Tim's strawberry blond hair would be a lot curlier, Sierra decided, if he let it grow longer. But he kept it short and often hidden under a baseball cap, as it was right now.

"What did you find out?" Sierra asked, catching up to the two guys.

"We exchanged all four tickets at no charge," Gregg said, "but the flight leaves later tonight. We won't get to Kalispell until a little after midnight."

"Does Jana know?" Sierra asked.

"No," Gregg answered. "I happened to notice your skirt as we were going by, and since there probably weren't two of those in the airport, I figured it was you."

"There probably aren't," Sierra said brightly. She noted Gregg's sarcasm, but it didn't bother her.

"We better break the news to Jana," Tim suggested. "It's going to be a long day and night."

"Unless," Sierra said, grabbing both guys by the arm before they had a chance to walk away, "we make a little detour out of the airport. We could all pitch in for a cab and go to the mall for the day."

"The Mall of America?" Tim asked.

Gregg's eyes lit up. "Perfect! I like the way you think, Sierra."

Sierra smiled. "Good. Now you get to convince Jana."

Chapter 2

Sierra crawled into the backseat of the cab next to Gregg. She couldn't believe the huge argument Jana and Gregg had gotten into when he told her they were going to the mall. At one point, Gregg said they would leave Jana at the airport and the three of them would go. That only made things worse. Then Sierra had told Jana to "lighten up" and "live a little," but Jana became so mad her face turned red.

Sierra hadn't realized how inflexible Jana was; this trip was turning out to reveal aspects of her that had remained hidden as long as they were safely tucked away in small-town Pineville.

Tim was the one who finally had convinced Jana to go. He had sat down next to her and had explained that the alternative would be to spend the whole day and half the night at the airport. Tim had suggested they call Jana's parents. She liked that safety precaution. After Mr. and Mrs. Hill had given their blessing, along with a handful of cautions and instructions, Jana was willing to leave the airport.

Sierra thought Jana's parents were more lenient than her parents would have been in the same situation. Although, if Sierra had been with her older brother, Wesley, she guessed her parents would have been fine with the arrangements. Wes had always been responsible, and Sierra imagined Gregg to be the same way.

Sierra considered calling her parents from the airport as the group made its plans. Her parents might appreciate knowing that she wouldn't arrive in Montana as scheduled. However, her parents had left that morning with her younger brothers to drive up to Portland to see Granna Mae. They probably were still on the road. She decided she would rather call them tomorrow, after her parents had arrived at Granna Mae's house, to let them know she was safely in Montana. Until she could make that claim, she didn't want to call.

Not until the driver dropped them off at one of the many mall entrances did Sierra realize what a gigantic place they were about to enter. Even though they had a good eight hours before they had to be back at the airport, they wouldn't be able to take in all this huge complex had to offer.

"We need a plan," Jana said. "We need a meeting place in case we get lost."

"Why don't we just all stay together?" Sierra suggested. "Then we won't have to worry."

"I don't know if the guys want to be with us the whole time," Jana said.

"Like we have a choice," Gregg said. "Don't you remember that was one of the rules Mom laid down? I'm responsible for both of you the entire time. So come on; I don't want to stand here wasting time. Let's find those rides the taxi driver told us about."

This was Sierra's idea of fun—a spontaneous detour to a mall with an amusement park. Jana looked miserable. She kept glancing to the right and then to the left, as if someone were lurking in the shadows, ready to jump out and steal her backpack.

"What are you so nervous about?" Sierra asked her.

"I'm not nervous."

"You're acting nervous. Or scared or something."

"I am not!" Jana snapped.

Sierra backed off. She fell into step with Gregg and let Jana walk with Tim.

"Don't let her get to you," Gregg said to Sierra. "She's like that whenever she's out of her comfort zone."

I guess I haven't seen Jana out of her comfort zone very often. This may be a more challenging weekend than I thought. What if she ends up being mad at me the whole time?

The four of them headed toward the complex's center. As they rounded the corner, a wide, open area of the mall stretched out before them. Sierra stood next to Gregg at the railing and looked down one level to survey an entire amusement park with a roller coaster, log ride, Ferris wheel, food stands, trees, and half a dozen other rides.

"Look at that!" Sierra exclaimed. "It's Disneyland in the middle of a mall."

"It's not Disneyland," Tim corrected her, pointing to the right. "See the sign? It's Camp Snoopy."

Sierra laughed. "Come on. I have my camera. Maybe we can find Snoopy and get a picture with him."

"I don't think so," Jana said.

"Come on," Gregg said, pulling his sister by the arm. "Lighten up and have some fun, will you?"

Jana glared at Gregg, as if to say, "You too?" She yanked her arm from his grasp and said, "Can't we get something to drink, first?" Jana cast a glance to Sierra. "I never got my lemonade."

Sierra tried to brush off Jana's biting words. Sierra's sister, Tawni, acted the same way when she was out of her comfort zone. Sierra knew it was best not to react or it would only make the conflict grow.

"Okay, food and drinks first, then the roller coaster," Sierra suggested.

"Not food," Jana said. "Who wants to go on a roller coaster with a full stomach?"

"You decide, then," Gregg challenged his sister. "What's it

going to be? Ride first or food first?"

Jana reluctantly gave into the consensus and headed toward the rides. She found a drinking fountain along the way and stopped for what Sierra thought was a dramatically long drink.

But then they were off. Tim figured out the ticket machine, and they each fed money into the slot at an alarmingly fast rate and then received in return a small ticket with a credited amount encoded on a thin magnetic strip.

"So much money," Gregg remarked, "and all we get is this!"

"What should we go on first?" Sierra asked.

Tim made the decision; they headed for the Kite Eating Tree. In the center of the ride was a huge tree with individual swings hanging from the ends of the reinforced limbs. Riders sat strapped in the seats, and the tree spun them in a great circle.

The four of them stood in line, watching as the centrifugal force pushed the riders away from the base of the tree and outward in a spin. Some riders made their swings twist and buck as they spun around. Sierra noticed that most of the riders were little kids, but she didn't care. It looked like fun.

"Come on," Sierra said to Jana when it was their turn to ride. "This should put you in a better mood."

Jana turned to Sierra with a hurt look and said, "And what's wrong with my mood?"

"You're a little grumpy, that's all."

"I am not!" Jana snapped.

"Are you two going to stand there and fight or get on the ride?" Gregg asked.

Sierra and Jana stared at each other as people walked past them and scrambled to grab what could be considered the best seats on the ride.

"I'm not going on this ride," Jana announced, walking to the exit gate and leaving Sierra to stand there alone.

Chapter 3

Sierra's feet dangled freely as the ride took off. She hated the way she felt. Part of her wanted to yell at Jana and tell her to grow up and stop being so stubborn. Another part of Sierra understood and felt a little compassion. She knew Jana was against this detour to the Mall of America, but did she have to ruin it for the rest of them?

As soon as the ride ended and they joined Jana, Gregg suggested, "Why don't we buy something to eat?"

"Look, they have funnel cakes here," Tim said, pointing to a small snack window.

"Funnel cakes?" Jana questioned. "They're loaded with sugar, no doubt."

"Should we find a restaurant?" Sierra suggested, trying to be diplomatic and not to be irritated with Jana.

They found a directory, and with more discussion than Sierra thought was necessary, finally agreed on where to eat. In Sierra's opinion, they wasted nearly an hour of their limited time, sitting down to order and eat. As the others munched a plate of nachos as an appetizer, Sierra consulted a brochure she had picked up at the directory and made suggestions of where they could go next.

By the time Jana had eaten half of her chicken Caesar salad, she was acting like a different person. When they hit the mall again, her attitude was much improved. Almost too much, because now Jana wanted to make the decisions.

"I think we should go shopping first and then go on more rides," Jana said.

"I think we should use up the tickets first," Gregg said. "They weren't cheap."

"I know, but we have plenty of time." Jana looked more cheerful, but she also looked determined.

"What about you, Sierra?" Gregg asked.

"Log ride would be at the top of my list. But I can go along with what everyone else wants to do." Sierra realized that growing up in a big family and not being the youngest certainly affected her attitude in situations like this. It was more important to be a team player than to get one's own way.

"And what do you want, Tim? Shopping or log ride?" Gregg asked.

"LEGOLAND," Tim answered with a quiet smile.

"We have to all stick together," Jana reminded them.

"But that doesn't mean we have to do what you want to do the whole time." The moment the words were out of her mouth, Sierra regretted them.

Jana looked hurt. "We're not exactly doing what I want. I wanted to stay at the airport, where it was safe."

"We're here now," Sierra said before Gregg had a chance to say anything. "Can you just make the best of it and not ruin the fun for everyone else?"

"How am I ruining everyone else's fun? I'm not ruining anything! All I suggested is that we go shopping. After all, this is a mall, not just an amusement park. And shopping is fun."

"Fine!" Gregg said, stepping in and showing by the tone of his voice that his patience had run out. "Let's go shopping and stop wasting our time arguing about it."

"Well," Jana stammered in a calmer voice. "We can go on

a ride first, if that's what you guys want."

Sierra closed her eyes and let out a frustrated huff. *Why does everything have to be so complicated?*

"How about this," Gregg said, regaining the control of the situation. "Why don't we go to LEGOLAND first and then the log ride? That should use up all our tickets, and then we can go shopping."

"Fine," Sierra said.

"Fine," Jana answered in a high-pitched voice.

"LEGOLAND!" Tim said with a little-boy grin on his face. He began to tell them how LEGOLAND would have been a dream come true to him ten years ago. He led the way into the maze of walls, tables, and castle arches all made of LEGOs. Half a dozen areas were set up in the corners where people of all ages sat making LEGO creations. Tim immediately plopped down and finished a helicopter someone had left on the table.

"Can you make another one of those, only a little larger?" Sierra teased. "Then we can fly it to Montana."

"Don't laugh," Gregg said, looking up at the large LEGO airplanes strung overhead. "It's probably been done. This is amazing. If I were six, I'd want to spend the whole day here."

"Good thing you're not six," Jana muttered.

"I'm almost done," Tim said, searching a mound of loose pieces. "Help me find a little red one shaped like this." He held up a tiny, square, red bit of plastic. Sierra found the needed piece, and Tim snapped it into place.

"There," he said. "What do you think?"

"A work of art," Sierra said. She had to bite her lip to keep from adding, "And now can we go on the log ride?"

Tim smiled at Sierra. "I couldn't have done it without you," he said, playfully overdoing his admiration for her.

As Sierra glanced at Tim, she noticed he was still looking at her and smiling. Warmly. It was different than the way he had ever looked at her before.

Why is he looking at me like that? He and Gregg are both too old for me. Or I'm too young for them.

"Log ride," Gregg reminded them. "You ready, Tim?"

Tim nodded. He seemed to be having a hard time walking away from his completed helicopter.

Sierra felt like laughing. None of her four brothers had ever expressed such loyalty to any of their LEGO creations, at least not that she could remember.

Tim rose, and to Sierra's surprise, he wrapped his arm around her shoulders and said, "Thanks for finding the missing piece. You made my day."

Sierra could feel her cheeks flush. She laughed and said, "Doesn't take much to make your day, does it?" Sierra noticed that Jana wasn't laughing.

"Can we go now?" Jana asked, stepping closer to Tim. He had taken his arm off of Sierra's shoulder and now Jana stood right beside him. She cast a glance at Sierra that Sierra knew all too well. Jana had switched into her competitive mode.

What are you doing, Jana? Do you think Tim is showing interest in me so you have to step in and challenge my right to his attention? It's not like that! Tim and Gregg are only "baby-sitting" us. I think. But what was Tim's look about?

Jana moved closer to Tim as they walked to the line for the log ride. "This should be fun," she said.

Tim gave her a startled look. Her sudden transformation from group grump to sweet flirt was a little too fast. He gave Jana a quick nod of agreement and echoed, "Yeah, it should be fun." Then he caught up with Gregg's long-legged strides and asked him if he still had the tickets.

"What are you doing?" Sierra asked, coming up beside Jana.

"I'm trying to relax and have fun. Isn't that what everyone has been telling me to do?"

"Yes, but what's with the flirting?" Sierra asked.

"I wasn't flirting."

"Jana," Sierra paused, not sure what to say next. She felt like lecturing Jana the way Tawni often lectured Sierra, but she already knew from personal experience how much good that did. "Jana, he didn't have his arm around me as a boyfriend thing."

"I know."

"This isn't a sports event. It's supposed to be vacation."

"I know!" Jana looked at Sierra with exasperation. "I'm just trying to find my comfort zone, okay? Sorry if it seemed like I was competing with you."

"That's okay," Sierra said. "I've just never seen you like this before. I don't know what's going on."

"I don't know what's going on, either, and all this random stuff is driving me crazy."

They stepped into line behind the guys at the log ride. "It's fun," Sierra said. "An adventure."

"How can you enjoy this?" Jana asked. "You never know what's going to happen next."

"That's what I like about it," Sierra said.

Gregg elbowed Tim and motioned with his eyes for Tim to look at something to the left of them. Sierra kept talking to Jana but followed Tim's and Greg's line of sight.

Two girls who were probably close to Gregg and Tim's age were standing there. They both had on shorts and were studying a map and then looking around. One of them pointed in the direction she apparently thought they should go. She had beautiful blond hair, and her legs were a dark, golden tan.

Sierra watched Gregg's and Tim's unsubtle glances at the girls and the guys' elbowing each other. She felt sure that if Gregg and Tim weren't "baby-sitting," they would have left the line for the log ride to help the lost girls find their way around Camp Snoopy.

The girls took off, and Gregg turned his head, watching them go.

"Don't strain your neck," Sierra said sarcastically.

Gregg quickly looked at Sierra. He seemed surprised at having been caught. But then he bounced back with a tease for Sierra and said, "Be patient. One day that will be you, and you'll be glad someone is watching."

"What are you talking about?" Jana asked.

"Nothing," Gregg said. He gave Sierra a smile, and with his expressive eyes warned her not to explain.

Sierra felt warmed. Gregg had just paid her a compliment. He thought one day she would be the kind of girl who turned heads. No one had ever hinted at such promise. It was always Tawni people raved about.

Sierra liked being away from her sister. She liked being around these older guys and being taken into their confidence in these odd little ways. She loved being on her own and having such freedom.

Jana nudged Sierra. "What were you guys talking about?"

Sierra leaned over and said quietly, "They were just looking at some girls."

"You?" Jana asked.

"No, they weren't looking at me. They were checking out some older girls that walked by. It was nothing."

Jana seemed upset. "I think that is so rude. I can't stand it when guys do that."

"I know," Sierra agreed. But she was thinking, *Unless you're the one they're looking at*.

Chapter 4

Jana seemed to relax after the log ride, even though they got wet when the log made a splash landing. As soon as they hit some of the shops, she was even more at ease. When she found a pair of sandals she liked and the store had them in her size, she cheered right up.

"You know," Jana said as she and Sierra left the shoe store to join the guys, who were sitting on a bench in front of the shop waiting for them, "I think I owe you an apology, Sierra. I was acting a little too neurotic about coming to the mall."

"Don't worry about it," Sierra said. "It is kind of bizarre when you think about it. This morning we woke up in Pineville, this afternoon we rode a log in Minnesota, and tonight we'll sleep in Montana."

"Don't say it that way," Jana said. "It makes me freak out all over again. I like things nice and slow and predictable."

"Where to now?" Gregg asked, checking his watch. "We should only stay another hour—or less."

"Let's go this direction," Jana suggested.

Sierra saw a Christian bookstore and convinced the group to check it out. Gregg and Jana's family went to the same church as Sierra's family, which was one of the reasons her parents had agreed to let Sierra go on this trip. Tim attended the youth group at Sierra's church even though his parents didn't come to the services.

Once they walked into the store, they all found things they wanted to buy and ended up spending more time than they had planned. Gregg left with three new CDs, and Jana was happy to find the next book in a series she liked. Sierra was tempted to purchase a T-shirt but decided her budget couldn't handle the expense. Tim didn't buy anything, either.

Sierra wondered if he was on a limited budget like she was. Gregg and Jana's family was well off and had paid for Tim and Sierra's airfare so they could come on the trip. Sierra's spending money for the weekend had decreased greatly after she had pitched in for the cab ride and her portion of the Camp Snoopy ride ticket. Plus, they still had the expense of the cab fare to the airport.

"We should head back," Gregg suggested.

"Could we go to one more store?" Jana asked. "I saw a candy store on the way in."

"You want to go to a candy store?" Sierra questioned.

"I wanted to get some licorice. It's fat free. And maybe they have some sugar-free chocolate."

"Do you mean the candy store that was right where we first entered the mall?" Gregg asked. "That's the opposite direction of where we are now."

"We have to go that way to get a taxi, don't we?" Jana reasoned.

"I don't know. It seems we could catch a cab anywhere. If that's what you want to do, let's start walking that way."

"Maybe we should call a cab," Tim suggested. "I didn't notice any hanging out by the entrance when we came in."

"Good idea," Gregg said.

They hoofed it through the mall back to where they remembered entering. But no candy store was in sight.

"I know it was here," Jana said.

"It didn't move in the last five hours." Gregg was beginning to sound irritated. Sierra guessed he felt responsible for getting them back to the airport safely, and time was slipping away from them.

"Let's find a phone and call a cab," Tim suggested.

"There's one." Gregg took off at a fast clip for the pay phone. The others hurried to catch up.

"I know what the problem is," Jana said. "We're on the wrong level. We have to go down a level."

"Let's call the cab first," Tim suggested. It was the only opinion he had expressed all day, aside from LEGOLAND, but he was holding firmly to it.

"Would it be okay if you guys called while Sierra and I go down one level to the candy store? We'll come right back up and meet you here," Jana said.

Gregg was flipping through the phone book in search of a number for a cab company. "Just come right back," he said. Turning to Tim, he said, "Do you suppose it would be under something other than 'cab'?"

"Try 'taxi,' " Tim said.

Sierra and Jana took off at a jogging pace and caught the elevator down to the next level.

"I should have brought some from home," Jana said. "They have this diet chocolate at the grocery store that's pretty good. I didn't think to buy any before we left, and I'm sure they won't have any where we're going in Montana. Thanks for coming with me, Sierra."

From the high-pitched tone of Jana's voice and how fast she was speaking, Sierra guessed Jana was nervous. They were doing the one thing they weren't supposed to do—splitting up from the guys. Not that anything bad could happen in five minutes while they bought candy, but now that Sierra thought about it, it bothered her that they had so quickly broken the rule Jana's parents had been so firm about.

"I think we should go back," Sierra said a moment before

they entered the candy store. "We told your parents we would stay together the whole time."

Jana stopped and gave Sierra a stunned look. All her insecurities about the mall seemed to come rushing back. "I forgot," she said in a small voice. "Oh, you're right. We should go back."

The candy store forgotten, Sierra and Jana hurried to the elevator but had to wait for the door to open.

"Come on, come on," Jana chanted nervously. "This is not good. If we miss that plane and it's my fault, I'll be so mad at myself."

"We haven't missed the plane yet," Sierra said.

The elevator door opened, but they had to wait for a woman with a stroller to come out. Jana hit the button twice.

"The guys better be right by the phone," Jana said.

"Don't worry. They will be," Sierra said.

But they weren't.

"Oh no. This is bad," Jana said, looking right and left. Her expression showed her panic. "Should we go outside? Or back down to the candy store? Do you think they thought we were supposed to meet at the candy store? What if they're already outside, sitting in a cab waiting for us?"

"I think we should wait right here," Sierra said. "That was the plan."

Just then Sierra spotted Gregg hurrying toward them. "Hey, come on!" he called out. "We had to use a different phone. That one wasn't working. They told us there's a taxi area where we can catch a cab. Let's go."

Sierra and Jana ran after Gregg. They found Tim waiting by the pay phone near the rest rooms. They all hurried to the designated area in the parking complex where a number of taxis were lined up waiting.

When a taxi pulled forward, they all climbed in. Gregg directed the driver to take them to the airport and checked his watch.

"Are we going to make it back in time?" Jana asked.

"I think so," Gregg said.

Sierra couldn't decide if it was okay to enjoy the thrill of this little adventure, or if she should be frantic like Jana. She decided to sit back and go for the ride. She couldn't do anything to change the situation. But she was glad she had suggested to Jana that they cancel the candy store. Knowing Jana, they probably would still be in there trying to decide what to buy.

Once they arrived at the airport, they broke into a full sprint. But then they arrived at the metal detector and had to halt for a long line. Gregg checked his watch again. At the gate, Gregg went up to the desk and spoke for all of them since he had the tickets. Sierra noticed no people were in the waiting area, and no one seemed to be boarding the flight even though the doors were open.

Are we late? Has everyone already gotten on? Or did we miss the flight?

"I'm sorry," the ticket agent said to Gregg after reviewing their tickets. "You were given the wrong information. These tickets were re-issued by another airline agent."

"We were told the tickets were good for this airline and for this flight," Gregg said.

"Yes, our airline will honor the tickets, but the other airline didn't have our current schedule when the tickets were issued," he said. "We no longer service Kalispell."

"What does that mean?" Jana asked, stepping forward. "The flight already left?"

"No, our airline cancelled that route. We used to fly to Kalispell, but we don't anymore. The change was made on the first of July, so it's easy to see why the other airline didn't know. The computer must not have given them the current information." As he was talking, the agent was typing busily. "There's a 6:15 flight with Partner Airlines."

"You mean 6:15 in the morning?" Jana asked. "We have to stay here all night?"

The agent typed in some more. "Yes, that's what it
like. There was an earlier flight at 7:23 this evening, but now
there's nothing until 6:15. You can take these tickets and go
directly to Partner Airlines' ticket booth on the Blue Concourse, and they'll honor them for you. There won't be any ad-
ditional charges, I don't think."

"Thanks," Gregg said, gathering the papers.

They all turned to find the Blue Concourse, and Jana said,
"I knew we should have stayed at the airport."

"It wouldn't have made any difference," Gregg said. "We
thought we had the right information, and we didn't. No biggie.
Get over it. We'll have these tickets re-issued, and then we'll
call Mom and Dad."

"You can call Mom and Dad. I don't want to be the one to
tell them," Jana said.

Gregg looked irritated. "I'll call them. Don't worry. It's only
a few more hours. Come on, Jana. You're all paranoid again."

"I am not," Jana said.

Oh boy! Here we go again!

Tim walked in stride with Sierra and said, "None of this
seems to bother you."

Sierra shrugged. "It's the modern world. We're at the mercy
of others all the time." To herself she thought, *And if I'd realized
that I'd spend the weekend at the mercy of Jana's many moods, I'm not
sure I would have come!*

Chapter 5

Gregg exchanged the tickets, called his parents, and used a bank machine to get some extra money. By then it was after 11:00.

Everyone managed to fall asleep rather quickly on the benches in the waiting area except Sierra, who couldn't find a comfortable way to lie on the narrow bench in her tie skirt. She tried to sleep sitting up but soon gave up that idea and fished in her backpack for something to eat.

She discovered a granola bar, but eating it made her thirsty. It didn't seem necessary to wake any of the others to tell them where she was going, so Sierra quietly left them in search of a vending machine. The huge airport was so empty in the middle of the night it seemed spooky. She found some vending machines by the rest rooms. The piped-in music, which floated from the speaker above Sierra's head, played a song she recognized, and she began to hum along, hoping the sound of her own voice would take away the eerie feeling.

Sierra dropped her coins into the machine. Behind her she heard one of the rest room doors open. She didn't turn to see who was coming out but pushed one of the buttons on the drink machine and listened to the loud rumble as the can fell into the metal tray.

Suddenly, as she bent to pick up her can, a pair of hands grabbed her around the waist. Responding with raw instinct, Sierra spun around with the can held firmly in her hand. With all her might, she slugged her attacker right under the jaw with her fist and the cold can of soda. Then she screamed.

The uniformed night janitor lay on the tile floor at her feet, knocked out cold. Beside him was a yellow stand-up warning sign that said, *Caution. Wet floor. Slippery.*

It took Sierra only a moment to realize the janitor, who was a rather small man, had slipped on his own wet floor and grabbed at Sierra on his way down. He was down now, all right. Down and out.

Kneeling beside him, Sierra gently tapped the man's cheek. "Sir? Can you hear me, sir?" She saw that his jaw was already swelling from where she had slugged him.

Looking around and trying not to panic, Sierra patted the man on the arm and said, "I'll be right back. Just stay there. What am I saying? Of course you're going to stay right there. I knocked you unconscious!"

She hopped up and ran back to the waiting area. "I can't believe this!" she muttered breathlessly as she looked to her right and left for any sign of a human who could come to her assistance.

"Gregg!" she called out, dashing into their waiting area and waking all seven people who were trying to sleep in that quiet section. "Tim! Jana! Come quick, you guys! I knocked a guy out!"

They all sprang to their feet, asking a dozen questions. "You did what? What happened?"

"Just come with me, you guys!" Sierra took off running, and they followed. She entered the area where she had left the janitor on the tile floor and stopped.

"He was right there," Sierra said, looking right and left. "Honest."

"What happened?" Gregg asked.

"Why did you leave us without telling anyone?" Tim wanted to know.

"Sierra, what are you talking about?" Jana asked in a groggy voice.

Catching her breath, Sierra explained. "I was thirsty. I couldn't sleep. I came here to buy something to drink, but when I had my back turned, this guy grabbed me."

"Grabbed you?" Gregg asked, stepping closer to Sierra as if he were ready to defend her honor.

"It was the janitor," Sierra explained. "But I didn't know that. My back was turned like this." She demonstrated, leaning over at the vending machine. "I was getting my drink, and I felt someone grab me, so I spun around like this."

Gregg leaned back just in time as Sierra's empty fist came flying in his direction.

"And I hit him in the jaw with the can in my hand. I hit him hard, and he was just lying there." She motioned to the ground, next to the wet floor sign. "I think he slipped. That's why he grabbed me. I tried to talk to him, but he didn't open his eyes."

Just then the door to the men's rest room opened. The janitor came out on shaky legs, holding Sierra's cold can of juice to his swollen jaw. The moment he saw Sierra, he pulled back in fear.

"Are you okay?" Sierra asked. "I'm so sorry. Do you want us to help you to the first aid center?"

The janitor held up his hand. He was shorter than all four of them and probably weighed less than Sierra. She felt awful.

"It's okay," the man said calmly. "I'm sorry I startled you. I didn't mean to—"

"I know," Sierra interrupted him. "It's just that I thought—"

"I know," he interrupted her. Then he turned to Tim and

Gregg and in a calmer tone said, "You don't have to worry about this one taking care of herself."

They all laughed nervously.

The janitor held the can of juice out for Sierra.

"Oh no. Please. Keep it. It's the least I can do for you."

"Okay," the janitor said. "I think it's about time for my break." He shuffled past them, being careful to keep his distance from Sierra.

The four of them went the other direction, heading back to their gate. Sierra's heart was still pounding fiercely.

Gregg came up beside her, and slipping his arm around her shoulder, he asked, "Are you okay?"

Sierra nodded.

"I know I told you back at the mall that you were going to be a knockout someday, but this isn't exactly what I meant."

Sierra laughed and with her laughter came a wave of relief.

Just then Jana turned around and saw Gregg with his arm around Sierra and Sierra laughing. Jana gave Sierra a stunned look. Then Jana grabbed Tim's arm and pulled it around her shoulders, resting her head against his chest. Sierra knew the competition had begun.

Chapter 6

At that point the dynamics among the four travelers became strained and awkward and stayed that way the rest of the journey. The morning flight took them directly to Kalispell with no mishaps. Mr. and Mrs. Hill were waiting for them, as was the luggage, which had arrived the day before, having been rerouted on the 7:23 flight out of Minneapolis. The group took off for the cabin, with Jana and Sierra in the Suburban's backseat, not speaking to each other, and with Gregg and Tim pretending to be asleep in the middle seat.

"You kids must be exhausted," Mrs. Hill said, smiling at the girls.

No one had mentioned the knockout incident, and Sierra was glad.

"Once we get to the cabin, you can all unwind. That's what we do best at the cabin. The weather has been beautiful."

Sierra smiled her appreciation back but didn't have any words in response. She was so tired—not only from lack of sleep but also from the lack of understanding. How could Jana have given Sierra such a look of disapproval when Gregg had his arm around her? Did Jana seriously think Gregg was flirting with Sierra? And why did Tim let Jana walk through the airport holding on to him the way she did? Didn't he realize she was a young, impressionable teenager and she liked him? He was only encouraging her.

Sierra knew she also was an impressionable teenager. But in this situation, she felt she was much more aware of what was going on than either Jana or Tim. Gregg had put his arm around Sierra to comfort her and to tease her a little, but that's what Gregg did with everyone. Teasing wasn't the same as flirting. It wasn't as if they were on a double date.

Closing her eyes and resting her head against the back of the seat, Sierra decided to enjoy the fresh air blowing in from the open front window. It seemed like a long time since they had had any fresh air. The air that now blew over Sierra's face smelled cool and clean. She wished she could feel the same way inside. It would be so nice if she and Jana could clear the air.

Without intending to, Sierra was lulled into a deep sleep as they drove. Unfortunately, it ended abruptly when the Suburban pulled onto a bumpy gravel road and then stopped.

Sierra tried to focus her bleary eyes as she looked out the window at a cabin nestled in a round of tall evergreen trees. She had seen pictures of the cabin that Mrs. Hill had framed and hung behind the couch in the family's living room. Sierra knew that the lake and dock were at the front of the house and that the car was parked by the back door.

Everyone climbed out, and Sierra felt herself moving like a robot, carrying her gear to the downstairs bedroom to the left of the living area. The small, simple bedroom had an open window that looked out on the lake. Two twin beds with light yellow spreads awaited them. Jana announced that she would take the bed on the right. Sierra gladly took the bed on the left, and just to prove how accepting she was of it, she flopped on her back and said, "Wake me in a hundred years."

"Come on," Jana said. "You can't sleep now. We have to go down to the lake. It's tradition. Whenever we arrive, we drop off our stuff and go right down to the water. Even if it's the middle of the night."

Sierra considered telling Jana to go ahead and uphold her tradition without her, but she heard the openness and enthusiasm in Jana's voice and realized none of the earlier tension seemed to have followed them into this room. Sierra didn't want to be the one to invite the tension back into the weekend.

"Okay," she said, pulling herself up.

Jana already had pulled her bathing suit from her bag and had it on. She was wrapping a towel around her waist and smiling brightly. Sierra was amazed how different Jana's outlook was on life when she was in familiar surroundings and back in step with comfortable routines and traditions. This was the Jana Sierra knew and liked back in Pineville.

"Come on!" Jana urged.

"Are we going to look at the water or get in the water?" Sierra wanted to know.

"It's your choice," Jana said with a twinkle in her eye.

"I'm coming to look, not to touch," Sierra said. She followed Jana out the front door and saw that Jana's parents and the guys were already out on the dock. Mrs. Hill was sitting in one of the wooden lawn chairs with her camera in hand. The guys were at the end of the dock, both wearing swim trunks. Gregg seemed to be explaining something to Tim.

"Wait for us!" Jana called out, running across the grassy area toward the dock.

Sierra let Jana jog ahead. She watched as Jana joined the guys, and then on the count of three, they all ran off the end of the dock and made three huge cannonball splashes in the water. They came up hooting and hollering about how cold the water was. Mrs. Hill snapped their photos. By the time Sierra arrived on the dock, the three jumpers were wrapped in beach towels, sitting in the sun with their teeth chattering.

"You should have joined us," Gregg said to Sierra.

Sierra laughed. "Oh yes, you all make it look like such a pleasant experience."

"It's much nicer in the afternoon," Mrs. Hill said. "It's still a little early for swimming."

"But we had to keep up our tradition," Jana said happily. "Gregg and I always jump in within five minutes of getting here. Once we jumped in at ten o'clock at night with our clothes on after we had driven two days. Then we went inside the cabin, put on our pajamas, and sat by the fire until our hair dried. Do you remember that?" Jana turned to Gregg, looking for affirmation.

"I think I was ten," Gregg said. "I remember it." He looked as if all the stress from the long journey had washed off his face.

Sierra almost wished she had jumped in with them. But right now her preference was to sit in the empty padded lawn chair next to Mrs. Hill and catch a few winks with her face to the sun. She was still wearing her tie skirt, a T-shirt, and a thin sweater. It didn't feel warm enough to take off her sweater, but she slipped off her shoes and tucked them under the chair as she settled in.

Gregg started to tell a story about their flight to Minneapolis. "I think the flight attendant wanted to see if anyone was paying attention when they went over the emergency procedures."

"Oh, I know," Jana jumped in. "It was so funny."

Gregg talked over his sister, taking the story back. "When she got to the part about the oxygen mask, she held that sample one up and put it over her nose and mouth and then her eyes bugged out, and she started to turn red, as if she was trying to breathe but no oxygen was coming through."

They all laughed at the memory.

"I'm surprised the airline let her get away with that," Mr. Hill said from his lawn chair on the wide dock. "You would think they would monitor the instructions to know if the procedures are being upheld to the full extent of the law."

His words sounded serious, but something in his tone told Sierra he was teasing. Gregg's wry wit obviously came from his father.

"Oh, and then that emergency instruction card they hold up," Jana said. "She held it upside down." Jana laughed. "Remember that time we were on the plane to Arizona, Gregg? You pulled out that card and pointed to the picture of the guy who had his head between his legs in the emergency crash position, and you said, 'This is a picture of the last guy who ordered the lasagna on this flight. We better order the chicken.' "

Gregg laughed, too. "Remember that flight attendant? He gave us such a dirty look. I didn't think he was going to give us lunch when the cart came down the aisle."

Sierra thought it was great the way everyone had let go of the tension that had silenced them earlier. This is how she had imagined the vacation. Maybe yesterday was just a bad beginning. The tension was gone, and the "experimental flirting" was likely to be over, as well. They could all settle in and have fun. Jana was in her comfort zone now. She could go back to being the steady, sure, predictable friend Sierra was familiar with.

Tim reached over and grabbed Sierra's bare toes with his cold hand. "You're sure the pacifist," he said.

"Hey, I didn't get any sleep in the airport," she protested.

"She was too busy knocking out janitors," Gregg teased.

"You did what?" Mr. Hill asked.

Jana, Gregg, and Tim laughed as Mr. and Mrs. Hill waited for an explanation.

"I went to buy a can of juice while these guys were sleeping," Sierra explained.

"No, you have to stand up," Gregg said, "and show them everything the way you showed us."

Sierra reluctantly complied. She stood near the end of the dock, out of the way of the others so she wouldn't accidentally hit anyone. As she continued her story, Gregg sat in her chair, holding the cushion instead of sitting on it.

Everyone laughed as Sierra related the humiliating experience all over again, complete with arm motions and facial expressions.

Gregg rose and took center stage next to her when she reached the part about the janitor coming out of the rest room. Still holding the cushion, Gregg used it as a prop for a can of juice, holding it to his jaw and giving a terrified look when he saw Sierra. They all had another great laugh.

Then Gregg said, "Oh, and I just remembered another line the flight attendant used." He handed Sierra the cushion, and she took it, assuming he needed both hands to act out his next joke.

She was right. As soon as Sierra took the cushion, Gregg announced, "And remember, in the event of a water landing, your seat cushion may be used as a flotation device." With that, he grabbed Sierra and jumped into the water.

Chapter 7

"My skirt!" Sierra cried when she surfaced from the brisk lake water.

Jana was standing at the edge of the dock, looking down on Sierra sympathetically. Sierra quickly realized that she hadn't been the first "little sister" Gregg had tricked into the water.

"Did it ruin your skirt?" Jana cried. "Gregg, if you ruined her skirt, you're going to have to pay for it. She made that, you know! It's not like she can just go buy another one."

Gregg had paddled to the ladder on the side of the dock and was back on deck as Jana continued to rail him about the skirt.

"My skirt!" Sierra cried out again, her teeth chattering as she tread water.

"You better come out," Tim said, directing her over toward the ladder.

Sierra paddled toward the ladder, too cold to say what she wanted to. Suddenly a strange, multicolored, bulbous creature popped to the surface and hovered ominously like a deformed jellyfish between Sierra and the dock.

"What is that?" Jana shrieked.

"My skirt!" Sierra yelled for the third time.

"Oh, you poor dear!" Mrs. Hill said, hurrying over to the

ladder with a dry beach towel. "Turn your heads, boys. Sierra has lost her skirt."

She had been concerned that her skirt had sunk to the bottom of the lake, never to be retrieved. Now that she saw it floating, she was relieved.

The guys turned around. Sierra grabbed her floating skirt, pulled herself up on the ladder and onto the dock, where she let Mrs. Hill wrap her in the warm towel.

Jana took the wet skirt from Sierra and carefully wrung it out. "Such tiny snaps," Jana said, examining the skirt. "No wonder it came undone. Maybe you should have used a zipper."

"Can we turn around now?" Gregg asked.

"Yes." Sierra sunk into the lawn chair still shivering, holding the towel tightly around her.

Gregg chuckled cautiously. "I honestly thought that floating thing was some creature from the deep lagoon, awakened from his primeval slumber."

"You wait, Gregory Hill," Sierra said. "You're going to be wakened from your primeval slumber before this weekend is over."

"Only you, Sierra," Mr. Hill said, awkwardly patting her wet head.

"That's what my dad always says," Sierra said through chattering teeth. Then she drew in a shallow breath. "Which reminds me. I need to call my parents."

"The phone line went out this morning," Mrs. Hill said. "Why don't you put on dry clothes, and we'll take a trek into town."

Sierra slipped her shoes on her cold feet and picked her way down the dock and back to the cabin. Jana went ahead of her and hung Sierra's skirt on the clothesline, which was strung from two trees on the left side of the yard area. Sierra appreciated Jana's being so concerned about Sierra's tie skirt. Jana apparently knew how much Sierra liked that skirt and how much it was a symbol of her personality.

As she changed, Sierra thanked Jana for hanging the skirt.

"I'm serious," Jana said. "If it's ruined, Gregg should have to pay you for it. So try to figure out what it's worth."

Sierra thought about that as the three women drove into town. What would that skirt be worth? What was her personality personified worth on today's market? Was she a fun and interesting person because of how she looked and acted? Or was she just a big klutz who knocked out innocent janitors and was too naïve to see a push into the lake coming?

On one hand, Sierra was glad Gregg had pushed her in. His action showed that he accepted her, that he liked her in a big-brother way. He wouldn't have tried so hard to set up the perfect opportunity to tease Sierra if he didn't think she could take it and if he didn't enjoy it. Not just enjoy it for the sake of the joke, but enjoy it because it was the way one buddy treated another buddy. She was the freckle-faced tomboy and everybody's kid sister.

On the other hand, what if she wanted more? What if she felt ready to encourage more in a relationship with a guy? Was that what Jana was doing when she put her head on Tim's shoulder at the airport? What if Sierra had done that to Gregg? How would he have reacted? she wondered.

And she wondered some more that afternoon after lunch. The guys had gone off fishing in the boat, which left Sierra and Jana plenty of time to lounge in the sun and catch up on their lost night of sleep.

When the guys came back with three fish, they were pretty proud of their catch. Sierra thought there wasn't enough meat on those three little silver-scaled fellows to feed all six of them. However, Mrs. Hill prepared lots of rice and vegetables and then mixed the diced pieces of cooked fish in with the whole batch.

Sierra had plenty to eat, as did the others. The cleanup went quickly, and then everyone put on a sweat shirt and went back out to the dock to enjoy the close of the day.

"Can we make a rule that you can only throw a person into the water once? And can we recognize that I've already had my dunking?" Sierra asked.

"Sounds fair," Mrs. Hill said.

Sierra noticed that Gregg didn't voice his agreement. Of course, he and Tim were busy with some project they had started after they came back with the fish. They had six long cattails that they had cut from the bulrushes of the fishing cove they had boated to that afternoon. The cattails were the longest Sierra had ever seen, with stalks as thick as broom handles. Gregg had the bulblike end of the cattails dunked in a white bucket at the end of the dock.

Everyone chatted and watched a family of ducks come quacking up to the side of the dock. Mrs. Hill was ready for them and offered Sierra and Jana several pieces of dried bread.

Sierra broke the bread into bits and cast it on the water. The energetic baby ducks paddled quickly over to where the bread landed.

"They are so cute," Jana said, tossing her bread to them. "I think we had three duck families last summer. Are these the only ones that have been coming?"

"Yes," Mrs. Hill said, "these are the only ones we've seen. Who knows, maybe once the word gets out that we're offering free food, we'll be swamped like we were a few years ago. Do you remember that? We had more waterfowl than we could feed. I think the Morrisons got here before we did this year, and the ducks made it a habit to go there."

When Jana's mom mentioned the Morrisons, Sierra noticed that Jana's expression changed. She looked surprised or hopeful. Or both.

"I didn't think they were coming until August this year," Jana said.

"No, they're here. I saw Corinna in town the day we arrived."

"Did their kids come this year?" Jana asked.

"Some of them," Jana's mom answered.

That's when Sierra knew what was going on with Jana. Sierra had heard about Danny Morrison, who lived in Oklahoma. His parents were wealthy and owned a lakefront house—not a cabin but a house—and it was located only a few hundred yards through the woods from Jana's family's cabin. Danny was thirteen when Jana had seen him two summers ago, but she had returned to Pineville with a secret summer crush she had told Sierra about. Jana had lamented that Danny wouldn't be at the lake this summer so she wouldn't have a chance to see if he had grown into a stud like his older brother, Michael.

"Is this the family that vacationed in Australia last summer?" Sierra asked.

"Yes," Mrs. Hill said. "That's where Corinna is from. They didn't come at all last summer, and we thought it was such a pity for that beautiful home to be locked up the whole season. How do you know about the Morrisons?"

Sierra shot a smile at Jana and teased her by saying, "I heard they had a good-looking son."

Jana's glare was ice and nails. Sierra was a little surprised. She didn't think Jana's intrigue with Danny Morrison was a big secret.

"Oh yes, Michael, their oldest son, is very nice looking. He played football for a big school in the South. I don't remember which one. Corinna said he may turn pro when he graduates next year."

Sierra glanced at Jana and knew she was saved from Jana's wrath since her mom thought Sierra meant Michael.

Jana leaned forward in her lawn chair. "You said only some of the Morrison kids came this summer."

"Yes?" her mom replied.

"Did Danny come?"

Sierra leaned forward, too, just as curious to hear the answer.

Chapter 8

"Yes," Mrs. Hill said, "Danny is here with them."

"And Cassie?" Jana asked.

Sierra vaguely remembered Jana mentioning Danny's annoying little sister, Cassie, and figured Jana was asking about her to cover up for her interest in Danny.

"Yes, Cassie is here, too. She was at the store with her mother. She's really grown."

Sierra wondered if Jana was thinking about whether Danny had grown since she had seen him. As Sierra looked over at Jana, she noticed Jana's dark eyes practically sparkled. As a matter of fact, they were reflecting a soft light. Sierra looked out at the end of the dock and saw the reason for the glow in Jana's eyes. Gregg had pulled one of the cattails from the bucket and lit the end of it. He now held the natural tiki torch over the water, and they all watched the flame from their lawn chairs.

"It's burning a long time," Sierra commented.

"They soaked them in kerosene," Jana said.

Now Sierra understood why it had smelled like gas when they came down to the dock. She thought it had come from the boat.

The cattail torch continued a little longer before snuffing itself out. Once the flame extinguished, Sierra noticed the sky. It was beginning to fade into a soft peach, and the first star was already visible.

Sierra wondered which star it was. She knew she could ask Wes, if he were here. He would know. Gregg, Tim, or someone else on the dock might know also, but Sierra didn't feel like asking the name of that twinkling star because none of them had noticed it. It was her star. She could enjoy it without having to know it on a first-name basis.

Gregg and Tim lit two more cattail torches and held them high, joking about being conquering warriors.

"I want to light one," Sierra said, getting out of her seat. "Do you want to light one, too?" she asked, turning to Jana.

Jana was daydreaming and didn't hear Sierra. *I bet I can guess what she's thinking about. Just because I'm such a nice friend, I won't disturb her.*

Sierra shuffled to the end of the dock and asked if she could "play" with one of the torches, too.

"We're not playing," Gregg said. "This is . . . ah, necessary. Yes, necessary for ah . . ."

"Keeping away the mosquitoes," Tim filled in for him.

"That's it exactly. We're keeping the mosquitoes from biting you guys, and our job is to hold the torches and wave them just right." Gregg gave his lit cattail a little loop in the air.

"That's right," Tim said, copying Gregg's loop.

"You guys, come on. I want to play, too. I mean, I want to keep the mosquitoes away, too. Besides, don't you think it's too cold for mosquitoes?"

"It will warm up as the summer goes on," Gregg said, using his most authoritative voice. "And we're letting those early mosquito scouts know that this dock and this cabin, with all its surrounding property, are off limits."

Sierra ignored Gregg and reached in the bucket for one of the cattails. "Got a match?"

"Not since Superman died," Gregg joked.

Sierra gave him a puzzled look.

"Don't you get it?" Gregg said, reverting back to his regular voice. "A 'match,' as in 'an equal'? No, I don't have a match since Superman died."

"When did Superman die?" Sierra asked, glancing at Tim to see if this was really funny.

"Never mind," Gregg said, shaking his head. Then looking over at Tim, he said, "Kids these days. About all they're good for is knocking out janitors."

Sierra had an awful feeling she wasn't going to hear the end of the janitor episode for as long as Gregg was around to tease her. At that moment, she wanted very badly to push him into the lake. She realized she didn't have any warm and snuggling feelings toward him.

I'm tired of Gregg's jokes. Tim is so much nicer. And cuter, too. He doesn't act as if he's my guardian all the time. He was really kind not to pull back from Jana after she put his arm around her at the airport. And he let her put her head on his chest. Tim is much more understanding and compassionate than Gregg. Gregg pushed me in the lake, but Tim was the one who told me where the ladder was.

"Here you go, Sierra," Tim said, holding his still lit cattail next to hers until the flame from his lit hers. The gesture seemed romantic. As Sierra stood there, feeling the warm glow from the fire on her fresh, freckled face, she couldn't help but wonder if Tim hadn't just lit more than her cattail.

For the rest of the night, Sierra paid special attention to Tim. When they finished lighting all the cattails, and the stars had all come out, Mr. and Mrs. Hill went inside, leaving the four teens sitting in the lawn chairs arguing over the rules to a word game Gregg wanted them to play.

Sierra listened as Gregg and Jana worked out the rules. Sierra's brothers and sister often acted the same way so the banter didn't bother Sierra, but Tim seemed to be trying to bring resolution.

Sierra knew that Tim had only one brother, and he was deaf. She thought Tim probably had developed a deeper sense of understanding and compassion toward people because of having to learn another way to communicate with his brother. The thought made Sierra feel an equal sense of compassion toward Tim. Without realizing it, she was staring at him while a happy smile played across her lips.

"Did you get that?" Jana asked, nudging Sierra.

"I think so," Sierra said, snapping herself back to the group. "Why don't we try a practice run? Just start the game and explain what we do wrong as we go along."

"That's a great idea," Gregg said. "Why didn't we do that in the first place?"

Because you're a controlling big brother, Sierra thought. *And you like to have everything your way, just like Jana likes to have everything around her nice and familiar. I've figured it out. Why can't the two of you see it?*

Suddenly Sierra felt that she and Tim were outsiders. Gregg and Jana had their games and traditions from every summer when they came to the lake. Why did Sierra and Tim have to go along with their rituals? Why couldn't Sierra and Tim start their own little traditions?

She couldn't think at the moment what such a tradition might be, but as soon as she thought of something fun that just she and Tim could do, she was going to tell him, and they would break away from the Hill family and make their own memory.

The game lasted far too long, in Sierra's opinion. It was fun once all the technicalities were ironed out, but three of the four people playing were fiercely competitive. Tim was the one who lost nearly every round because he didn't have the killer instinct that Sierra, Gregg, and Jana had. That only made Sierra feel more compassion for Tim.

By the time they finally went to bed, it was well after midnight. Sierra's bed felt comfy, and she was ready to drift off to dreamland the minute her head hit the pillow. But Jana had other ideas.

"Did you hear what my mom said?" Jana asked as soon as she was in bed and the light was out. "Danny is here!"

"I heard," Sierra said. "I watched your face when your mom told you. You looked dreamy."

"Oh no! Do you think my mom knows I want to see him?"

Sierra laughed quietly. "I think everyone here knows you want to see him."

"Are you serious?"

Jana sounded so distressed that Sierra reevaluated her comment. "Maybe not everyone. I know more about the whole thing than anyone else, so I'm sure I picked up on more than they did."

"I can't wait to see him," Jana said. "I wonder how much he's changed."

Sierra propped herself up on her elbow to make sure she wouldn't fall asleep. Obviously this conversation was important to Jana.

"I've been trying to figure out the best way to see him. I thought maybe you and I could go berry picking tomorrow morning in the woods and end up at their property. Hopefully, he'll be outside, and we can just start to talk."

"I thought we were going river rafting tomorrow," Sierra said. "Isn't tomorrow the Fourth? Saturday, right?"

"Oh, rats. I forgot. I feel like we're a day behind because it took us so long to get here. Yes, my mom made reservations, and it's one of the busiest weekends so I know we shouldn't cancel."

It was quiet a moment. Suddenly Jana switched on the light.

Sierra blinked at the brightness and said, "What?"

Jana was sitting straight up in bed looking bright-eyed. "I have an idea."

Chapter 9

Sierra flopped back in bed and stared at the ceiling. She was certain she didn't want to hear Jana's idea. And she was certain she could guess the general direction the idea would take. Yet against her better judgment, Sierra said, "What's your idea?"

"We'll go berry picking early, and that way we'll see Danny, and when we do, you'll mention that we're going rafting, and then I'll say, 'Hey, do you want to come with us?' That way it will be really casual, and he'll say yes, and he'll come, and it'll be great."

Sierra wanted to laugh. This was so unlike Jana to make elaborate plans in an attempt to be casual. Of course, there was a sobering side to Jana's scheme, too. If practical, non-risk-taking, likes-everything-set-in-a-non-threatening-routine Jana could fall into such illogical thinking and scheming for the sake of being with a guy, Sierra knew very well that the same thing could happen to her one day.

"You know what?" Sierra said, taking a rabbit trail off of Jana's plan to conquer via the woods. "I always thought of you and me as being the slow ones to blossom."

"The slow ones to blossom? What does that mean?"

"You know how Mikayla and Dave are already preengaged or promised or whatever it is?"

"Yes."

"And Jennifer has gone out with about every guy in our school."

"Yes."

"And Becca has that boyfriend who's in college."

"Yes, yes. I know the life of every girl in our class, too. What's your point?" Jana said.

"They all have boyfriends or have had boyfriends, even though we've only just finished our sophomore year."

"Not everyone has a boyfriend or has had a boyfriend. Misty doesn't."

"Yes, she does. Sharla told me," Sierra said. "My point is, all through junior high, when everyone paired up except us—"

"Not everyone," Jana protested.

"Okay, almost everyone. And in high school when everyone started going out and getting serious, you and I were slow to blossom. Do you see?"

"Yes, I see," Jana said in a sulking voice. "And I don't like it one bit. You're sounding like we should be proud of being looked over."

"All I'm saying," Sierra said with a sigh, "is that if you really like Danny, then something might change this summer, and I don't know if I'm ready for that change."

"Sierra, you are so melodramatic sometimes. You do realize, don't you, that we're fifteen years old? In some countries that's old enough to be married! It's natural for us to chase guys and flirt—in the right way. Not only is it natural, it's practically unnatural that we haven't gotten boyfriends yet. We're fifteen! I know sixth graders who are more experienced than we are when it comes to guys."

"And that's supposed to be our goal? Our role model?"

"No," Jana said, sounding exasperated. "You're not trying to understand what I'm saying. It's time, Sierra. So blossom already, will you? And even if you don't want to blossom or you don't think you're ready to, I am. And I'm going to this summer. My first step will be to get Danny rafting with us tomorrow. You can go berry picking with me or not. But even if you don't, I'm going into the woods tomorrow and coming back with Danny Morrison, or I'm going to die trying!" With that, Jana snapped off the light.

Sierra wanted to laugh into the darkness and say, "Now who's being melodramatic?" But she kept quiet until she could tell that Jana's breathing had calmed down.

"Jana?" Sierra whispered into the cool space of air that hung between them. "Jana, I'll go with you. I don't think I was clear about what I was trying to say. I didn't mean to upset you. It could be you're ready to blossom, and I'm not. But I'm not saying you can't or you shouldn't. I'm just . . ."

Sierra realized she was heading for dangerous territory if she continued to speak her mind. It was awfully hard for her to pull back. There was so much she wanted to say, and it all seemed clear to her now. Instead, Sierra said, "I'll go with you tomorrow."

"Thanks." Jana didn't say anything else, even though Sierra must have stayed awake half an hour, waiting for Jana to add a final comment the way she usually did when she and Sierra debated. But it never came.

Having been awake most of the night before and then sleeping in the afternoon, Sierra's internal clock seemed confused. Not to mention that she hadn't slept much the night before the trip because she had put off her packing until the last minute. Still, she couldn't sleep now, so she quietly pulled on her jeans and jacket. She peeled through the layers of clothes in her bag until she touched her Bible. Then she found her flashlight in her backpack and tiptoed out of the room and out the front door. She grabbed an old blanket off the clothesline. It was damp with the night dew, as was her skirt. She decided to let her skirt remain hanging until tomorrow morning, but the blan-

228

ket would feel warmer than nothing.

Stepping onto the grass with her bare feet was exhilarating. It made her feel fully alive and wide awake.

The night's silence around her enabled Sierra to hear sounds she hadn't heard in the day. She stopped moving and stood still, her feet planted on the blades of wet grass. She could hear the dock creaking like an overgrown baby being rocked in an antique cradle. Overhead, a bird, most likely an owl, effortlessly flapped its way through the darkness. Sierra was certain dozens of night creatures had stopped their scuttling about when she walked out of the house. They were all transfixed in their hiding places, waiting for her to make the first move so that her human noise would mask their padded comings and goings.

If her feet weren't so cold, Sierra might have tried to wait out one or two of those creatures so she could see them scamper to new hiding places. But she couldn't wait, and so she was the one who scampered down to the dock.

Seated with her feet under her on the padded Adirondack chair, Sierra tucked the blanket all around her and then leaned back, breathing in the glory of the night sky.

"Oh wow," she whispered as the thousand vibrant points of light came into focus. There were too many. Too many to take in. Too many to imagine. Too many stars in God's great heaven.

The longer she sat, quietly watching the night spectacle, the more she thought about a verse she had heard many times. She knew it was in Psalms somewhere.

She tried to recite it in a holy whisper. " 'When I consider your heavens, the moon and the stars which you ordained, what are humans, that you are mindful of us?' "

Sierra pulled her warmed arms out of her cocoon and reached for her flashlight and Bible, which were on the chair next to her. She wanted to make sure she had quoted the verse right.

Holding the flashlight in her teeth, she checked her concordance in the back of her Bible, looking under "stars." Another reference that caught her eye was listed in Daniel 12:3. All the concordance said was . . . *like the stars forever and ever.* It reminded her of a song she liked, and she wondered if the song was inspired from this verse.

Turning to the book of Daniel, she found the verse. Then, taking the flashlight out of her mouth and pointing the light's beam at the page, she read, " 'Those who have insight will shine brightly like the brightness of the expanse of heaven, and those who lead the many to righteousness, like the stars forever and ever.' "

Sierra liked that. She glanced back up at the stars, and the sight of the "expanse of heaven" again took her breath away. " 'Those who have insight will shine brightly,' " Sierra repeated. More than anything, she wanted to have insight. Schoolwork had come easily for her. Whenever facts entered her brain, they seemed to stick around, and she could pull them out when necessary, like on a test. What she wanted more than knowledge was wisdom. Insight. Understanding.

It was sort of like the discussion she and Jana had just had. What Sierra had wanted to communicate was not just which girls in their class were dating which guys. Sierra had wanted to say that she didn't want to be like everyone else. She wanted deeper insight when it came to relationships. She wanted to reach higher. For the stars, maybe?

Why not? Sierra pulled off her blanket, stood up, and lifted her arms as far as she could stretch them. With her face toward the heavens, she said aloud, "I'm yours, Lord. Let my life shine for you, like a bright star in a dark world."

She twirled around and did a barefooted dance on the dock. Just as she was about to break out in song, she heard *plop-splash* right beside the dock.

Sierra froze. It could have been a fish. The fish were jumping earlier that evening, but she hadn't remembered hearing any such sound since she had come out on the dock.

Scanning the dark water as her heart pounded, Sierra tried to imagine the various kinds of creatures that could make plop-splash sounds in the water, like the sound of a rock when it's thrown into the water.

Sierra couldn't see anything.

Suddenly a second *plop-splash* came from nearly the same spot, followed by the gentle stroke of a paddle.

"Jana?" a male voice called out softly.

Sierra's heart jumped to her throat as she saw a kayak emerge from the shadowy reeds along the lake's edge. A guy was in the kayak. His blond hair caught the light from the night sky, and Sierra knew who it was.

Chapter 10

"Danny," Sierra whispered.

"Jana?" he whispered back.

"No."

He paddled closer to the dock, and when he came completely out of the shadows, Sierra's first thought was, *Oh yes, Jana, I think he's grown up a little since last summer.* The buff guy coming toward her in the kayak made both Tim and Gregg look like wimps.

Sierra, still frozen in place, bit her lower lip as Danny paddled closer. Nervously she stammered, "Uh, Jana isn't here right now. But I'll tell her you called. Or rather, that you came by. Or should I say, that you came out of the shadows?"

Sierra found a boost of courage in those last words, and suddenly she was mad at this hunk for lurking in the shadows, spying on her private conversation with God.

"What are you doing out at this time of night, anyway?" Sierra snapped, placing her hand on her hip. "This is private property, and you have no right to be lurking around, spying on people."

"What are you doing up in the middle of the night?" Danny

asked her. He was now at the bottom of the ladder, bobbing in his streamlined kayak.

"I couldn't sleep," Sierra stated.

"Neither could I. You want to go for a ride?"

"No, of course not," Sierra said with a light laugh. "You don't even know who I am."

"Let me guess. You're a friend of Jana's."

"I'm going in now," Sierra said, picking up her Bible and tucking it under her arm. She had heard people refer to their Bibles as their "sword," and as soon as she picked it up, she felt armed and ready for this night stalker. If he so much as dared to take one step out of that kayak and up the ladder, Sierra would knock him on the head with her Bible and send him sprawling into the cold water.

But Danny didn't move. "You're going in?" he repeated.

"Yes," Sierra stated firmly. "Good night." She almost added, "I'll see you in the morning," but that would be giving away Jana's plan.

Sierra fumbled for her flashlight. As soon as she had it, she took off at a clipped pace. She heard Danny call out in a controlled voice so as not to wake everyone, "Hey, tell Jana to come out here."

Sierra kept striding through the cold grass. Each blade felt like a tiny needle on the bottoms of her feet. She didn't turn around. Hopefully Danny would think she hadn't heard him. He didn't call out again. She entered the cabin as quietly as she could and tiptoed on her numb toes back to her bed, where she crawled right in, still wearing her jeans and jacket.

For several long, dark, agonizing moments, Sierra lay in bed with her heart pounding. *What do I do, Father God? What do I do?* She thought about the verse she had just read. What was the part about having insight and shining brightly? That was all she could remember. Except something about leading others to righteousness.

If I wake Jana up and tell her Danny is waiting, I sure won't be leading her to righteousness. But he's out there waiting. If I hadn't heard him say to tell Jana, I wouldn't be having this tormenting decision to make. But I did hear him. I can't pretend that I didn't. And I can't have insight if I'm not honest with myself and others.

"Ohh!" Sierra growled through her clenched teeth. She knew that if she woke Jana, Sierra would have to explain why she was outside in the middle of the night, and Jana might tell her parents, and they might be so upset with Sierra that they would put her on a plane back home. The only one home this weekend was Tawni, who was staying at her friend's house. That meant Sierra would have to face her sister, and she didn't want to have to do that.

Or she could tell Jana, and Jana would sneak out, and then the two of them would have to keep that secret from Jana's parents. Sierra really didn't want to do that, either.

But if she didn't tell Jana until tomorrow, when they went berry picking, Danny would say something about seeing Sierra dancing around barefooted on the dock in the middle of the night. Then Jana would be furious with her because Danny would say he had told Sierra to get Jana, and then the rest of the weekend would be a disaster.

What am I thinking? The rest of the weekend is going to be a disaster no matter what. I can't win here.

It dawned on Sierra that if she merely gave Jana the message, then Jana would have to make her own decision about whether to see Danny. Sierra believed she knew her friend well enough to trust that Jana would make the right choice. It was Sierra's responsibility to tell the truth, not to try to manipulate the outcome of the situation.

Drawing in a deep breath, Sierra crawled out of bed and walked on still numb feet over to the light switch. She closed her eyes, turned on the light, and then gently shook Jana's shoulder.

"Jana, wake up," she whispered.

234

"What? What's wrong?" Jana pulled the covers up over her eyes.

"I'm really sorry to do this to you," Sierra said. She glanced at the clock. It was almost three in the morning. "I have to talk to you."

"Can't it wait?"

"No, listen. I couldn't sleep so I went out on the dock, and I was reading my Bible and looking at the stars and . . ."

Jana pulled back the covers and opened her eyes, staring at Sierra. "You went out on the dock?"

"Yes, but wait. I was having this really wonderful time with God, and then I heard this plop-splash sound, and it was Danny!" Sierra tried to calm herself and act with wisdom and insight as she told the next part.

Jana stared at her in disbelief.

"Danny talked to me, and he asked me to go for a ride with him. He didn't even know who I was."

"Did you go?" Jana asked in a small voice.

"No, of course not. I came back to the cabin. But on the way, he asked me to tell you to meet him out there."

"Now?" Jana asked, sitting up in bed.

Sierra nodded. "I didn't know if I should tell you or not, but I knew that if I told you, then you would know and wouldn't be mad when we go meet Danny tomorrow, in case he acts like he already met me. Which he didn't really, but, well, now you know and we can go back to sleep."

Sierra stood and turned off the light.

"Sierra Mae Jensen!" Jana said loudly. Then, lowering her voice to a whisper, she added, "You turn that light back on this minute."

When Sierra turned it on, Jana already was out of bed, pulling a pair of warm-up pants on over her flannel pajama bottoms.

"What are you doing?" Sierra asked.

"What do you think I'm doing? I'm going to see Danny. Help me find my shoes."

"Jana, I don't think you should—"

"What? It's okay for you to go out and carry on with him in the middle of the night, but I can't?"

"I didn't carry on," Sierra said. "And I didn't go out there to see him." Then, because she thought it added a nice spiritual touch, Sierra added, "My appointment was with God."

Jana stopped dressing and turned to look at Sierra long enough to give her the most pathetic "oh brother" look she had ever delivered. "Come on. You're coming with me."

"No, I'm not," Sierra said.

"What? You can go outside in the middle of the night for God, but you won't go outside for me?"

"Jana, this is crazy. Wait until the morning."

Jana looked at the alarm clock. "It is morning. What difference will a few more hours make?"

"A lot! The rest of the world will be awake then. Jana, don't go out there."

"Why?" Jana stopped to scrutinize Sierra's expression. "Did he say something? Anything?"

"No."

"You saw him. Does he still look like the picture I showed you?"

Sierra couldn't help herself. A grin broke through, and she said, "No, he looks much better." As soon as she said it, Sierra slapped her hand over her mouth and scolded herself.

"That's it; I'm going," Jana said decisively, zipping up her jacket. "Are you coming?"

"No," Sierra said, standing firm. "And I don't think you should go, either."

Without comment Jana slipped out of the bedroom and quietly went out the front door. Sierra turned off the light and rushed over to the window that faced the lake. She wanted to look out without being seen. She also thought that if Danny saw the light go out, he might take it as a signal to go away.

In the dim starlight, Sierra could see Jana—steady, predictable, non-risk-taker Jana—running toward the dock as if the winning goal for the soccer game depended on her.

"What have I done?" Sierra muttered, throwing herself on her bed. She considered running after Jana. At least if she had gone with Jana, Sierra might have been able to convince her to only stay a few minutes.

Sierra got up and paced the floor. Maybe it wasn't too late. Maybe she should run out there just to make sure that all Jana did was say, "Hi, do you want to go rafting tomorrow?" He could say yes, just the way Jana had planned it before they went to bed. Then the two girls could go back to the cabin and sleep in tomorrow since there wouldn't be any reason to explain why they felt a sudden urge to pick berries at the crack of dawn.

Sierra peered out the window once more. This time she saw nothing. No Jana. Only the form of the four Adirondack chairs on the dock. She didn't see a kayak anywhere, either, although she knew Danny was good at hiding.

"I have to go down there," Sierra convinced herself. If Jana had gone off for a ride with Danny, Sierra knew she would have to make another decision about whether to tell Jana's parents. But first, she had to try to stop Jana.

Sierra left the house, and she wasn't real quiet about it this time. She closed the door too quickly, and it made a lot of noise. As soon as she was out the door, she took off at a sprint fast enough to match Jana's dash across the grass.

When Sierra reached the dock, she spotted Jana. Not on the dock. Not in a kayak. But on the shore, walking toward Danny's house.

"Jana!" Sierra called out.

Jana stopped, turned to see Sierra, and then stood still.

"Come back," Sierra called to her.

It took Jana a moment, but she turned and came back along the shore. Sierra waited for her.

"Did you make it all up?" Jana asked.

"No, of course not! He was here."

"Well, he was gone when I got here," Jana complained. "How long did you wait before you told me?"

"I don't know. Not very long. A little while. I had to think about what to do."

Jana began to walk back to the cabin. Sierra trotted after her. Jana didn't speak again until they were almost up to the cabin. "I can't believe I came out here."

"I can't believe it, either," Sierra said.

"Neither can I," came a male voice from the cabin's front door.

Chapter 11

It took almost an hour for Sierra and Jana to explain the situation to Jana's parents. They weren't happy, but they weren't mad, either. Sierra wondered how her parents would have responded. The Hills seemed pleased enough that Sierra and Jana had both told the truth and had admitted that they hadn't made wise choices, although Sierra still wanted to think that her alone time with God had been special and not foolish or dangerous.

They all went to bed and slept well past nine o'clock the next morning. The proposed berry-picking trip was, of course, canceled.

The guys were up first, and Tim was making pancakes when Sierra meandered into the kitchen.

"Your pancakes woke me up," she mumbled, lowering herself into a straight-back wooden chair.

"I was making too much noise?" Tim asked.

"No, you were making too much smell. It smelled too good to stay in bed."

Tim laughed and scooped up two fresh pancakes from the griddle. "Here. See if they taste as good as they smell."

Sierra smiled her thanks and went to work decorating the

pancakes with two dots of butter for eyes and a happy face smile from syrup. "See? Even Mr. Pancake is happy this morning."

Tim smiled, lifted his hand to his nose, and then moved his first two fingers together quickly, as if he were flicking something away.

"What was that?" Sierra asked.

Tim stopped and looked at the hand sign he had just made. "Oh, I do that sometimes. I sign without thinking about it."

"What did you just say?"

"That was the sign for 'funny.' "

"Like this?" Sierra said, trying to imitate the finger movements.

"No!" Tim quickly corrected her. He looked as if he were trying to keep from laughing. "You just said 'nerd.' "

"Whoops!" Sierra said, picking up her plate and heading for the refrigerator for some milk. "I better not try to say anything else until I've at least had my happy pancakes. It was a rough night last night."

"So I heard," Tim said. "You better pull yourself together, though, because we're supposed to go rafting in an hour, which means we need to leave here in forty minutes at the latest."

"No problem," Sierra said. Getting ready quickly was her specialty. It was one of the few perks of not wearing makeup and having uncontrollable hair. Her hair did its crazy, curly gyrations all over her head no matter what she did to curb its exuberance. Sierra kept it long so that its weight would hold down the curl some. She had learned long ago that it didn't matter if she spent an hour on it or one second—it always looked the same.

"Thanks for the pancakes, Tim," she said, standing in the kitchen and eating them with vigorous bites. "They're really good."

"Glad you like them," Tim said. "You know, it's refreshing to see a girl enjoying food the way you do."

Sierra licked the syrup off her lower lip and tilted her head, hoping he would explain that statement.

"The last girl I went out with never ate," Tim said. "It wasn't fun to go out with her because if I ordered anything to eat, she would just sit there watching me with this longing look in her eye, but she wouldn't eat a thing."

"At least she was an inexpensive date," Sierra suggested.

Tim laughed and smiled at Sierra.

"Are you going out with anyone now?" Sierra asked.

"No." Tim turned back to the stove and flipped two more pancakes onto a plate. "Is Jana up yet? These are for her."

Sierra rinsed her empty plate and placed it in the sink. "I'll go check on her."

Sierra found Jana in the bedroom. Jana's bed was made, and her clothes for the day were neatly laid out on the smooth bed-spread. Sierra's bed and her side of the room were a disaster.

"Tim made pancakes," Sierra said, quickly stuffing her dirty clothes in her bag and pulling up her bed's covers. "They were good."

"I feel so strange about last night," Jana said, sitting on her bed and sighing. "What am I going to say to Danny when I see him?"

"Hi?" Sierra ventured.

"And what about my parents? They're used to my being so dependable. What was I thinking last night?"

Sierra decided it was best not to answer that one. She was actually having a hard time concentrating on what Jana was saying because Sierra was thinking about Tim. It was pretty great the way he found his way around the kitchen and felt at home enough to make pancakes.

"You know what I mean?" Jana asked.

Before Sierra had to come up with an answer, they heard a knock on the closed door.

"Jana, you want anything to eat?" her mom asked.

"Yes, I'll be right there." Jana dressed quickly. Then she told

Sierra that if she got any more wacky notions about running out to the dock in the middle of the night or even going berry picking in the woods, Sierra was supposed to slap some sense into her.

"You don't have to really slap me," Jana said, turning at the door before she left. Sierra guessed that Jana was remembering the janitor at the airport. "All you have to do is talk me down."

"That's what I tried to do last night," Sierra said.

"Well, try harder next time." Jana slipped out and closed the door.

Sierra shook her head. A long strand of wavy blond hair fell over her face, and she flipped it back behind her ear. Things were never this intense or complicated with Jana back home. *What is it about summer vacation that brings out the crazies in a person? I'd never go outside barefooted in the middle of the night at home, would I?*

Sierra knew the answer. She might. If the conditions were right, she would have done exactly what she did last night, even at home. She was given to fanciful whims every now and then.

Stretching out on her not-so-smoothly made bed, Sierra thought about how, so far in life, she had no regrets. She liked that feeling. And she wanted to finish her life with that same confidence.

So what was she supposed to do with all these confusing feelings about guys? Just feel them? Or was she supposed to act on them?

I don't think God would have made my emotions this way if this wasn't a good and useful thing. But what am I supposed to do? Acknowledge my impulses but tame them? Or do I learn by acting on what I'm feeling?

Sierra closed her eyes and saw Tim in her imagination, standing in the kitchen with the spatula in his hand. She remembered the way he had smiled at her when she showed him her Mr. Pancake happy face. Was he smiling because he thought she was attractive and fun? Or was he smiling at her the way he would smile at an adorable little kid?

And he had smiled at her in such a wonderful way when she found the LEGO piece at the mall. She liked his smile. She liked it when he smiled at her. She liked Tim. There, she had said it. Or rather, she had thought it. She liked Tim. Now, what was she supposed to do about that?

Jana burst back in the room, and Sierra shot upright in bed.

"Sierra, we're almost ready to go. What have you been doing?"

"Daydreaming," Sierra admitted, hopping up and dressing in a flash. "I was thinking about feelings and what we should do with them."

"What do you mean?" Jana asked, reaching for her sunglasses and a bottle of sunscreen.

Sierra slung her backpack over her shoulder and grabbed the beach towel she had left wadded up on the floor. "Eww! This is still wet."

"There might be a dry one on the line," Jana suggested as she headed out the door. "Don't forget to bring dry clothes to change into."

"Oh yeah, I forgot," Sierra said. She scooped up a pair of shorts from the floor and dug in her bag for underwear and a clean T-shirt.

Jana stopped and, closing the door, lowered her voice. "I've been thinking about some things, too. And I decided something a few minutes ago."

"What's that?"

"First, let me ask you a question," Jana said. "What do you think of Tim?"

Sierra smiled a gleeful grin at her friend. *Was I that obvious? Did Jana figure out that I was daydreaming about Tim?*

"He's wonderful," Sierra said openheartedly.

"That's what I think, too," Jana said. "I mean, if I'm going to fall victim to a summer romance, it might as well be with someone I already know pretty well."

"Like Tim?" Sierra said quietly, her eyes widening in disbelief.

"Yes," Jana said triumphantly. "Like Tim, exactly!"

"What about Danny?" Sierra asked.

Jana paused, shrugged, and said, "I think I want to concentrate my efforts on Tim first." She turned to hurry out to the Suburban, leaving Sierra standing in a stunned daze.

Now what am I supposed to do with all these feelings? Stuffing them in her backpack, along with her change of clothes, Sierra hurried out to join the others.

Chapter 12

Gregg drove the four of them to the river-rafting meeting point. He was unusually perky and full of jokes. Sierra wondered where he had been all morning and why he had left his friend to make the pancakes.

Jana wasn't bothered by any of Gregg's teasing about her escapade in the middle of the night. She was too wrapped up in Tim, who was sitting next to her in the middle seat.

"How did you learn to make such great pancakes, Tim?" Jana asked, ignoring a comment Gregg had just made about how tired Jana looked.

Sierra was glad Gregg wasn't harassing her about her midnight jig on the dock. But she wasn't glad that Jana was trying out all her flirting charms on Tim. He was too nice of a guy. He would be sweet and considerate back to Jana, just as he had been when she had put his arm around her in the airport. He wouldn't realize what all this was beginning to mean to Jana. And what was worse, Tim wouldn't realize that Sierra was the one he was supposed to be interested in.

Unless . . .

Sierra began to devise a plan. The more she thought about it, the more sense it made. Jana and her family stayed at their cabin most of the summer. This year they were staying until the first of August. Sierra and Tim were only here as weekend guests. They were going to fly home together, and they would be together in Pineville for almost a month before Jana got home. It made no sense for Jana to start something that could only last a few days. Sierra had the definite edge on this one.

As her competitive spirit kicked in, Sierra turned to face the middle seat and said, "Tim, how do you say 'river rafting' in sign language?"

Tim thought a moment and then said, "I don't know. I'd probably sign it like this. This is 'river,' and then I'd spell 'raft.' " His fingers moved quickly as he spelled the word.

"Do that slowly," Sierra said, trying to imitate the letters with her fingers in the air. "Is this an 'r'?"

"Like this," Tim said, reaching over and readjusting the way she had her first two fingers crossed.

Sierra smiled. She knew she had just scored a point. Tim had touched her.

As quickly as the thrill of scoring came over Sierra, it left. This was Jana. They had competed for years in school and in sports but never when it came to guys. It felt different with guys, like it was unfair because in relationships a person's heart and soul were involved. Sierra didn't like what she was feeling. She turned back around in her seat just in time to see Gregg pull into a gravel driveway and park the car in front of a log cabin. To the right was a sign carved in wood that said, "Mountain Bob's River Rafts."

"Everybody out," Gregg said. Then, turning to Jana, he grinned and said, "Get ready to have an especially good time."

Sierra hoped that didn't mean Gregg was planning to topple their raft or some other such practical joke.

They were about to walk toward the office when Jana grabbed Sierra's arm and pulled her back behind the large Suburban. "Look!" Jana squeaked.

Sierra looked around the side of the car. Then she turned

back to face her friend, just as red-faced as Jana was. "It's Danny!" Sierra said. "What's he doing here?"

"I don't know, but I'm not ready to face him."

"You're not ready to face him?" Sierra said. "What about me? I'm the one he watched doing a little star dance on the dock last night."

Gregg noticed the girls weren't with them, and he came back to get them. "What's going on?"

"What's Danny doing here?" Jana whispered.

Gregg looked over his shoulder and gave a friendly wave to Danny. "Mom invited him. He's your surprise."

"My surprise? Why would Mom invite him?"

Gregg shrugged. "She sent me over to their house this morning, and I was supposed to ask him to come rafting with us."

Jana gave Sierra a look of agony and said, "This is just like my mother! I'm sure she thought that if she arranged my social life, I wouldn't have any reason to sneak out in search of my own adventure. She's done this our whole lives, Gregg, have you noticed? She organizes everything to the last detail—even this."

Sierra knew her mom would never do something like this to ensure that Sierra had a budding social life. But then, Sierra's mom had never been as concerned about Sierra's social life as Jana's mom apparently was. Or at least as of last night.

"You're making a big deal out of nothing," Gregg said without a pinch of understanding or patience in his voice. "Now, are you coming in or not? You can spend the whole day waiting for us in the car if you're going to act like this."

Jana straightened her shoulders and put on a fierce expression. "Don't treat me like that, Gregg."

"Don't act like that."

"You don't understand."

"You're right. I don't. There. End of argument. Now, are you coming or not?"

Jana brushed past Gregg, bumping his arm on purpose as

she strode ahead of them to the porch where Danny stood talking to Tim. Sierra was about to march after her when Gregg caught her by the arm and held her back a minute. "Why don't we give her a chance to get her feet wet?" he said in a gentle voice. "You know, my parents have been kind of concerned about her being so slow to start liking guys. They don't want her to date yet, but they like Danny and they want to encourage this relationship."

"Then why were you so rude to her?" Sierra challenged, pulling her arm from his grasp.

"That's the way we are. You know that. And you can't tell me you and Wesley don't act the same way sometimes."

Sierra looked away from Gregg and his expressive eyes. The truth was, she and Wesley had had their moments. And she and Tawni had tiffs all the time.

Sierra calmed down a little, realizing that Gregg was trying to look out for his little sister. Sierra knew all too well that that's what big brothers did.

"You know what?" Gregg said, leaning closer to Sierra and talking softly. "I'm glad you came this weekend. You're good for Jana. You're fun and smart and not nearly as serious as my little sis. I wish you were staying all summer with us."

"Thanks," Sierra replied softly. She had to look away from Gregg. His expression and the light in his eyes were so tender. Sierra found she was changing her opinion of him, and she wasn't sure she wanted to. Especially when she was still feeling drawn to Tim.

With a quick glance back at Gregg, Sierra took off to join Jana and Tim with Danny. Gregg followed her as she walked up to Danny and smiled at him.

"Hi," Sierra said, stretching out her hand in an effort to appear mature and formal and not at all intimidated by this guy who had spied on her in the starlight. "I'm Sierra."

His hand was huge, and his grip hurt as he squeezed her hand and shook it. "Danny," he responded.

Sierra tried not to stare. He was even more buff up close in the daylight. And very good-looking. His hair was almost white, and Sierra wondered if he had it colored that way. She had never seen hair like that on a guy before.

"Are we ready?" Gregg asked.

Sierra noticed that Danny was acting as if nothing had happened the night before on the dock. She wondered what Jana had said to him. Or if she had said anything to him. Perhaps this was all a fresh beginning and nothing needed to be said. Sierra liked that idea.

"I'm ready," Sierra said, glancing at Tim. "Have you ever been white-water rafting before?"

"No," he said, falling in step with her as they entered the office to sign up. "I'm looking forward to this."

"Me too," Sierra said, smiling her best smile at Tim. It was all she could do not to say, "Will you sit by me?"

"I've been before," Jana said, stepping in between Tim and Sierra while leaving Danny in the dust with Gregg. "There's only one rapid on this river that's a challenge. The first time we went down it I was scared. But the last two times it seemed less threatening."

Sierra felt someone tug on the end of her hair. She hated that and turned around with a fierce expression. Danny held a lock of her hair in his hand and wore a sly expression. He waited until Gregg went past them and then said quietly to Sierra, "Did you tell her we met last night?" He looked as if he was enjoying their shared secret.

Sierra held back her shoulders and said, "Yes. And in actuality, we didn't meet. Not formally."

"Now we have," he said, reaching over and touching one of her long curls. "Is this real?"

Sierra jerked away, and with a scowl she said, "Of course it's real. Is yours?"

"No," he replied.

Sierra tried not to be surprised by his response. She turned to join the others at the check-in desk, and Danny leaned over and said, "I like your hair."

She didn't thank him for the compliment. It felt awkward having this overwhelming, good-looking guy flirting with her. Sierra guessed that Danny didn't know that Jana had come out last night looking for him, and it was just as well. A guy so cocky and confident shouldn't have the satisfaction of Jana's running to meet him when he snapped his fingers.

When Sierra looked up, she saw Jana flirting with Tim. They had been handed life vests, and Jana was helping Tim fasten the front snaps on his. By the way she was giggling and tilting her head, Sierra knew Jana wasn't acting like her normal, level-headed self.

Jana's actions sent Sierra's mind spinning. If only Jana would go back to wanting to be around Danny, then she would leave Tim alone and Sierra would be free to pursue her little daydream with him. As for Gregg, he would have to keep himself occupied. Although, he had been awfully sweet to her when he said he wished she were staying the whole time. Was that merely so she could be with Jana, or was Gregg trying to tell Sierra he liked her?

She felt as if her head might burst from all the sporadic, crazy thoughts bouncing around at an increasing velocity. She was relieved when she was handed a life vest and told to sign a paper and wait out front. At least out in the fresh air she could breathe and hopefully think more clearly.

This is crazy! I've never been so perplexed in my life. What's going on here?

"This way, people!" Mountain Bob, their guide, said, motioning for them to follow him down to the river. He gathered them together on a pebbly inlet in front of a large, gray inflated raft. "How's everybody today? You all ready for a wild ride?"

Sierra didn't answer aloud the way the rest of them did. As far as she was concerned, she had been on a wild ride for the past ten minutes. She doubted Mountain Bob had anything on this river that would compare.

Chapter 13

Sierra was wrong. Mountain Bob and his river had plenty to offer. And the friends she was riding the white water with had plenty to offer, as well.

First they were instructed to sit on the raft's bench seats. Sierra climbed in, but before she could turn and give Tim a welcoming smile to come sit next to her, Danny had snuggled right up next to Sierra. Jana stood on the shore adjusting Tim's life vest for him once again.

"Hey, Danny? It's Danny, isn't it?" Mountain Bob asked. "I need you to move back to the last bench. I'm going to have you help me out."

Danny moved as Mountain Bob said, "That's it. We're going to put all the brawn in the back."

Oh brother!

"Then you probably want all the brains in the front," Jana said, stepping into the front. "Come on, Tim. That's us."

Oh brother and sister!

Sierra thought the overly expressive grin on Jana's face was comical, but Sierra couldn't laugh because she would be the only one who saw the humor in the situation. Less than twelve hours ago this same Jana Hill was chanting to Sierra that she would "go into the forest and come back with Danny or die trying." Now she had Danny right there, and she was ignoring him and feeding her sudden flourishing interest in Tim. Sierra knew it was all fake. Jana didn't like Tim. Jana didn't know what she wanted—beyond being noticed by every guy who came within flirting distance.

What's going on with you, Jana? Are you trying to qualify for the fickle woman of the year award? Jana's behavior reminded Sierra of a little silly tongue twister her Granna Mae used to say whenever one of the grandkids was being fickle. "You want what you want when you want it. But once you've got what you want, you don't want it!"

Sierra could see how easy it would be to get caught up in the flirting thing, especially with her competitive nature. But she wanted to be removed from all the guy-girl dynamics whirling around their raft. She had a feeling the day would be more fun if she were.

Gregg slipped into the raft and teasingly said to Sierra, "Pardon me, is this seat taken?"

"All yours," Sierra said.

"I guess they're putting brawn in the back and brains in the front," Gregg said, smiling at Sierra. "That leaves beauty for the middle row, which is obviously why they put you here."

"Awww," Mountain Bob said, pushing them off into the gently gurgling river. "We have a poet on board." He hoisted himself into the raft and took his place behind Sierra. Tapping her on the shoulder, Bob asked, "Are you two going together?"

"No!" Sierra croaked.

"Well," Gregg said, "there could be worse plagues in life."

Sierra laughed. The situation felt so foreign. *Flirting? Pairing up? Being labeled "going together" simply because Gregg said something nice?*

Fortunately, Mountain Bob didn't ask any more questions. Instead, he started to bark instructions. Everyone had a paddle, and everyone was expected to use it when the time came. He had them practice paddling forward for speed, back paddling to slow the raft, and paddling on either side to steer the great rubbery beast that was quickly transporting them down the river.

Sierra had carried her baseball cap with her and laid it on the bottom of the raft when they got in. The way they were paddling, the raft floor already was wet. Sierra scooped up the wet cap and shoved it on her head. As the others paddled, Sierra struggled with her hair, trying to convince the majority of her blond mop to come out the open loop in the back of the hat. A few renegade tendrils in the front refused to participate. She gave up and let them hang down.

As soon as she picked up a paddle, she felt someone messing with her ponytail. She spun around and let out an "ouch" when several of the strands were yanked out as she turned. "Do you mind?" she snapped at Danny.

He pulled his hand away and looked at her sheepishly. "I was trying to help. You had a bunch of hair caught in the back there."

"You did," Mountain Bob concurred with a nod. "I saw it."

Sierra turned back to her designated position. She didn't like Danny touching her hair. The physical contact with a guy who seemed to like her was new to her. New and not completely comfortable.

Comfortable. That was the feeling that was missing. She was comfortable in most situations she ventured into, but on this trip she felt less and less comfortable with herself and with the people she was around.

Bob directed them to stop paddling and to let the raft float through the calm waters on this stretch of the river. Sierra laid her paddle across her knees and drew in a deep breath.

For the first time she paid attention to the beautiful scenery around them. This section of the river cut a calm course through a jagged, dramatic canyon with tree-studded sides that rose far above them to the bright blue sky. The raft bobbed along comfortably, letting the water carry it, and Sierra loved the sensation. She wished she could calm herself down enough to float through this weekend and let the Holy Spirit carry her effortlessly. She seemed to have paddled so hard to get away from where this river was taking her.

Why can't I relax and just float through life like this? Why all the ups and downs? Why can't it all be effortless like this?

Sierra soon found out that life may be a river, but it's not all a leisurely float. The section through the canyon may have been a slow and effortless ride, but no sooner were they out of the shadow of the great cliffs than the river took a turn to the right, and Mountain Bob instructed them to get their paddles ready. On his command, they were to paddle with all their might.

Yes, life consisted of whirlpools, pockets of dead water, and rapids. It was never the same for very long but always changing. She was changing, too. Sometimes the best choice was to sit still and let circumstances take her onward. Other times, it was up to her to paddle for all she was worth.

"And now!" Mountain Bob yelled.

Sierra dug her paddle into the water and gave it all she had. The raft flexed its way over the bumpy river current and bounced into a large boulder. Mountain Bob pushed off from the boulder and yelled for them to keep paddling.

The nose of the raft lifted into the air. Underneath her feet Sierra could feel the smooth boulders they were jetting over. She stopped paddling and held on to her seat for dear life. Jana screamed as they came down, nose first, into a loud, whirling pocket of white water. The splash doused them all, filling the bottom of the raft with water.

They all paddled as the raft spun around twice before Mountain Bob had them headed in the right direction. As soon as he did, he hollered for them to paddle out toward the middle of the river.

"Great job," Mountain Bob praised them all as they floated into calmer waters.

That rousing venture paralleled what Sierra's emotions had been doing the past few days—tossing her up and down and dousing her good.

Mountain Bob began to call out directions again. He wanted the guys on the left to paddle, and he wanted Jana to grab the bail bucket and bail out the bottom of the raft in the front.

"What about me?" Sierra asked.

"You? You sit for the moment."

Sierra made another mental note that while going down the river of her life, at times she would be still while everyone else was busy with what they were instructed to do. That didn't mean she was being left out, but that rather, for that place and time, she was supposed to sit.

"Okay," Mountain Bob called out, "now everyone, including Sierra, paddle—except for Jana. Keep bailing, Jana. Our biggest rapid is just ahead."

This time they could see the white water before they hit it. Boulders were on either side and one was straight ahead.

"Guys on the left, when I give the word, you dig into it because we have to get to the right of the boulder as soon as we hit the white stuff. You ready?" Mountain Bob asked.

Sierra could feel her heart pounding. For the first rapid she hadn't known what to expect. But now that she had experienced the sensation of their raft seemingly spinning out of control and being lifted by the powerful water, she had more respect for what they were about to paddle into.

She bit her lower lip and silently prayed. They hit the white water before they felt anything sensational, but as soon as the raft was all the way into the fray, the frantic water's noise was so loud they could barely hear Mountain Bob's instructions.

Sierra thought she heard him tell Jana to stop bailing, but Jana obviously didn't hear him. When she should have been paddling, she was scooping up water and holding the bucket by the handle over the raft's side.

At that moment, the raft veered to the right. The bucket instantly filled with the rush of water coming at them. Jana screamed, but instead of letting go of the now full and heavy bucket, she held on to it with both hands as the raft tipped to the right. While Sierra watched, powerless to do anything, Jana went over the side, still holding on to the bucket.

Chapter 14

Sierra screamed and rose to her feet.

"Sit down!" Bob bellowed. "Keep paddling!"

In a minute and a half of furious paddling, they had steered the raft past the dangerous boulder, out of the white water, and to the side of the lake where the water rippled quietly over tiny, well-worn pebbles.

"Where is she?" Gregg yelled, standing up and calling out behind the raft. "Jana! Jana!"

"I'll go in and get her!" Danny announced, throwing down his paddle.

"No, wait!" Bob told them. He stood and pulled out a bullhorn and a rope from a box in the back of the raft.

"Jana!" Tim and Gregg called at the same time.

Sierra spotted Jana clinging to a shelf that jutted out on the big boulder in the middle of the river. "There she is! Jana!"

Mountain Bob stood and yelled at Jana through the bullhorn. It was the same instructions he had given them at the beginning of their float—what to do in case of an emergency. Sierra wondered if Jana had been paying attention then, or if it was like when they were on the airplane and the emergency instructions seemed more useful as joke material than as actual warnings.

"Let go, Jana!" Bob yelled at her. "Float on your back and keep your feet in front of you with your toes up."

They could hear Jana screaming that the water was cold.

"Let go, Jana!" Mountain Bob yelled, repeating the instructions.

Sierra's heart was pounding. "Come on, Jana!" she yelled with Bob. "Let go!"

The others began to yell the same instruction until they saw Jana release her grip and begin her float toward them on her back, with her toes up.

It took only a few seconds before she floated right to the raft. They all began to talk at once, cheering and reaching to help her climb in.

Shivering and still shook up, Jana slumped onto the seat next to Sierra, which Gregg had vacated when he had moved up next to Tim. Everyone pelted Jana with questions until she finally managed to say, "I lost the bucket."

They all laughed, and Gregg said, "You almost kicked the bucket is more like it."

"Why did you hold on to the bucket?" Danny asked.

"I thought that was my job."

"I don't think she heard you," Sierra said, turning to Mountain Bob. "When you told her to put down the bucket and start to paddle."

"I guess not," Bob said. "Glad you're okay, Jana."

"I'm okay," she said, still shivering.

"We'll get you out in the sun, and you'll warm up nicely," Mountain Bob said. "We only have one more rapid, and that one is about fifteen minutes down the river. You have a fairly easy float between here and there."

Sierra liked the sound of floating in the sun for the next fifteen minutes.

"I hope you guys all saw in this situation the importance of listening to instructions and following them. If anyone else goes over, remember to get on your back, keep your toes up, and let the river take you downstream. Let your life vest carry you. That's what you put it on for."

As the river took them into a sunny stretch of calm water, Jana seemed to catch her breath. Sierra put her arm around Jana's shoulders. "You okay?"

Jana nodded. Water still dripped from the ends of her dark eyelashes.

"That must have been pretty scary."

"It happened so fast," Jana said.

The two friends leaned close and talked quietly while the others leisurely paddled. Danny was stretched out along the side of the raft, soaking up some sun.

"Do you want to lay across the bench so you can get the sun all over you?" Sierra asked.

"Where will you sit?"

"I'll just squish up front with the guys." Sierra carefully moved off the bench so Jana could stretch out.

"We can stop for a while if you guys want to," Mountain Bob said. "Up ahead on the left is a nice sunny cove."

"That sounds great," Sierra said, answering for all of them. She balanced on the edge of the raft as Bob directed them into the cove.

Sierra thought the water looked as if the sun had poured out all its summer riches into the liquid blue, like a bagful of gold coins that now glittered with each swish of the paddles.

"This is beautiful," she murmured.

"It sure is," Tim agreed, casting a shy smile at her. He looked up at Bob and said, "We can go swimming here, right?"

Mountain Bob nodded. "It's the best place on the river to swim. The water is much warmer, and see those high rocks over there? The water is about twenty feet deep. Safe enough for jumping. But everyone hear me on this: Jump feet first only, no diving!"

"Got it," Gregg said. "Do you want me to get out and pull the raft up on shore?"

"This is shallow enough," Bob said. "How about if everybody gets out here, and I'll park this buggy."

The moment Sierra's feet went into the shallow water, she felt even more sympathetic toward Jana. If this was the warm water, Jana must have been freezing back in the white water.

Tim waded into the water and, without warning, stretched out and began to swim toward the jumping rock.

"Isn't it cold?" Sierra called to him.

"Not once you get all the way in," Tim called, turning to float on his back. "It's nice. Are you going to come jump?"

"Sure," Sierra said. "Do you want to come, Jana?"

"No way. I want to get warm." She had made a smooth place on the pebble beach to stretch out in the sun and waved Sierra to go on without her.

"I'm coming," Gregg said.

"Me too," Danny said, making the biggest splash when he went all the way into the still cove water. "Yee-haa!" Danny hollered as he surfaced. "That'll clear your sinuses."

Gregg went in with much less noise and splash. He followed Danny and Tim around the corner with strong, steady strokes.

Sierra was having a hard time working up the nerve to dip into the cool water.

"Are you going in?" Jana asked her.

"I'm talking myself into it," Sierra said.

"You know," Mountain Bob said as he tethered the raft and was about to stretch out in the sun on the middle bench, which was the longest. "You can walk to the jumping rock. See that trail over there? It'll take you right to the top. First jump is always the best when you're dry going in. And remember, feet first."

"Okay," Sierra agreed. "If you hear a shriek loud enough to start a landslide, that will be me."

"Try to keep it down," Bob said, stretching out. "Some of

us around here will be sleeping, right, Jana?"

"Quiet," Jana teased. "I'm trying to sleep."

Sierra took off on the trail. She was glad to see that Jana was joking with Bob. Sierra took it as a good indicator that Jana was feeling better.

At the end of the trail, Sierra could look down on the guys, who were just emerging from the water and climbing up the rock. She was tempted to stay in her fairly hidden spot above them and listen to what they said. But they weren't talking; they were jumping.

Tim went first, quietly jumping into the water and coming up with a wide-eyed expression that showed just how brisk the water was.

Gregg went next, clowning by plugging his nose as he jumped. Danny was last. He hesitated, started to get in position, then stopped. Sierra knew how he felt.

As Gregg climbed out of the water, he called up to Danny, taunting him to jump. When Gregg looked at Danny, he noticed Sierra standing there.

"How did you get up there?" he yelled.

"There's a trail," Sierra said.

"Are you going to jump, or are you out for a stroll?" Gregg taunted.

"I'm going to jump," Sierra said, edging her way down. Her wet tennis shoe caught on some foliage, and she nearly slipped but managed to correct her balance and remain standing.

Danny applauded and yelled out, "Make way for the Queen of Coordination."

"Hey, be nice. I've come to offer you some moral support."

"You really going in?" Danny asked when she joined him on top of the jumping rock.

"Yes, of course I am. But you first."

"Oh no," Danny said, his smile swelling with overdone charm. "My mama always taught me to let ladies go first."

"Well, these are modern times, Danny boy. Women and

men supposedly have equal rights," Sierra said, smiling back. "So you have the right to go first."

"How about we jump together?" Danny suggested. He offered Sierra his large hand.

Sierra placed her hand in his. It felt sweaty. She wondered how sweaty hers was.

"On the count of three," Danny said.

"And it has to really be three," Sierra said. "None of this two and a half stuff or pulling back at the last minute."

"Right. I hate that, too."

"Okay, then on the count of three," Sierra said.

They shouted in unison, "One, two, three!" With hands tightly clasped, Sierra and Danny leaped into the air.

Chapter 15

"You didn't have to hold his hand," Jana said, giving Sierra a whap on the thigh. They were lying on the dock in the late afternoon sun, resting up for the evening events. It was just the two of them, with no one around to hear. Gregg and Tim had gone over to Danny's to combine their fireworks and set up everything on the Morrisons' dock for a combined Fourth of July fireworks show.

"Ouch," Sierra said. "You don't have to hit me."

"There I am, recovering on the beach from my traumatic experience—"

Sierra broke in laughing and repeated, "Your traumatic experience."

"And I gaze up from where I've washed ashore, looking like a beached whale, I'm sure."

"Not even close to a beached whale," Sierra said.

"I look up and there, against the perfect, pristine blue of the wide Montana sky, what do I see but you holding hands with Danny Morrison!"

"We were jumping!" Sierra protested. "What was I supposed to say? 'Oh, thank you for the offer to hold your hand while we jump, Danny. You're a kind, considerate gentleman, but you know what? My friend Jana over there might see us, and it would be more traumatic than the last traumatic experience she had when she wouldn't let go of the bail bucket—' "

"Hey!" Jana jumped in, sitting up and socking Sierra again in the thigh. "At least I don't go around knocking out poor, innocent airport employees!"

They both laughed.

"You gave me a bruise," Sierra whined. "One good bruise deserves another. Where do you want yours?" She sat up and faced Jana with her fist ready to strike.

"You already gave me a bruise! You bruised my poor heart when you let Danny hold your hand!" Jana wailed playfully. "Life is so unfair!"

"Oh, listen to you! You changed your mind about him faster than anyone I've ever seen."

"I did not," Jana said.

"You did, too! How am I supposed to keep up with you? Yesterday it was, 'I'm going into the woods, and I'm going to bag me one Danny Morrison and bring him home on a silver platter.' Then you see him, and you realize his body has grown faster than his social skills."

Jana laughed. "I got a little spooked being around him at first."

"I guess," Sierra said with sarcasm.

"He's younger than I am, you know," Jana said.

"So? That didn't seem to be a problem for you in the middle of last night."

"What do you think about Danny? Honestly," Jana asked.

"I think he needs another year to grow up."

"Unless maybe he had someone to help him along," Jana suggested.

"Let me see, who could we find to take on such a project?" Sierra struck a pose, as if she were thinking hard.

"All in all, I think he's a nice guy," Jana said.

"I think so, too," Sierra agreed. "I admit, once he quit pulling my hair he was a lot of fun. Jumping off the rock with him was great. But what about your plans for a summer romance with Tim?"

"I think Tim thinks I'm too young for him. Which I'm not, but my brother makes me look that way in front of him."

"I think that's the way Tim views me, as well," Sierra said.

"He really is a nice guy," Jana said. "And cute in a snuggly kind of way."

"Is it my imagination, or is one of us changing her mind every twelve seconds?"

"Come on, Sierra. Don't be so critical. This is all part of it."

"Part of what?"

"Part of figuring out life. You know, leaving childhood and venturing into the wild, wonderful world of womanhood."

Sierra laughed. "What is that supposed to mean?"

"You know what I mean. You said it last night. It's time to blossom. I'm just trying to figure out what that involves. And if it means giving Danny another chance, then I should do it."

"Another chance? I never noticed you giving him a first chance."

"I told you. I got spooked."

"Oh." Sierra paused for a moment and then with a giggle turned to Jana and said, "Boo!"

"Very funny. You can stay on the little girl side if you want, Sierra, but I'm going to step over into womanhood this summer."

"And what exactly does that mean?" Sierra said, examining Jana's expression more carefully.

"It's nothing outrageous. All I'm saying is that I want to figure out how to act around guys and maybe figure out how they feel about me. That's all."

"Take it slow," Sierra cautioned.

"Sierra!" Jana said with a twinge of irritation. "I think I have taken this whole guy thing pretty slow when I'm sixteen and just now trying out my relationship wings."

"Well, I think there are some definite advantages to lingering on the girl side a little longer. Once we step over to the woman side, it's not likely we can ever turn around and go back," Sierra said, stretching out her legs.

"And why would we want to go back?" Jana asked.

"Good point."

They lounged contentedly in the warm sunshine, with the soothing sound of the lake echoing off the underside of the dock. Overhead the wide Montana sky spread its gorgeous blue wings.

"I never told you about the verse I read last night when I came out here on the dock," Sierra said. "It was in Daniel. If I remember correctly, the verse said, 'Those who have insight will shine brightly like the expanse of heaven, and those who lead others to righteousness, like the stars forever and ever.' Isn't that poetic?"

"Poetic?" Jana said.

"Yes. I thought it was last night. And today I thought the trip on the river seemed like our journey through life. Some parts of the trip are easy floats and some parts we have to paddle over the rough stuff."

"And what about the parts when you go over the side?" Jana asked.

"I guess that's when you follow the emergency instructions and keep going, feet first."

"Now that's poetic," Jana said. "You're becoming a shining star of insight, Sierra."

They both laughed. A contented silence came over them for a few minutes before Jana's mom called to them from the grass. "We plan to leave in fifteen minutes to go over to the Morrisons'."

Jana jumped up and said, "They sure didn't give us much notice!" She took off for the cabin while Sierra reluctantly left her perfect napping spot on the dock.

They were both ready to go in the allotted fifteen minutes.

Jana put her hand on the doorknob of their room and stopped. She leaned closer to Sierra. "I think I'm ready to be around Danny and not get spooked. Wish me the best."

Sierra smiled at her friend but felt sad and a little out of order inside. Jana was ready to move ahead without Sierra. And Sierra wasn't sure how she felt about that.

Chapter 16

The big Montana sky was fading from blue to a deep lapis shade as the group congregated on the dock in front of the Morrisons' big house. Sierra settled in, cozy and contented, on a lawn chair with a blanket around her. Danny and his dad were at the end of the dock with Gregg and Tim, preparing to set the night sky on fire with their combined fireworks.

"We need a little cannonball music," Mr. Morrison said over his shoulder to the audience lined up for the show.

Mr. Hill began to hum the *William Tell* Overture.

"I don't think that's what he means," Mrs. Hill told her husband.

The "pyros," as Mrs. Hill called the guys, had strung up a long line of fireworks and appeared to have a definite plan of attack.

"Are we ready, gang?" Mr. Morrison asked.

"Ready!" they answered.

Sierra looked up into the star-flecked sky. The first star of the night was there again, winking at her. She winked back. For a brief moment, Sierra thought what a pity it was to ruin what she considered to be a much better light show than anything these guys could come up with.

An echoing boom sounded from somewhere across the lake. The first fireworks of the night. The boom served as a starting gun for Mr. Morrison, as he lit three punks with his pocket lighter and ceremoniously handed a punk to Danny and one to Gregg. Mr. Morrison held the third one, and the guys lifted the long, slow-burning punks in the air as proudly as if they were holding the Olympic torch in their sweaty fists.

"Let the show begin," Mr. Morrison declared.

With that, the three of them bent down in unison and lit one firework after another after another. Three seconds later, the first one exploded above the lake, sprinkling its red and white twinkles into the thin air.

The first one had barely begun its descent when the second one burst dazzlingly before their eyes. Then the third and the fourth and so on, until Sierra lost count somewhere after the fourteenth one.

Without even a moment's pause to "ooh" or "ahh" before the next spray of colored glitter in the sky, Sierra stopped trying to find the little-girl wonder that she usually felt every Fourth of July. Instead, she felt sadness like the cloud of smoke that was forming over the end of the dock and was more visible with each firework that lit up.

Am I more woman than little girl? I'm away from home and my family for a holiday. That's the first time I've ever done that. I'm traveling almost on my own. I'm almost, sort of, kind of being noticed more by guys. I guess in some ways, I am leaving my girlhood behind.

The thought made her sad. She didn't want to rush into anything, especially a relationship that was more than just buddies. She watched Tim and remembered how he had lit her cattail the night before. That had seemed like such a romantic gesture to her then. Right now, Tim was just one of the guys. Nothing he did or said held special interest for her.

Back and forth, off and on. Feelings sure are funny. But I think everything I'm feeling is normal.

Sierra glanced over at Jana, who had joined Danny at the

end of the dock. She was saying something to him, pointing to the fireworks that had just gone off. Danny appeared to be enjoying the attention.

Sierra noticed that Jana's mom was watching Jana as she interacted with Danny. Her mom had a happy, proud look on her face.

Look at Jana. She got over being spooked pretty easily. I wonder if being six months older than I am makes a difference in how she feels about guys.

Whatever the reason, Jana looked as if she was about to blossom. And she was going to blossom before Sierra did. Or maybe they were both blossoming, but in different ways. It could be they were both finding their voices, their styles, what was really important to them but just via different rivers. Sierra realized she was content to float for a while. She knew there would be plenty of significant rapids ahead.

What she wanted most from her blossoming season this summer was insight. She wanted her life to shine like the stars forever and ever. And that's what she told God in her whispered prayer as the fireworks grand finale blazed across the sky. She had started this vacation expecting to have a little adventure and some fun. In her opinion, there was still room for more of both.

"Bravo!" Sierra said, standing and applauding after the last sprinkling of color fell from the sky. "Perfecto! Magnifico! Brilliant-o!" With each word, she took a step closer to Gregg, who was overdoing his bow for the audience.

Sierra was right next to him at the end of the now empty dock as Gregg took his last bow.

"As they say in show biz," Gregg said, "thank you. Thank you very much. Thank you, ladies and gentlemen. Thank you. Thank you very much."

"You know what else they say in show biz?" Sierra asked, moving closer.

"No, what?" Gregg said, giving her one of his "I'm so cool" smiles.

"Don't they also say, 'In the event of a water landing . . .' " Sierra didn't need to finish her line. Her one solid push had worked easily, and Gregg's big splash was too loud to hear the part about the seat cushion being used as a flotation device.

Gregg surfaced laughing and tried to splash Sierra, but it didn't work. "One of these days, Sierra!" he threatened.

"Yes," Sierra murmured to herself while laughing with the others. "One of these days I'll stop acting like a freckle-faced tomboy and start acting more like a woman. But not today."